DAUGHTER OF
DELIVERANCE

BOOKS BY GILBERT MORRIS

THE HOUSE OF WINSLOW SERIES

1. *The Honorable Imposter*
2. *The Captive Bride*
3. *The Indentured Heart*
4. *The Gentle Rebel*
5. *The Saintly Buccaneer*
6. *The Holy Warrior*
7. *The Reluctant Bridegroom*
8. *The Last Confederate*
9. *The Dixie Widow*
10. *The Wounded Yankee*
11. *The Union Belle*
12. *The Final Adversary*
13. *The Crossed Sabres*
14. *The Valiant Gunman*
15. *The Gallant Outlaw*
16. *The Jeweled Spur*
17. *The Yukon Queen*
18. *The Rough Rider*
19. *The Iron Lady*
20. *The Silver Star*
21. *The Shadow Portrait*
22. *The White Hunter*
23. *The Flying Cavalier*
24. *The Glorious Prodigal*
25. *The Amazon Quest*
26. *The Golden Angel*
27. *The Heavenly Fugitive*
28. *The Fiery Ring*
29. *The Pilgrim Song*
30. *The Beloved Enemy*
31. *The Shining Badge*
32. *The Royal Handmaid*
33. *The Silent Harp*
34. *The Virtuous Woman*
35. *The Gypsy Moon*
36. *The Unlikely Allies*
37. *The High Calling*
38. *The Hesitant Hero*

CHENEY DUVALL, M.D.[1]

1. *The Stars for a Light*
2. *Shadow of the Mountains*
3. *A City Not Forsaken*
4. *Toward the Sunrising*
5. *Secret Place of Thunder*
6. *In the Twilight, in the Evening*
7. *Island of the Innocent*
8. *Driven With the Wind*

CHENEY AND SHILOH: THE INHERITANCE[1]

1. *Where Two Seas Met*
2. *The Moon by Night*
3. *There Is a Season*

THE SPIRIT OF APPALACHIA[2]

1. *Over the Misty Mountains*
2. *Beyond the Quiet Hills*
3. *Among the King's Soldiers*
4. *Beneath the Mockingbird's Wings*
5. *Around the River's Bend*

LIONS OF JUDAH

1. *Heart of a Lion*
2. *No Woman So Fair*
3. *The Gate of Heaven*
4. *Till Shiloh Comes*
5. *By Way of the Wilderness*
6. *Daughter of Deliverance*

[1]with Lynn Morris   [2]with Aaron McCarver

To Charles Collier—
who has oft refreshed me.

GILBERT MORRIS spent ten years as a pastor before becoming Professor of English at Ouachita Baptist University in Arkansas and earning a Ph.D. at the University of Arkansas. During the summers of 1984 and 1985, he did postgraduate work at the University of London. A prolific writer, he has had over 25 scholarly articles and 200 poems published in various periodicals, and over the past years he has had more than 200 books published. His family includes three grown children, and he and his wife live in Alabama.

PART ONE

RAHAB

CHAPTER

I

Rahab's hands flew across her loom effortlessly, weaving scarlet and blue wool. She had become so skilled at her work that she no longer needed to watch her hands. The shuttles from her loom and those of the five other women in the room filled the air with a clicking cadence, an incantation that made Rahab's eyes droop as she fought off sleep. Outside the small window she could see the last shadows of the day fading in the streets of Jericho. Her mind wandered to another place and time—far from the bleak workroom of Gadiah to a field that she and her family had visited during the spring. She could see it all now with perfect clarity, green grass so fresh it almost hurt her eyes, the sparkling waters of a stream curling across the plain. She could hear birds singing and the sibilant whispers of the breeze. She could even smell the pungent aroma of acacia trees lacing the warm air with sweet, musty odors.

A pleasant memory of her younger sister Zayna warmed her when suddenly a groping hand brushed across Rahab's body. Dropping the shuttle, she threw up her hands in self-defense. "Don't do that, sir!"

Her master, Gadiah, was a thin, wiry individual with lustful eyes and hands to match. His eyes glittered as he laughed deep in his throat and leaned closer. "A woman needs a little loving, Rahab."

Rahab quickly got up and pushed him back. "It's time to leave." Glancing around, she saw that the other weavers were averting their eyes. What could they do? Gadiah took liberties with all of them.

The little man leaned in again, his intentions written plainly across his face. Rahab picked up a small knife used for cutting threads. She held the blade in front of her, not speaking but with flashing eyes.

Gadiah glared at Rahab, then changed the subject. "What's in that box?" he growled, gesturing at a small box on the floor.

"Scraps of wool."

"There are no scraps. Use them for something. I can't afford to waste money." He waited for her to answer, but she just stood quietly holding the knife. Finally he snapped, "Be here early in the morning," and whirled on his heels.

After he left, a tall, thin woman with hollow cheeks laughed. "That's the way. Cut his heart out, the dirty old man!"

A faint smile played across Rahab's face. It had become a normal part of her life to fight off her employer. She picked up her scarf, put it over her head, and walked out into the other room, where Gadiah was seated at the table. "I'd like to have my wages, sir."

Gadiah glared at her but slowly shrugged and reached into his tunic. Pulling out a leather bag, he opened it and pulled out several coins. "You'd better learn to be a bit more friendly, Rahab. There are plenty of others who would like to have your job."

Not bothering to answer, Rahab took the coins and hastily left the weaver's shop. Shadows were growing longer now, but as she made her way through the streets of Jericho, she found there was still plenty of activity. She had never lived anyplace except in the city, and she was completely at home with the crowded streets and the babble of voices.

From time to time she would greet someone who called out her name, and more than one young man tried to speak with her. Her fresh, glowing beauty had begun to draw men when she was barely more than a girl. Now at seventeen, she had a wealth of brown hair, her complexion was as clear as any in Jericho, and her eyes were a startling hue, almost violet. Her mother, who had been bought as a slave from somewhere up north, had given Rahab her unusual eye color, as well as the slight dimple in the center of her chin and her pleasing figure. Overtures from men were so common she paid little attention to them.

She stopped at several shops and bargained carefully for a few vegetables. Moving on, she stopped at a butcher's shop, where sheep carcasses hung upside down from large hooks. Only wealthy people could afford a whole sheep. Instead she looked over the carcasses of four rabbits, trying to decide which one was the plumpest. Then she began to bargain with the woman who ran the store. They knew each other well, but it was still the custom in Jericho to bargain. No one paid the asking price. Finally the woman threw up her hands. "All right, you can have it at your own price if you're determined to starve an old woman to death!"

Rahab laughed at Mari, one of the fattest women in Jericho. "Little danger of you starving to death. You've got enough meat on you to last through the winter, Mari."

Carrying the freshly wrapped rabbit and the vegetables, Rahab hurried toward home, anxious to share the bounty of fresh meat with her family. She stopped abruptly, however, when she heard her name called.

"Rahab! Rahab!"

Turning, she saw a young woman leaning against the wall of one of the temples of the goddess Ishtar. The woman wore heavy makeup and revealing clothes, the attire of a temple prostitute. Her attitude had the boldness characteristic of the profession. Rahab knew this young woman—Deziah. She also remembered her as she had once been—a childhood playmate, a simple, cheerful girl who had taken a wrong turn, at least in Rahab's mind.

"Stop and have something to eat. Our supper's almost ready," Deziah offered.

"Oh, I'd like to, but I've got to hurry home. I've got to cook supper for my family."

"There's no hurry about that. They won't starve."

"No, I really must go."

Deziah pouted, her full lower lip sticking out and her eyes dissatisfied. "You never have any time for me."

"Well, I work long hours, Deziah. You know that. And I have the family to think about."

"You're working yourself to death." Moving closer, Deziah grasped Rahab by the arm. "We've talked about this before. You're crazy to work yourself to death working for that old devil Gadiah. Everybody knows what he is."

"I have to work."

"You can join us here."

"Become a temple prostitute?"

"What's wrong with that? I make a good living," Deziah said defiantly. Her eyes were outlined with color, her cheeks redder than nature intended them to be. "What's wrong with the way I live?"

"I . . . I couldn't give myself to men like you do."

"Oh, there's nothing to that. You'll do it when you get married."

"That's different."

"Not different at all. If you join us, you'll have an easy life. No hard work, plenty to eat, the best of food, and all you can drink. Fine clothes. Besides," Deziah said, her eyes narrowing, "it's a good thing to serve the goddess."

"What do you mean by that?"

"Why, I mean if you're the servant of Ishtar, she'll hear your prayers first."

Something about that struck Rahab as wrong, but she

merely shook her head. "I've got to go."

"You'd better listen. You've been praying for that little nephew of yours for a long time, and he just gets sicker. We could pray together, and we could get our customers to pray for him. He'd get well."

"I don't think the men that visit this house have praying on their mind," Rahab said dryly.

"Well, aren't you a pure woman now!" Deziah snapped.

"Don't be angry, Deziah. I love you. We were childhood friends and we still are, but you have gone your way and I'll have to go mine."

Deziah sniffed. "Go on and work yourself to death, then, if that's what you want."

Rahab watched as her old friend turned angrily and stalked through the doors of the temple. She stayed still for a moment, thinking about the life that Deziah now lived. Any man could walk in and sleep with her and would leave money for the goddess. Something about the whole thing just wasn't right. Rahab had discussed her misgivings with others, but temple prostitution was a respectable profession in Jericho, and most people scoffed at her squeamishness. Still, it gave Rahab a queasy feeling to think that any man could claim a woman for a few coins. Shaking off her thoughts, she turned and headed toward her house.

Rounding a corner, she climbed a long set of stone steps that led to the wall of Jericho. She hurried along and, as always, thought of the immense labor that had gone into the wall. It circled the whole city and was built with a solid stone base topped with sturdy mud bricks. At its widest point it was some thirty feet wide, and according to all wisdom, no enemy could ever break down such a wall!

The outer side protected the city from surrounding enemies, such as the Hittites. On its inner side, the wall of Jericho served as a dwelling place for many. Houses were built along the wall in many places, and there were scattered shops and stalls.

As she arrived at just such a row of houses, Rahab spoke to several people who were sitting out in the front. She knew many others were up on their flat roofs. A few leaned over and called to her. Without warning a young man appeared at her elbow and took her arm in his. "Hello, Rahab. How about you and I take a walk?"

"You take the walk yourself, Emir."

"You need a real man."

"Well, if I do, I wouldn't choose a child like you."

"Child! I'm almost sixteen years old. Give me a kiss."

Rahab laughed and pushed the boy away. "You'll come to a bad end, Emir. Now, go away."

She knew the boy had a crush on her, but she had little patience for such things.

Near the middle of the row, she stepped through the door of a two-room house. Most of the living, cooking, and eating was done in the first room. There were several rough stools and a rough-plank table. The other room was primarily for sleeping. At one end of the living area, a window gave access to the outside. One could stand by the window and see the sharp stones and rocks at the foot of the wall far below. In the far distance, one could see mountains forming a cordon around the whole area.

As she called out "I'm home" her twelve-year-old sister, Zayna, and four-year-old nephew, Oman, rushed to greet her. Oman, her sister Romar's son, was a sickly little boy. His legs were like sticks, and he had a frightening cough. Rahab laid down her package and picked Oman up. "How's my big boy today?"

"I'm fine, Aunt."

"Have you been a good boy?"

"No!"

Rahab laughed and winked at Romar. "He's a truth-teller. What's he been into?"

Her older sister shook her head. Fondness was in her eyes, but worry too. She was a plain woman with black hair and brown eyes, not at all pretty like Rahab. They had the same father but different mothers. "He's been good as gold. Why do you tell lies to your aunt, Oman?"

"I thought I was bad."

"You're never bad." Rahab kissed his cheek and put him down. She turned to her other sister and hugged her. "Have you been good?"

"Good as gold," Zayna said.

"No she hasn't," Romar complained. "She's been naughty."

"Did you take a stick to her?"

"No, but I should have."

Zayna was laughing, for they never punished her with a stick. She was a budding beauty with the same wealth of brown hair and unusual-colored violet eyes that Rahab had. And also like Rahab, she was beginning to shine.

A man came out of the sleeping area, swinging himself on a crutch. "Hello, Rahab," he said, smiling.

"How are you today, Kadir?"

"I can't complain." Rahab's brother-in-law, Kadir, had once been a tall man but was now stooped. His black hair was streaked with gray, and his dark eyes were sunken. He had been fine-looking once, but years of work in the mines had worn him down, and an accident had crippled him. He was in pain most of the time, though Rahab never heard him complain.

Turning to the package she had brought, Rahab pulled out the rabbit. "See what I have. We'll have rabbit tonight."

"That will go down good," Romar said, "but meat's so expensive."

"We deserve it. I brought some fresh vegetables too. We'll have a feast."

"Can I help cook?" Zayna pleaded.

"Of course you can. Come along. We'll get started."

Preparing the meal was a family affair, all of them doing a little. The fresh meat and vegetables were a relief from some of the things they had been forced to eat recently.

Kadir laid aside his crutches, sat down, and began carefully cleaning the vegetables while he spoke to his sister-in-law Rahab. "I don't know what we would have done without you." He smiled at her. In his face were traces of the handsome man he had once been.

It hurt Rahab deeply to see how he had been beaten down by life. She went over and patted him on the shoulder. "We're a family, Kadir," she said. "We have to take care of each other."

"Well, I don't do much, but you work such long hours. I worry about you."

"Don't worry. I'm all right."

Across the room Zayna and Oman were playing a game on the floor. She studied her younger sister, and her brow wrinkled for a moment. *She's very beautiful,* she thought. *The men will be coming around her soon enough, as they did to me, and it's hard for a young woman to resist.*

Rahab went to join the two. As she sat down and began to play the simple game, Oman smiled at her. His face was thin, and from time to time he would cough deeply. The rasping cough cut her like a knife.

When the meal was ready, they all sat down at the crude table. Zayna's eyes turned toward the door. "Father's coming," she said.

Rahab noticed that some of the joy went out of the young girl's eyes. She turned to face the door, bracing herself for the entrance of her father. He was that kind of a man.

"So, you couldn't wait for me?"

Makon stood framed in the doorway. He was short and scrawny, and one of his eyes was cocked so that you could never be quite certain whether he was actually looking at you or not. He had a high-pitched nasal voice and was careless about trimming his beard and washing himself. He came to the table, slung himself into a chair, and whined, "You could wait for the head of the family before you start a meal."

"I'm sorry, Father," Romar said. "We didn't know how late you'd be working."

Makon sniffed, his nostrils flaring. "What's that I smell?"

"Fresh rabbit. Rahab bought it," Kadir said.

"Let's have it, then. I'm starved."

Rahab got the rabbit that had been roasted on the fire and set it down before her father. She watched as he cut off the best parts for himself and shoved the platter away. He began to eat greedily, making a great deal of noise.

Rahab took the rest of the rabbit and divided it as evenly as possible. It was a fair-sized rabbit, but it didn't go very far, and she tried to see that Oman got the best pieces.

"Did you get paid, Rahab?" Makon snapped.

"Yes, Father, I did."

"Let's have the money," he said, sticking out his hand.

Reluctantly, Rahab removed the coins from a small leather bag around her waist. "I need to keep some to buy more food for tomorrow."

"No, I need it," Makon grumbled. "Give it to me."

With a sigh, Rahab dropped the coins into his hand.

Turning toward Makon, Romar pleaded, "Father, please don't gamble this away. It's hard enough to live without your losing money at the games."

"You're telling me, your father, how to live?" Makon barked. "You think you can boss me around?" He began devouring his food even more noisily, trying to take everything within his reach.

Very seldom did Kadir have anything to say to his father-in-law. He himself wasn't able to bring home very much money, but now he said quietly, "We all need to be very careful. Times are hard."

Romar, sitting close to her father's side, quickly agreed. "Yes, it's—"

Without warning Makon extended his arm and struck his oldest daughter. He was not a powerful man, so the blow was more insulting than harmful.

In a soothing voice, Rahab said, "Let's not argue. I've brought some fresh figs."

Makon glared at his son-in-law and Romar, but he accepted a lion's share of the fresh figs. Between bites he began speaking roughly. "Everybody's talking about those Israelites. They're terrible people! Terrible!"

"What have you heard?" Kadir asked.

"Why, they're invincible," Makon snorted. He paused just a moment to plump a juicy fig into his mouth and savor the juices. Then he waved his hand. "They're like locusts, and they're terrible warriors. They're killing everything in their path." He continued, but in a few moments he pulled a small flask out of his tunic and drank from it. As the fermented liquid hit his stomach, he began to weep, growing maudlin and whining that the Israelites would kill them all.

Finally he got up and lurched toward the sleeping room. "You mind what I say. Those murdering Israelites will kill us all."

Everyone sighed with relief as the old man disappeared. Rahab went to get a few figs she had set aside. "Here, one for you and one for you." She smiled as she gave the figs to Oman and Zayna.

When they had finished, Romar said, "You must all be tired. Time to go to bed."

"I think I'll go up on the roof and enjoy the cool air for a while first," Rahab answered.

She ascended the ladder to the flat roof, the place where they all went to relax. Rahab sat down and gazed out over the teaming city of Jericho, thinking of the thousands of people who lived there. Then she turned her eyes outward toward the west and thought of the terrible Israelites that everyone was talking about. She leaned back as the thoughts played in her mind. She had heard that the Israelites had only one god, not many. In Jericho there were hundreds of different gods. Each city and town in Canaan had its own god or goddess, and some, like Jericho, had many.

Her eyes grew thoughtful, and she murmured, "How could there be only one god, as the Israelites say? How could one god alone protect the whole world?" Not able to wrap her mind around the idea of such a big god, and truly tired at last, she went downstairs to bed.

CHAPTER

2

Rahab was awoken out of a restless sleep by the sound of coughing. She sat up, rubbing her eyes in the faint daylight that came down from a small, high window. Oman's shoulders were shaking. Alarmed, she got up quickly and went over to put her hand on his forehead. *He's got a fever, and the last time it took him two weeks to get over it.* A spasm of coughing shook the young boy very hard, as if it were going to rip him apart. Rahab held him to her breast, wishing desperately she could do something to help him.

"I'll get you a drink of water, Oman."

Getting up, she went into the other room, walking quietly to avoid waking the others, and picked up a large earthen jug. She filled a cup with water, tepid in the hot weather, went back into the sleeping room, and pulled the boy up to a sitting position. "Drink this," she whispered. His hands were hot in hers as she held the cup and he drank thirstily.

"That was good, Aunt."

"You lie still now and try to sleep."

Oman nodded, but his body was hot as a furnace and he kicked off his cover. She picked him up and carried him into the living area, where she laid him on a pallet, then filled a pan with water. Dipping a cloth in it and wringing it out, she began applying it to his thin limbs and body.

"That feels so good!"

"I'm glad. Just be still now."

"Tell me a story."

"No, you need to sleep."

"But I'll go to sleep if you tell me a story."

Rahab whispered, "All right, I'll tell you a story about a little bear and a little deer that became friends out in the forest. . . ."

Somewhere in the middle of the story, Rahab turned at a noise and saw Romar coming out of the sleeping room. "How is he?" she asked, dark circles under her eyes.

"He had a fever," Rahab said, "but I think it's finally going down."

"Why didn't you wake me?" Romar said.

"I knew you needed your sleep," Rahab replied with a smile.

"But what about you? You're the one who's been up with him, and now it's almost time for you to go to work again. Oh, how I wish you didn't have to go work for that awful man!"

"It's not that bad."

"Yes it is. Couldn't you find something else to do?"

Rahab shook her head. There was no point even discussing it because work was scarce. She had been working for the weaver for three years and had become quite an expert. There were other weavers in town, but despite his roaming hands, Gadiah did pay a little more than the others. "It doesn't matter," Rahab said, shaking her head.

Romar reached for her son. "Here, let me hold him while you eat a good breakfast."

Rahab fixed a simple meal of rice cakes and dried fish. The larder was almost empty, so she did not eat as much as she wanted.

"I've got to go now," she said. "I'll stop by the market

and see if I can get something that will be good for him to eat."

"Don't let Father see it," Romar said bitterly. "He'd take food out of a starving child's mouth."

Rahab did not have an answer for that. She knew that the words were literally true. Things had been a little easier when their mother was alive. To be sure, Makon had abused both her sisters, but Rahab had had enough strength of character to resist him and had been able, at times, to keep him from the worst excesses. No one, however, had been able to keep him from gambling. It was a wild sickness in him, and he lost every bit of money that came into his hands to other gamblers.

"I'll try to be back early, Romar," she said. She leaned over and kissed Oman and saw that he was asleep. "I'll stop by the temple and leave a gift and pray for his healing."

"Little good that will do," Romar said bitterly. She had no confidence in the gods. Rahab herself had little, but what else was there to do?

Leaving the house, she turned and headed toward the weaver's shop. By the time she got to Gadiah's dwelling, the sun had turned a brilliant red and was lighting up the city. Outside the shop she paused for a minute, dreading to go inside. She knew that her employer had been a womanizer for a long time. He had slept with almost all the women who worked for him. The few who refused to give in to him did not last long in his employ, and Rahab knew that sooner or later she would have to face up to this.

She entered the house through a small room and then stepped through a door that led into the work area. Three of the other women were already there, and Gadiah was with them. He was laughing and had his hand on the neck of one of them. "Well," he said, "you're here on time for a change." He stepped over to Rahab. "It'll be a good day if you're nice to me and go fetch some fruit from the stand."

Rahab faced him squarely, and her hand went to the pocket in her robe where she carried the knife. "No thank you," she said sharply. "I've had breakfast already."

"Always stubborn! Well, go hungry, then. Now go on and get to work."

Rahab waited until he left, then glanced at the other women. "He never stops, does he?"

"He never will," the woman named Alma said bitterly. "I wish he'd drop dead."

"He's too evil to die," the third woman said. She was the oldest of the three, and gray streaked her hair. "Evil people live forever."

"No they don't," Alma said. "It just seems that way."

Rahab sat down at the loom and began to work. She was paid by the piece, so her hands flew fast and skillfully over the loom. The other workers also came in, and soon there was a steady hum of clicking shuttles, back and forth, back and forth, and the soft voices of the women murmuring to one another. Outside a dog could be heard howling as if in pain, and indeed all the many sounds of the city waking up filtered in.

As the morning slowly passed, Rahab thought about Oman, worrying about him. There was so little one could do for a fever! There were some physicians, but most of them she considered frauds, and besides, who had the money to pay for such care?

At noon she ate the lunch she had brought. Gadiah came in and passed out some fruit to his favorites but offered none to Rahab. As he was talking to one of the younger women, his hand caressing her back, his wife suddenly stuck her head in through the door. She was a fat, greasy woman who hated her husband, knowing well of his dalliances with the women in the shop. "You have a customer if you can leave the women long enough."

"Who is it?"

"I don't know, but he has money."

Gadiah straightened up and left the room. He was gone for some time—a relief to all the women—but came back accompanied by an obviously wealthy customer. His robes were made out of pure silk, and as he passed close by, Rahab could smell the scent of an expensive ointment used only by the very wealthy.

"This cloth you see would do very well for the project," Gadiah was saying. He stopped by Rahab's area and picked up a piece of the work she had finished. The man took it and examined it closely. "Master Shalmanezer, you will not find finer workmanship in all of Jericho."

"It is very good, very well done." The man called Shalmanezer nodded. He studied it some more, held it up to the light, and then up to his cheek.

Rahab stole a glance at him. How like a hawk he was with his thin face and beak-like hooked nose. She also noticed his dark complexion and carefully tended fingernails.

"You did this, young woman?"

He was watching her now with his glittering dark eyes. His hair was black and oiled.

"Yes, master, this is my work."

"You are an excellent weaver."

"Oh, Rahab is the finest in the city," Gadiah said eagerly. "I'm very proud to have such a craftsman in my shop."

"How long have you been a weaver?" Shalmanezer asked Rahab.

"Three years, sir."

The rich man kept running the cloth through his hands as if to examine it, but his mind was evidently on Rahab. "Are you married, Rahab?"

"Oh no, sir."

"You have a family?"

"I have my father and two sisters and one small nephew."

"I see. You are the oldest?"

"No, my sister Romar is older. I live with her and her husband and my father."

"Your house is far from here?"

"It's on the city wall, master."

Shalmanezer continued to ask questions, and Gadiah did not interrupt, but he watched anxiously as he always did with wealthy customers.

"Is the work very hard?" Shalmanezer inquired.

It was indeed hard, but with Gadiah standing there, Rahab said carefully, "I grow tired sometimes, but then all work is tiring, I suppose, if you do it long enough."

"You are right, I know."

How he would know about work of any kind Rahab couldn't imagine. He looked as if he had never lifted a finger in his life but had only experienced pampered luxury. As he ran the material through his hand, she watched the glittering rings on several of his fingers and noticed a gold chain around his neck with a green stone that reflected the faint light in the workroom.

"I will take this piece and give you this reward for outstanding work." Shalmanezer pulled a heavy leather purse out of an inner pocket. He opened it and laid two coins down before Rahab.

Her eyes widened, and she gave an involuntary gasp, for it was as much money as she usually earned in a week of hard work. "Oh, you are very kind, sir."

Shalmanezer fixed his eyes on her while a smile turned the corners of his lips upward. "Workers should be rewarded. I will, perhaps, see you again." He turned and left the workroom with a fawning Gadiah close behind.

Once they were gone, Alma said, "Well, you made a conquest there. How much is it?"

Picking up the two coins, Rahab stared at them. They appeared to be newly minted, of pure silver. She said, "They're worth at least ten monias."

"I wish he liked my work," Alma muttered with a shrug.

Five minutes later the sound of voices ceased, and Gadiah came rushing back in. "Well, this is a good day for me. I think he's very happy with the work."

"Who is he?" Alma asked.

"A wealthy man."

"I can see that. Where does he get his money?"

"He has many interests, I understand. I think you owe me half of that money, Rahab."

"What makes you think that? He gave it to me."

Ordinarily Gadiah would have argued and shouted, but he had gotten such a fee himself from Shalmanezer that he let it go. "He's going to come back. All of you will have to do your best work. We'll be working for a very rich man now."

———————

After work that evening, Rahab exchanged the silver coins for smaller coins but did not mention her windfall at home. She knew that her father would demand the money if she did. Instead, she bought some healthy food and medicinal herbs for Oman.

On the third day after this event, in the late afternoon, Shalmanezer returned to the weaving room, wearing a gorgeous robe of green and white silk. The turban on his head had a large jewel in the front. He glanced around the room and then walked over to Rahab, smiling. "Well, Rahab, you are busy, I see."

"Always, sir."

"And how is your family?"

"Very well. Thank you for asking, master."

"Your employer tells me that you have a nephew who is ill, a child?"

"Yes. My nephew, Oman. He has some sort of sickness of the lungs."

"And the boy's father. I understand that he is an invalid."

"Not so bad as that, but he is frail."

Once again Shalmanezer inquired about Rahab and her life. "I have a very fine physician," he said. "Perhaps he could see the boy."

"Oh, I could never afford such a thing."

"Well, perhaps I could help. I'll tell you what," he said. "Why don't you come to my house after you get off from work? We will talk about it. Perhaps we can make an arrangement. I could pay the physician, and you could work out his fee at my house. I always need help there. It's a large establishment."

"Yes, sir, I will gladly do that."

"Good. I live in the inner city by the canal. You may ask anyone. It's a large white house with some pink stones set into the outer wall. Very striking. Anyone in that area can tell you where Shalmanezer lives."

"I . . . I'll be there as soon as I get off from work."

"Very good." He picked up another piece of her work and shook his head. "It's always a mystery to me how anyone can be patient enough to sit and work at a loom."

"It can be a pleasure, but sometimes it is tiring."

"Well, I would imagine so. I will see you later."

Shalmanezer left, and once again Gadiah appeared, a look of satisfaction on his oily face. "The man's made out of money," he said. "I've got enough orders here to keep us busy for at least a month. I'm probably going to have to hire another weaver or two."

Rahab did not speak. In her mind she was turning over the possibility of having a real physician see Oman. *If only he could be well, I would be happy,* she thought. She continued to work steadily all afternoon. When it was time to get off, she noticed that a pile of bits she had saved was growing. She would not think of stealing from Gadiah, but these were bits that were usually thrown away. She was clever, however, and had pulled them apart and each evening had taken some home, where she was using them to make a long, strong rope. She had no idea what it would be used for, but it was simple and kept her hands occupied. She took the scraps, stuffed them into her bag, got her fee, and left the weaver's. She turned toward the inner city to find the rich man's home. She managed to get lost more than once, for Jericho was a huge city with soldiers and tradesmen and beggars all jostling one another in the streets.

At last she saw a house that had some pink in the front. It was a magnificent structure built of imported stone, she thought. It glistened in the fading light of day. She stopped a woman who had a large basket on her head and asked, "Please, is that the house of Shalmanezer?"

The woman glanced at her coldly. "Yes," she said briefly.

"Thank you."

"I'd stay away from there if I were you."

The remark took Rahab off guard, but she had no time to ask the woman's reasoning, for the woman turned and walked away in long strides.

Approaching the doorway, she knocked timidly. She had to knock three times, but then the door swung open. A tall woman had opened the door. She wore an expensive blue gown and her eyes were made up in the Egyptian fashion. "What is it, girl? What do you want?"

"A man named Shalmanezer told me to come here. Is this his house?"

"Yes." The woman hesitated, then shrugged. "Come in."

As soon as she stepped inside, Rahab was struck by the beauty of the interior. The walls were smooth and glowing with faint colors. The furniture was of richly carved wood, some with marble tops. She smelled the incense and saw the faint rising smoke trails.

"Wait here," the woman said. "I'll see if Shalmanezer will see you."

"Yes, mistress."

The woman disappeared, and Rahab stood filled with apprehension. She had never been in the home of a wealthy person before, and surely this man had money such as she had never even dreamed of.

The woman came back and said crossly, "Come along, girl."

Rahab followed the woman down a hall that made two turns, and then the woman drew back a curtain. "Go in there," she said with a nod.

"Thank you."

Stepping inside, Rahab saw Shalmanezer rising from a couch. He had on a different garment this time. Flowing trousers gathered around his ankles, and his shoes were of soft leather with a jewel on the top of each. His multicolored robe flowed gracefully as he came toward her. "Have a seat. I was just about to have some refreshment. Could I offer you some?"

"No, thank you, sir." Rahab took her seat and sat tensely watching him.

"Oh, don't be shy," he said. "Here, try this fruit. It's delicious. I have it imported from quite a distance."

Rahab took one of the small round grapes, bit into it, and nodded. "It's very good."

"Eat all you want. They're quite refreshing, especially after a hard day's work." Shalmanezer seated himself to her right on a couch covered with pillows and ornate coverings. "I expect you're tired after such a long day."

"I'm fine, sir."

Shalmanezer shook his head. "You're very young. I would guess you're not much over sixteen."

"I am seventeen, master."

"Well, you're a beautiful young woman." The compliment slid easily from his tongue. "But you know how it is with hard work. That beauty will quickly fly."

Rahab sat there anxiously, but Shalmanezer gave every appearance of enjoying himself. His eyes remained fixed on her as he urged her to eat more fruit and drink a glass of wine, which was unlike anything she had ever tasted before. "I hope you like that wine."

"It's . . . very good."

"Now, then . . ." Shalmanezer said as he leaned forward, his hawklike face turned to face her, "you have a nephew that needs to see a physician. I will be most happy to work out something with you."

"I'm a good cook and I can clean. I'll do anything to help my nephew."

"I have a better proposal than that. I would like for you to stay at this house."

"Stay here, sir, as a servant?"

At this Shalmanezer got up smoothly and easily, in an almost animal-like way. He stretched out his hand and laid it on Rahab's cheek, startling her with his touch, but she could not draw back without offending him. He left his hand on her cheek for a moment, then smiled and said, "We'll work out something. In a large house like this there are many things to do. I have a great many interests. I'm interested in you."

"I will think about it, sir, but I'm just a poor girl. There is little I know how to do. I'm afraid you would not be pleased."

Shalmanezer grinned. "You'll please me well enough."

Rahab just nodded, not quite sure of his intentions.

"I'll have the physician visit your nephew," Shalmanezer went on. "Tell me where you live." He listened as Rahab described how to get to her house, then nodded. "He'll be there tomorrow. I suggest you come back here after you get off work. We'll see about some way for you to repay me."

Rahab rose instantly. "Thank you so much, and thank you for the refreshments, sir." She bowed low before him, then left.

As she stepped outside into the corridor and started down the hall, she saw the woman who had admitted her to the house standing there waiting. "Well, did you have a good meeting?"

"I think so. He's offered to help my nephew, who is very ill."

"I hope it works out."

"Are . . . are you his wife?"

The woman laughed aloud. It was a harsh laugh without humor. "His wife? Shalmanezer doesn't have a wife. Don't you know what this place is?"

"This place? You mean this house?"

"Yes."

"Why, no—I assume it's his home."

"It's a brothel. We keep prostitutes here—for men. No, Shalmanezer doesn't have a wife. He doesn't need one."

Before Rahab had time to react, Shalmanezer appeared. "Well, Lamile, I see you're getting acquainted with Rahab. I've been trying to get her to stay with us."

Rahab was paralyzed now with fear. She knew about brothels and whores and the men who visited them, but she had never associated all that with such a fine house as this. She could not think what to say. "I must go," she said.

Shalmanezer lightly stepped closer and took her arm. "Why work yourself to death? It will be an easy life here. I'll see that your family is well cared for."

Lamile's eyes glittered and she smiled cruelly, but she said nothing.

"I must go, sir. I thank you for your offer, but I couldn't live here." She turned and hurried out.

As soon as the door closed, Lamile smiled, "Well, your charm didn't work this time, did it?"

Shalmanezer reddened with anger, but then he burst into laughter. "Oh, she will be back."

"I doubt it. She appears to be meek enough, but I think she has a streak of stubbornness."

"I can get any woman I decide on. I got you, didn't I?" he taunted her.

Lamile stiffened angrily. "You'll not get this one."

"You're very sure of that, aren't you? But there are ways." He ran his long, sensitive fingers over his beard, and his eyes glittered. "Yes, there are ways," he said. "I will have her here, Lamile. You can count on that!"

CHAPTER
3

Shalmanezer kept his word concerning the physician. The primary physician in all of Jericho came to see Oman the day after Rahab's visit. He prescribed medicine and was a cheerful, good-natured fellow. Before he left he turned to Rahab and winked lewdly. "Well, I've done my part. Now it's your turn."

The roly-poly physician left, and Romar, who was holding Oman in her lap, asked Rahab quizzically, "What did he mean by that?"

Rahab had concocted a story in her mind and said, "Well, I agreed to do some work for Shalmanezer in return for the doctor's visit."

"What sort of work?"

"Housework, I suppose. I can clean or cook." Rahab could not bring herself to look directly at Romar as she said this. She felt guilty for deceiving her sister, but it had to be done, and that was all there was to it.

The next evening when she went to the house of Shalmanezer, Lamile met her. There was a strange smile on the woman's thin lips, and she said, "Well, you're back."

"Just long enough to work off the debt I owe to the master for the physician's visit."

"You aren't going to join us permanently, then?"

"Oh no. I couldn't do that."

"You have something against harlots?"

The blunt question struck Rahab hard, and she did not know how to answer. Dropping her gaze toward her feet, she shook her head and murmured, "I just want to do housework or cleaning, something like that."

"Very well. There's plenty of that to do," Lamile said. "But you're a fool not to join us. It's an easy life here." When Rahab didn't answer, she shrugged and said, "I'll show you your duties."

Rahab threw herself into the work, happy that Shalmanezer was out of town on business. She did not think she could face the man again. She was aware that Lamile was watching her carefully as she worked at menial tasks for the next three evenings after her regular job at the weaver's. As she watched men coming and going for all the young prostitutes under Shalmanezer's care, she was convinced more than ever that she could never give herself to a life like this. She considered the men despicable, but she kept silent, especially around Lamile.

On the third evening, Lamile said, "That's enough. Your debt is paid, and I think you are a fool for working yourself to death when you could have an easy life."

Rahab lifted her head and said quietly, "It's not something I could do." She turned abruptly and left. It was dark, and she hurried through the streets lit only by dim torchlight. When she entered her house, she stopped dead still, for there was a man she did not recognize sitting at the table. Her father was sitting beside him, and Makon said, "Ah, here's Rahab. You remember her, don't you, Hamath?"

The man seated beside her father was thin and balding, about the same age as her father, or perhaps slightly older. He was apparently shortsighted, for he squinted and leaned forward, then smiled, exposing very bad teeth. "Why, she was just a baby the last time I saw her. She's grown up well."

"This is our kinsman Hamath, Rahab."

"How are your kinsmen?" Rahab asked politely. She did not remember meeting the man, but she had heard her father speak of him often enough. Hamath was his second cousin, but you would have thought they were blood brothers by the way her father had always bragged on their acquaintance. *"Why, he's the richest man in Bashan,"* he would often say. *"He's got money coming out of his ears. I wish he'd remember me with some of it."*

To Rahab, Hamath did not have the appearance of a prosperous man, though she bowed to him before going to embrace Oman. Zayna was helping her sister with the cooking, and Rahab whispered to them, "When did he get here?"

Romar's whisper was also low. "He just came about an hour ago. I hardly recognized him. The last time I saw him he was hale and strong and dressed in fine clothing. Now he looks like a beggar."

"What does he want?"

"He's fallen on hard times. It's easy to see that. I expect he'll tell us his story after he's eaten."

The two women prepared a meal, and Hamath ate like a starved wolf while he and Makon spoke of old times. Once the meal was finished and the single bottle of wine in the house was brought out, the two men drank and Makon asked abruptly, "You don't look well, Hamath. What's happened to you?"

"Don't look well?" Hamath snorted. "I guess I don't after what I've been through."

"You've had hard times. That's easy enough to see. Where's your family?"

"Dead. All dead."

Makon blinked with shock and shook his head. "That's a hard blow. How did it all happen? Why have you left your homeland?"

Hamath took a big gulp of the wine and then shook his

head sadly. His eyes were dim with the beginning of cataracts. "Cousin, you know how well I did after I left Jericho and moved to Bashan."

"I remember. Your father was against it. I guess we all were. After all, we didn't know anything good about those Amorites and people in that country. They're pretty vicious."

"Men are vicious everywhere, but it turned out all right. I made a lot of money there. We had a good king. His name was Og. He was a hard man but fair, as kings go. As long as you didn't displease him, he wouldn't cut off your head."

"Well, we heard word that you were prospering. What happened?"

Hamath finished off the cup of wine, then shoved it over to let Makon refill it. Everyone kept their eyes on the disheveled man who sat at their table. His clothes were filthy and patched. His cheeks were sunken in, and he had all the earmarks of a fugitive. Even sitting there in the safety of their home, he kept glancing back over his shoulder as if he expected someone to burst through the door and seize him.

"Everything was going fine—until those cursed Israelites came!"

"You mean the people we've heard about?" Rahab asked eagerly. "The ones who followed Moses out of Egypt?"

"The same bunch. They're a bloodthirsty, wicked bunch of cold-blooded killers."

"You don't say!" Makon said, shock etched across his face. "We've heard rumors but nothing definite."

"Well, I can tell you something definite." Hamath gulped down more wine, letting some of it dribble over his chin. "They came into the Amorite country like an army. It all started when they asked Sihon, the king of the Amorites, for permission to pass through his country. Sihon's a hard man. He told them to stay out. Well, that was a mistake. The Israelites came down like a bunch of ravening wolves. They killed everything that had breath, even the children, all the way from Arnon to Jabok.

They took all of Sihon's cities and all the villages. It's theirs now. But that wasn't enough."

"You mean they came to Bashan?"

"We heard they were coming, and if I had sense enough, I would have sold out and left. It just never occurred to me that Og could be defeated by a rabble of shepherds. Og did his best. He armed every able-bodied man, including me, and we went out to meet the Israelites. We had good arms and good leaders, but we were like children against them." Hamath began to shake and tremble. Putting his hands over his face, he even wept. "They killed us as if we were sheep. It was all the doing of their god."

"What's their god's name?" Rahab asked eagerly.

"They call him different names. Most of the time it's Jehovah. Sometimes simply the Holy One."

"What does their god look like?" Kadir asked, leaning forward, his eyes bright with interest.

"Nobody knows. That's what's frightening. We know all of our gods, for they're made out of stone or clay, but their god doesn't have any form."

Kadir shook his head. "I've never heard of a god without form. How do they know who he is, then?"

"Oh, I don't know anything about that. All I know is he's the strongest god I ever saw. I ran away when I saw everybody was going to get killed. I went back home, but the Israelites got there before I arrived. My family were all dead, and everything was burned or destroyed or carried off. Even the king was killed."

There was a silence around the table until Rahab asked, "What will you do now, kinsman?"

"I have nowhere to go. I came to beg you to take me in."

"Well, we have little enough here, but you can stay with us," Makon said. He was studying his kinsman with a critical gaze. "Do you think the Israelites will head this way?"

"I don't know, but if they do, I'm getting out. Nobody can

stand against that god of theirs!"

After the guest had been given a corner to sleep in and had fallen into a drunken stupor, the family talked about what he had said. "It sounds like a bad situation," Kadir said. "If the Israelites head this way, we're done for."

"Not our city," Makon boasted. "The walls of Jericho are famous throughout the world. Nobody could break them down."

Rahab was not so sure, but she kept silent. At first she listened to the men talk, but then she put the children to bed. She herself lay awake for a long time and was preoccupied with the idea of the god of the Hebrews. *A god with no form that cannot be seen.* Somehow this appealed to her, for the statues of the gods of Jericho were oftentimes crude, and it was all she could do to make herself kneel down and pray to hunks of stone. She drifted off to sleep, wondering what it would be like to have a god like that of the Israelites.

Rahab quickly put the idea of Shalmanezer out of her mind, but a week after Hamath's arrival, one of the prominent citizens of Jericho, a merchant named Joar, stepped unannounced into their lives. Joar met Makon during a gambling match, and the two had become close friends. Makon had returned home exultant. He had money in his pocket, and he flung it on the table, crying out, "See this! I won all this tonight. I have a new friend named Joar. Tomorrow we're going to the home of the richest man in Jericho."

"Who is that?" Kadir asked.

"His name is Shalmanezer. He's the one you worked for, isn't he, Rahab?"

"Yes." Rahab's heart fluttered, knowing that the meeting between Joar and her father was not accidental. "If I were you, I'd stay away from there. It's a bad place, Father."

"A bad place? But look at all this money," Makon boasted.

"Joar's good luck for me. You wait and see. We'll all be dressed in silks and drinking the best wine in the country. Just wait and see!"

———————

That was the beginning of more anxious times for Rahab's family. Makon went almost every day the following week to the home of Shalmanezer. He brought home money every night, most of the time so drunk he could barely walk. In fact, one night he had to be carried home by Shalmanezer's servants.

Rahab was deeply troubled about all this, and she said as much to Romar. "Father's going to get in trouble with Shalmanezer and Joar."

"Why do you say that? He's winning money."

"They're letting him win money. Father's a terrible gambler. You know that."

"Maybe he's just gotten lucky."

Rahab did not answer, but she knew better. She tried to speak to her father to warn him, but he merely laughed at her. "Are you afraid of being rich, girl? Look at this money I won. This family is going up, I tell you."

The next day Shalmanezer came to the weaver's establishment. As usual, Gadiah fawned over him, and when he led the rich man into the workroom, Shalmanezer came directly over to Rahab. "How's that nephew of yours?"

"He's doing better, sir. I thank you for your help."

"Nothing to it." Shalmanezer waved his perfumed hand. "And Lamile tells me you're a good worker. So I guess we're all even."

"Still, I must thank you, sir. I'm very grateful."

"It's nothing ... nothing at all," he insisted, then added, "I met your father. Perhaps he's told you about our acquaintance."

"Yes, sir, he has."

"Fine fellow, your father." Shalmanezer's eyes glittered as he smiled. "Have you changed your mind about becoming a part of my establishment?"

Establishment—that's sure a fancy name for a brothel, Rahab thought, then said, "No, sir, I will remain where I am. Thank you very much."

"Well, we will see. Give your family my best wishes."

When Shalmanezer arrived back at his home, Lamile greeted him. He smiled and said, "Well, the noose is tightening around the neck of our little pigeon."

"Who is that?"

"Rahab. You remember."

"What have you been doing?"

"I'm laying a trap for her. It's a little trouble, but I'm enjoying it."

Lamile shrugged her shoulders with disgust. "Why take so much trouble? There are plenty of beautiful girls to choose from."

Shalmanezer shook his head. "No, she shows too much pride." A touch of anger smoldered in his dark eyes. "She'll have little enough of that when we get her . . . and we will get her, you know."

Everyone was shocked at Makon's unexpected appearance in the middle of the afternoon. He was arrayed in a silk robe and a new turban that fairly glowed, and he had been to a barber, for his beard was neatly trimmed and he smelled of fragrant oil. "How do you like this outfit?" he crowed, turning around for them, eliciting their admiration.

"You look very nice," Zayna said. "Where did you get such fine clothes, Father?"

"Why, I bought them. I'll buy you some too, Zayna. All of

you are going to have to keep up appearances a little better, and I think we're going to have to find a better house. This one's not worthy of us anymore."

Rahab did not speak. Something about this frightened her. She knew deep in her heart that Shalmanezer was using her father, but there was nothing she could say. She simply sat there and listened while the others surrounded the old man and flattered him concerning his new raiment.

"Well, I'm going out to win our fortune tonight." From an inner pocket Makon pulled out a thick pouch. He rattled it, and the clink of coins was clear. "I've got a stake, and I intend to finish the game with enough money to do anything we please. Wish me luck."

Dutifully, most of the family wished him good luck—all except Rahab.

Kadir had been watching Rahab. He had noticed that she showed no pleasure at her father's new prosperity. "What's wrong, Rahab? Aren't you happy about your father's winnings?"

"They're letting him win."

Kadir blinked with surprise. "What are you talking about?"

"They're letting him win. You know Father's no gambler. Those men spend all their time at it. They're smart and they're wicked."

"But Shalmanezer's been so good to us," Romar exclaimed. "He sent the doctor for Oman, and he's been a friend to Father."

Rahab knew she could not keep the secret any longer. She lifted her head, and they all saw the despair in her eyes. "He runs a brothel, and he wants me to be a part of it," she said bluntly.

A dead silence filled the room, and Romar exclaimed, "You never told us that!"

"I hoped he would leave us alone. He's been after me for

some time now. It angers him when I refuse to do what he asks."

"You should have told your father this!" Kadir exclaimed. "He doesn't need to be with a man who's out to ruin his daughter."

"He wouldn't listen," Rahab said in despair. She turned away and fled.

After she had left the room, Kadir exclaimed, "What can we do about this, Wife?"

"Nothing. You know my father. He's stubborn. He won't listen to anything we say. The best we can hope for is that the man will give up and leave Rahab alone."

———

Four men—Makon, Shalmanezer, Joar, and a merchant named Magite—sat around the table playing a game with colored stones of different values. The players kept the stones they had won hidden in a box in front of them. The object of the game was to accrue the greatest value in stones. No player ever knew exactly how many stones the others had unless he was very sharp.

Makon's face was flushed—not only because he was half drunk, but also because his box was filled with stones. He had tried to keep track of what the others had in their boxes, but they had been playing now for a long time and the varied-colored stones had been exchanged many times. The game also involved a bone-white die that helped a player win when he threw the highest number.

"Here, Makon, my friend, have some more wine," Shalmanezer said smoothly. He himself had not drunk very much, and neither had the others. He smiled as Makon accepted the goblet and drank deeply. "You're lucky tonight," he said.

"Yes, I am, and it's about time!" Makon exclaimed. He always grew reckless when he won, and although he knew he could cash out now and go home with more money than he had ever seen at one time in his life, he still gazed avidly at the stones and the boxes of the other three players. "I feel like I'm going to make you all sorry you let me in this game."

"Oh, you're a gambler, you are!" Joar laughed. "Never seen better."

The man called Magite was tall and thin with glittering eyes. He shook his box, then said sadly, "You just about cleaned me out, but I've still got hopes of beating you, my friend."

"You can't beat me—not tonight. I feel it," Makon cried out. "Let's get on with the game."

The game proceeded until the stakes had grown so high that each player had to put up an equal amount, and now it was time to make the bet. Makon peered cautiously in his box, guarding it so that the others could not see. He saw that he had four red stones, and any game could be won with only three. Greedily he shook the box and leered across the table. "Let's bet."

The betting went on until Shalmanezer raised it so high that Makon was taken aback. "Why, you know I don't have that kind of money!"

"You'd better drop out, then. Of course you'll lose what you've put on the table."

"No, I won't do that. But you've got to give me a chance."

"Why, of course. We're friends, aren't we? I'll tell you what. You put up some security. I'll be glad to take that if you lose."

Makon tried to think clearly, but his mind was cloudy. "I don't have anything. I don't own any land and I don't even own the house I live in. You know that, Shalmanezer."

"Well . . ." Shalmanezer shrugged his shoulders and smiled. "You have a family."

"I have. What about it?"

"You could put them up for security."

"What are you talking about?"

"Why, people are worth a great deal for slaves, don't you know."

"Are you crazy?" Makon shouted, his eyes inflamed. "I wouldn't let my family become slaves."

"Of course you wouldn't," Joar said smoothly. "But you're almost sure to win. I can see the way you peered into that box. If you do, you're set for life. You'll never have to work another day."

"That's right," Magite said, nodding encouragement. "You've won all night. Why shouldn't you win once more?"

"I don't think there's really much risk. I don't have much, to be truthful," Shalmanezer said, peering into his box. "But it's up to you."

A silence fell on the room, and the other three players saw greed struggle with honor in the old man's face. None of them had the least doubt about the outcome.

With a sudden gesture, Makon struck the table with his fist. "All right, then. Let's play."

"Right enough."

The play went on, and when it came time to show what was in their boxes, Makon laughed with exultation. "See here, see this!" Makon was trembling with excitement. He had never been so sure about anything in his life. "Four red stones. It can't be beat."

Shalmanezer's thin lips drew into a cruel smile. "Ordinarily that's true, my friend, but five red stones beat four red stones." He upended his box, and the five red stones rolled out across the table.

A dead silence filled the room. Makon stared at the five red stones, then let out an agonizing cry of grief and ran from the room.

Shalmanezer laughed and was joined by the other two. "The fool! He'll probably kill himself, and I'll be out one slave."

"You don't need him. You have the girl. That's all you wanted."

"True enough," Shalmanezer said. He picked up one of the red stones and smiled fondly at it. "Men are fools," he said. "That old man had nothing, and now he has even less."

CHAPTER

4

Rahab had brought home a good portion of a lamb that a butcher had let her have cheap. The family had filled their stomachs with the meat and a few vegetables, and had even enjoyed a bottle of cheap wine Rahab had managed to find. Now they were sitting around enjoying one another's company.

"Sing another song, Rahab," Oman pleaded.

"Oh, you've heard me sing enough."

Kadir put his arms down and pulled the boy up onto his lap. "How about if I sing a song?" He winked at his wife and Rahab.

"No, you can't sing as good as Aunt Rahab," Oman said.

"Well, I'll sing one more, but that's all," Rahab conceded.

Rahab had a beautiful singing voice, and she knew a great many songs. This one was a song she had learned as a child that told the story of two rabbits trying to get away from a hungry wolf. As always, the rabbits escaped and the wolf fell into dire difficulty.

"I love that one. Sing it again!" Oman exclaimed, his eyes bright.

"No, that's enough singing for one night," Kadir said. "It's time for you young ones to go to bed."

"That's right," Romar agreed. "Come now." She left with

Oman and Zayna and came back soon. "They're exhausted, but it's been a good day for them," she said.

Kadir was feeling very happy, and it showed in the brightness of his eyes. He had found a job he could do sitting in a shop for a potter. It did not pay much, but it was steady work. "Let's have some more of that wine," he said, "to celebrate my new employment."

Romar went to get the wine, but before she could get to it, the door swung open. They all turned expectantly.

Rahab's heart sank as she saw her father. Tears were running down his face as he blubbered incoherently and stumbled into the room.

"What is it, Father?" Romar cried, going to him without hesitation.

"Lost ... lost ... lost!"

"What's lost?" Kadir demanded. "What's wrong, Makon?"

Makon shook his head. Then he began weeping uncontrollably and flung himself into a chair. He put his arms down and buried his face in them.

Rahab went and put her hand on his shoulder and waited until the paroxysm of weeping had stopped. "What is it?" she said, but somehow even before he spoke, a sense of doom touched her.

At last Makon straightened up and stared about wildly. "We're lost!" he wailed. "We're all going to be slaves."

"What are you talking about?" Romar whispered, fear showing in her eyes. "What do you mean we'll be slaves?"

"I had the game all won, but something went wrong. I bet all of us against Shalmanezer. If I'd won, we'd have enough money to do anything right now. But I lost!"

"You bet all of us, your own family?" Rahab cried. "How could you do such a thing?"

Makon could not answer for a while. Then he cried out wildly, "It's all my fault. Give me a knife. I'll kill myself."

"No need to talk like that," Kadir snapped. "Now tell us

what happened. Straighten up. We must know."

Rahab and the others listened as her father related the details of the game. He was such a foolish man he could not see how the other three had ganged up on him and cheated him. Now it was too late.

"Maybe he'll have mercy on us," Romar whispered.

"No, he won't." Rahab's face was pale. "He'll make slaves out of us all. Especially me."

"He's sending his servants tomorrow," Makon whispered. "We'll all be his slaves forever."

———

Rahab approached the front door of Shalmanezer's fine home. Her face was set, and her lips were drawn into a straight line. She knocked on the door, and Lamile greeted her. The woman stared at her and understood everything all at once. "I see he got you." Disappointment tinged her voice. "I thought you might be the one to stand up against him. How did he do it?"

"He tricked my father in a game of chance into risking the whole family as security, so now we'll all be his slaves."

Lamile was a hard woman, and there was little compassion or concern in her for anyone else. But something about the defenseless young woman before her touched a part of her she thought was long dead. She came over and put her arm around the girl and said, "You'll just have to do the best you can, Rahab. Don't cross him. I'll protect you as much as I can."

She waited for the girl to speak, but when she got no answer, she said, "He'll want to see you right now. Time to get it over with."

Numbly Rahab followed Lamile down the hall and into the chamber of Shalmanezer. As she had known he would be, he was waiting for her. He did not rise this time, nor ask her to be seated. "I'm here to ask you for mercy," Rahab pleaded.

"Well, of course you are, and I'm prepared to give it."

A shock ran through Rahab. "The gods would bless you, master, if you would show mercy to my family."

"I myself need all the mercy I can get. A man in my trade can't expect much," Shalmanezer said. He got up and came over to her and ran his hands across her face and down her body in the manner of a man inspecting a new horse he had just bought. "I'm prepared to be merciful. Of course I would expect something in return. After all, I must have a little consideration."

Rahab stood motionless, although she inwardly recoiled at the touch of his hands. "What do you want, master?"

"You work here, Rahab, in my house, and all the rest of your family will go free."

At that instant Rahab knew she had absolutely no choice. She had thought about her poor crippled brother-in-law being enslaved to a cruel master. She thought of her beautiful sister Zayna, only twelve, being sold to a brutal man who would abuse her. And Oman—what would happen to him and to her sister Romar? Strangely enough she did not think about what would happen to her father.

"I will have to do it, sir," she said. She held her head high, and although her face was colorless, there was a pride in her that even this could not extinguish.

"Fine, fine. You may not like this, Rahab, but your family won't suffer." He hesitated, then said, "In the event you had decided not to give in, I had already planned to take your younger sister into my house. A lot of men like young girls like that."

Shalmanezer waited for Rahab to reply, but she did not speak. He lifted his voice and called out, "Lamile." When the woman entered, he said, "Show Rahab the ropes." He thought for a moment and added, "You'll be in my bed tonight. I'll see what you have to offer our customers."

Lamile led the young woman outside and did not speak. She showed her to the quarters where the other harlots slept and introduced her. One of them, a woman with dyed red hair, winked at her. "Shalmanezer will try you out tonight. He always does. Do the best you can—that way you can make a better deal."

"That's enough," Lamile said. "Let's see about your clothes now."

"I have to go home and tell my family what's happened."

"Of course. When you come back, I'll have everything ready for you."

Lamile watched the young woman leave, and once again the strange sense of pity she had thought dead long ago stirred within her. "I can't be feeling sorry for her. We've all got our problems," she muttered, then turned to her affairs.

The family was waiting when Rahab walked in. "What did he say?" Makon cried out. He had felt hopeful when Rahab had agreed to go plead for mercy, but now as he saw her pale face, his heart sank. "He's not going to have any mercy, is he?"

Rahab gazed into their faces, then slowly scanned the room that had been her home as long as she could remember. When she spoke, her voice was as steady as she could make it. She had wept all the way home but had paused outside to clean her face and pull herself together. "You will all be free. You won't be slaves," she said.

Cries went up from the entire family, but Kadir, who had more discernment than the others, was watching Rahab. "What about you, Rahab?"

"I will be a . . ." She tried to say the word, but it was hard. "I will have to remain in Shalmanezer's house."

"In a brothel?" Romar cried out. "You can't do that!"

"I have to—otherwise, all of us will be slaves."

Romar turned to her father and slapped him across the face with all her might. The blow drove him backward, and he stumbled. She came to stand over him and when he tried to get up, she struck him again. "This is all your doing, you old fool!"

she screamed. "I don't ever want to hear another word from you as long as I live. You sold your own daughter into harlotry!"

The old man crept away, crawled into a corner, and pulled himself into a fetal position.

Kadir came over and put his arm around Rahab. "Is there no other way, my sister?"

"There's no other way." Rahab knew she could not stand to be at home any longer. She went over and kissed Oman, holding on to him tightly, and then embraced Zayna. The two clung to her. They were both weeping, although Oman did not understand what was happening.

She hugged her older sister, who clung to her, and then hugged her brother-in-law.

"You will see me again. I will see to it that you have no wants." She whirled and left the house, and when she stepped outside, the night was dark, but not as dark as her heart.

PART TWO

ARDON

CHAPTER

5

From the top of a high ridge thrust up from the level plain, Joshua stood, taking in the wonderful sight of the tabernacle of God, amazed, as always, at the structure. He had, of course, been there when the tabernacle was constructed under the guidance of Moses, and he thought back to those early days of glory. He remembered crossing the Red Sea on dry land and seeing the armies of Pharaoh drown in the same sea. He thought of the many miracles God had done to bring the children of Israel through the desert. Bitterness gripped him when he remembered how he and Caleb and ten others had gone to scout out the land. When they returned, Israel had defied the word of God and refused to believe that the land could be conquered.

"Forty years of wandering in this forsaken desert!" Joshua muttered. He was not a tall man but was strongly built, and even in his eighties he still had the full strength of his young manhood. He felt the burden of leadership that Moses had thrust upon him. Joshua had tried desperately to avoid the task, but Moses had insisted that God had appointed him, and who could argue with God?

Below him he saw the Israelite camp surrounding the tabernacle, which was itself surrounded by a wall of cloth held up by many pillars. The brazen altar was sending up a column of white smoke, almost like a pillar in the windless air, and between the altar and the tabernacle was the brass laver in which the priests washed their hands and bodies to purify themselves.

Joshua's eyes shifted then to the surrounding tents, and a smile of satisfaction spread across his face. They were camped exactly as God had instructed them from the very beginning. The twelve tribes were each divided into three smaller tribes, and within those divisions they were further separated. God had chosen to keep the identity of the tribes pure.

Joshua's eyes went to the north, where the tribes of Dan, Asher, and Naphtali were set in order. To the south, the tribes of Reuben, Simeon, and Gad flanked the tabernacle. On the east stood the tribes of Judah, Issachar, and Zebulun, and to the west were Ephraim, Manasseh, and Benjamin.

Joshua took pleasure in the order of the encampment, but then he lifted his eyes toward Canaan on the far side of the Jordan River and a cloud crossed his face. He was not a man of fear but of faith. Still, the commandment to conquer a land filled with strong kings, some of them within walled cities, was daunting.

"God will do it," Joshua said loudly. Raising his eyes and his hands to the heavens, he entreated, "God, you are the Almighty One. Nothing is too difficult for you, but you must help me, for I am weak."

Joshua's hearing was still keen, and he heard the sound of approaching footsteps. Turning, he saw Caleb rapidly striding toward him. Joshua smiled at his old friend, whom he so greatly admired. At the age of eighty-five, Caleb was still tall, lean, and strong. His piercing hazel eyes could see farther than anyone in all the tribes of Israel. Joshua noticed the missing forefinger on his left hand, remembering how it had been bitten off by a bear. Caleb had slain the bear with only a knife but had lost his finger. It was a story Caleb loved to tell to his children and grandchildren.

"Good morning, Joshua," Caleb said. His voice was high-pitched and could carry for miles, and his face was expectant. "Am I disturbing you?"

"Not at all, old friend," Joshua replied with a smile, "but we must face up to some facts. The big fact is that Moses is leaving us."

Caleb glanced at Joshua's face and saw the lines that the years had put there. "Are you worried about leading Israel?"

"Of course I am!"

"Don't be." Caleb shrugged his shoulders. He had sinewy arms and fingers, and by his side was the sword with which he was an expert. A knife hung on the other side. He was also an expert with a sling, able to bring down a deer at an unbelievable distance. "Jehovah will be with us," he said.

"He'll have to be," Joshua said grimly. He gazed down again at the camp. "Does it seem strange to you that we are the oldest ones who will enter the Promised Land?"

"Yes, I suppose it does. But God commanded that the old generation would have to die off in the wilderness. Only those who were twenty or younger when we came over the Red Sea are left now."

"Except for you and me. We're the old men."

"I'm as strong as I was when I was twenty, and so are you."

"Well, you don't lack confidence." Joshua dropped his face and studied the ground for a long moment, then said, "I miss those who are gone."

"So do I, but I love the new Israel. The men are strong and lean. They're ready for a battle. It's not like it was when you and I first brought back the news of the land that is to become ours."

"I was just thinking about that. We could have already been there for the last forty years if it hadn't been for the unbelief of the people."

"Well, that's all done," Caleb said with a shrug. "Now what?"

"When Moses leaves, we'll cross over the Jordan, and that's when the battle will begin."

"I'm ready for it!" Caleb replied. "We'll go forward in the power of God and watch Him give us the victory."

The two old men stood for a moment, bound by their past history, trusting and loving each other as only warriors who have been in battle together can. Then they turned and walked slowly back down the trail that led to the camp.

They parted, and Caleb went directly to the section of the camp occupied by Judah, of which he was a member. He found his own tent and his daughter Ariel, and his face brightened as always. Her real name, one given to her by her mother, was Acsah, but Caleb had chosen his own name for her. Legally she might be Acsah, but she was Ariel to him. He paused to study her for a moment, and a rush of pride filled him. She was, to him and to many of the young men of Israel, the fairest woman of all. She was as tall as he was, with a beautiful complexion. Her hair was as black as a raven, and she had almond-shaped, wide-spaced eyes of a peculiar gray color that was sometimes almost green. She had a provocative figure, which had drawn the young men. But despite her physical attractiveness, Caleb knew that Ariel had some severe faults. One was her pride. Pride was a good thing in some ways, but sometimes Caleb worried that his daughter, whom he loved so deeply and completely, was headed for trouble.

"Hello, Father," Ariel said, running up to him and kissing him on the cheek, her eyes sparkling. "You're the handsomest man I've ever seen."

"You must want something."

"Why must I want something?"

"That's the way you always begin when you want something you don't have."

"Well, I didn't want anything, but I'll think of something now."

"Where's Ardon?"

Ariel shrugged her shoulders and tucked her hair back up under the kerchief she wore. "Oh, he's over with the Levites. He and Phinehas are studying Moses' book, as always."

"I worry about your brother," Caleb said. "He's a fine soldier, but he thinks too much. That can be dangerous for a man of war."

"You think soldiers must be stupid? Why, you're not, and he's like you."

"No, he's more interested in the Lord than I am, I'm ashamed to say. He wants to know everything about God, and no man can ever know that. He just wants to be so righteous that I worry about it."

Ariel laughed. "I suppose you think I'm not religious enough."

"It wouldn't hurt you to have a little more religion."

Ariel slipped her arm in his, and the two walked together toward the tent. "I'm too much like you."

Caleb laughed. "I suppose that's true. That's why I call you Ariel. It suits you better—'the lioness of God.'"

"You think I'm vicious like a lion?"

"A little." As the two entered the tent, he turned and asked, "What about young Zuriel? Are you going to marry him?"

"I doubt it."

"Why not? He's a fine man. He has plenty of large herds. He'll have more when his father dies."

"He's boring."

"What do you want, to marry a dancer to keep you entertained? You're too choosy. I'm going to find Ardon."

"Don't take too long. We killed a lamb, and I'm cooking it the way you like best."

Caleb started toward the tents of the Levites, who were the keepers of the Law, but a thought came to him. He changed direction and threaded his way among the tents until he came to the tent of Achan, a man of his own tribe. He found Achan sitting in the shade of his tent eating, which was not unusual. *The man's a glutton and a drunkard,* Caleb thought, *but even so he's well liked. I don't understand it.*

"Achan, I'm looking for Othniel," Caleb called out. "Is he here?"

Achan scrambled to his feet. He was a short, chubby man with a red, good-natured face and a wealth of curly black hair, both on his head and on his chin. "I don't think he is."

Caleb snorted abruptly. "He's either here or he's not. Now, which is it?"

"He was here a while ago, but I don't know where he went."

"Yes you do. You're lying to me."

Achan tried desperately to avoid telling the truth, but Caleb had an eye like a hawk, and there was no hiding the truth from him.

"Well, I know he's your nephew, so I don't like to get him in trouble," Achan whined.

"You're going to be in trouble if you don't let me know everything. Now, where is he?"

"He's taken up with that woman from the tribe of Dan. Her name is Carphina."

"She's a married woman."

"I know it, Caleb, and her husband is a rough fellow. I tried to talk Othniel into staying here, but you know how he is."

"Yes, I know how it is. Listen to me, Achan. The next time he starts to do something like this, you let me know right away. I won't have my nephew acting like he does."

"But I can't be a talebearer."

"Would you prefer to have your back scratched with a whip?"

"No, I wouldn't."

"Then you mind what I say. He's my nephew, and he's not going to bring dishonor to my family. If his father were alive, he wouldn't be acting like this. Now he stays with you most of the time, so you're responsible for him."

"I can't do anything with him, Caleb. He's strong-willed. He laughed at me when I tried to correct him."

"He won't laugh at me," Caleb said shortly, then turned and walked away.

Achan swallowed hard and wiped the perspiration from his forehead. He was deathly afraid of Caleb, for he knew the old man had a temper like a wildfire. He considered trying to beat Caleb to the woman's tent to warn Othniel but decided against it, knowing that he couldn't cross this man.

"Othniel, you're in trouble this time," he muttered, then went back, sat down, and took a long swig from his jug of wine.

The Levites were kept apart from the other twelve tribes because they were different. God had commanded Moses to separate the tribe of Levi to be His special servants. They were to be the keepers of the Law, to furnish the priests to minister in the tabernacle, to make sacrifices, and to serve God alone.

Caleb spotted his son Ardon talking with his good friend Phinehas, the son of Eleazar, the high priest. "Ardon," he said, "come over here."

Ardon turned. "Just a minute, Father. We're not quite finished here."

"Yes, you are. Phinehas, you're going to ruin my son's mind, filling it full of religious things."

Phinehas was a tall man, lean and strong. He had a trim beard and a pair of steady dark eyes. He smiled at Caleb, who was one of his favorites. "Why, I'm surprised to hear you say that. Most men want their sons to be men of God."

"He's already that." Caleb was always mystified by the work the Levites did. "What do you do with this book that Moses has been writing all these years?"

"We're preserving it, Caleb," Phinehas said. "We're making sure that it's kept absolutely accurate. Every letter is gone over by at least half a dozen Levites. Our scribes work night and day to preserve the integrity of the Law."

Caleb listened and, after a pause, said, "Well, Moses approves it, so it has to be all right. Ardon, come with me. You can do your study with Phinehas later."

"Yes, Father." Ardon walked away with his father. Physically, he was much like Caleb—tall, strongly built, with black hair and the same hazel eyes, a wedge-shaped face, and a wide mouth. "What is it?"

Caleb's mind, however, was on Phinehas. "You know, that man is unusual."

"He has a great mind, Father."

"Wasn't talking about his mind. He's got a strong arm. Has he ever talked about how he killed Zimri and Cozbi?"

"No, he's never mentioned it. What happened?"

"I suppose you were too young to remember, but that devil Balaam polluted our people back when we were wandering in the desert. He sent a harlot named Cozbi to tempt one of our princes, a man named Zimri. Zimri brought her into the camp, right in the sight of everyone, and began to commit fornication with her. God was ready to kill us all for permitting such a thing, but your friend Phinehas grabbed up a spear, ran into the tent, and thrust them both through." Caleb's face was grim. "Twenty-four thousand people died in a plague because of that sin, but God said that Phinehas would never be forgotten among our people. I remember clearly what God said: '*I am making my covenant of peace with him. He and his descendants will have a covenant of a lasting priesthood, because he was zealous for the honor of his God and made atonement for the Israelites.*'"

"Now that you mention it, I remember it vaguely, but I'm glad you told me the full story."

"Phinehas is a great man, my son. Better than his grandfather Aaron, really."

"How can you say that? God spoke to Aaron face-to-face."

"Aaron also made the golden calves that nearly got us all destroyed, but that's enough about that. We're going to be leaving this place soon. I want you to go find Othniel and bring him to me."

"What's he done now?"

"About the worst thing a man can do," Caleb said grimly. He stopped and turned to face his son. "He's dallying with that whorish woman from the tribe of Dan, the one named Carphina. According to the Law, she ought to be stoned. Maybe she will be yet. Go get Othniel and drag him out of there."

Ardon shook his head, his face registering the disgust he felt. "Othniel ought to have better sense."

"He should have, but he doesn't. I wish his father had lived."

"Othniel's not interested in anything but pleasure, Father."

Caleb, distressed, chewed his lower lip. He examined the stub on his hand where the finger had been bitten off by a bear, as he often did when he was troubled. "He can change."

"He hasn't changed since he was fifteen-years-old. When his father died, he started going downhill. Besides, men don't change."

Caleb stared at his son, puzzled. "You really believe that, Ardon—that a man can't change?"

"You've lived many years, Father. You've had a lot of experience. How many have you seen change?"

Ardon's reply caused Caleb difficulty, and he couldn't answer. "Well, go get him," he said.

"I'll bring him back if I have to knock him on the head."

Caleb watched Ardon leave. Then he turned and walked back toward his tent. He studied the people as he walked through the camp, especially the men. *I wonder if this new generation will be any more faithful to God than the ones who died in the wilderness.* He was not the man of prayer Joshua was. Still, he had faith in God like a rock. "God," he said, "we're going to need you. We can't do it alone, so be our helper in this battle that's shaping up."

CHAPTER
6

A stream of disgust rose in Ardon as he made his way to the section occupied by the tribe of Dan. His thoughts were consumed with Othniel, and they were not pleasant ones. The two had grown up as childhood playmates and had been inseparable. But as they passed out of childhood into early manhood, their pathways began to divide. Othniel was interested in having a good time and began seeking out young women early. He was a handsome, witty, and charming young fellow and had no trouble attracting their attention. He had little interest in religion, or in Moses' book of the history of Israel, and this was a matter of concern to Caleb, who had become Othniel's foster father after Othniel's father, Kenaz, had died.

Ardon was greeted by several of the members of the tribe of Dan. They were an unruly, quarrelsome group, and Ardon remembered the prophecy that Jacob, the grandson of Abraham, had given on his deathbed. He had identified the nature of each of his sons, and of Dan he had said, "Dan will be a serpent by the roadside, a viper along the path, that bites the horse's heels so that its rider tumbles backward." A grim smile touched Ardon's broad lips. "Old Jacob got it right that time. Dan has some good soldiers, but they are not to be trusted."

He stopped one of the young men he knew and said,

"Where's the woman called Carphina?"

The young man grinned at him and pointed. "That red tent over there, but I think she's busy right now." He snickered, and a wicked light touched his eye. "Her husband's gone on a hunting trip, but you'll have to wait your turn with that one."

Disgusted with this news, Ardon left the young man, despising his lewd smile. He was proud of his family, the family of Caleb. And now to have their own flesh and blood dragging their name in the dust stirred his anger.

Nearing the red tent that the young man had pointed out, Ardon stopped and thought about what to do. Then he heard Othniel's voice and, without hesitating, stepped into the tent. It was gloomy inside after the bright sunlight, but light filtered in through several openings.

Othniel was lying on a couch with a woman by his side. They were both drinking, but when Othniel caught sight of Ardon, he exclaimed in surprise, "Ardon, what are you doing here!"

"What are *you* doing here?" Ardon snapped back, anger boiling up in him. "You're a disgrace, Othniel, dallying with a married woman."

The woman was dressed in a clingy outfit that appeared to be blue silk. She had adopted the Egyptian method of cosmetics with the coal outlining her eyes, and she had arched her eyebrows. Her full, pouting lips were red with rouge, and her voice was shrill as she demanded, "Who is this, Othniel?"

"He's my cousin," Othniel said, somewhat shamefaced.

"Well, he's got some nerve coming into my tent like this. Tell him to get out."

Othniel swallowed hard and rubbed his hand through his thick reddish hair. "I think it might be better if you leave, Ardon."

"Don't let him leave, Othniel. I would say he's all right."

Ardon whirled around to see that another woman had entered the tent. She was past the first days of youth and was a little heavy. Still, there was a seductive light in her eyes, and she smiled and edged closer to him. "Introduce me to your friend, Othniel."

"This is Danzia," Othniel said hurriedly. "She's a friend of Carphina."

"There's just four of us," Danzia said with an inviting smile. "Just the right number for a party. We're late, but we can start in, Ardon." She pressed against him and ran her hand across his cheek.

Ardon pushed her away disdainfully. It was not a hard push, but it was insulting.

The woman stared at him for a moment, her eyes burning. "You think you're too good for me?"

Ignoring the woman, Ardon turned and said, "Othniel, we're leaving."

"Too good for me!" the woman called Danzia shrilled in a piercing voice. "I heard about you. Othniel said you're so good that you wouldn't eat an egg laid on the Sabbath. A holy man."

"Close your mouth," Ardon said sternly without even turning to face her. He took a step forward and said, "Othniel, you're going one way or another." He heard the woman leave the tent shouting curses at him, but his eyes were fixed on Othniel. "Get up!"

"Wait a minute, Ardon, I'm not ready to go yet."

Ardon stared down at the young man with whom he had been so close for so many years. Bitterness rose in him, and he shook his head, a painful expression on his face. "Don't you have any shame?" he demanded, his voice cutting like a blade. "My father's given you everything. He's treated you like his own son, and what's the thanks you show him? You make our name a disgrace in Israel. . . ."

Othniel dropped his head and hunched his shoulders. It was almost as if he were receiving physical blows. Ardon continued to lash at him with his words.

Finally Othniel shook the woman's hand away from his arm

and muttered, "All right, all right, I'm coming. You don't have to make such a bad thing out of it."

"It is a bad thing," Ardon said grimly. He gave one disdainful look at the woman and said, "You have a husband. That should be enough for you."

Ignoring Carphina's curses, Ardon waited for Othniel, who grabbed his cloak, slipped on his sandals, and then shamefacedly crept out the door of the tent.

As soon as they stepped outside, Ardon became cautious. The woman he had rejected was there with three men, big fighting men.

"That's the one. He said I wasn't good enough for him and he hit me."

"Nobody hit you," Ardon said, not taking his eyes from the three men. "We're leaving."

The three burly men all carried knives in their belts, and one of them had a club in his hand. He, apparently, was the oldest, and he scowled. "You're not going anywhere, fellow. You can't treat our sister like a whore."

"Back off," Ardon said. He had a knife in his belt, but he did not want to enter into a knife fight with three sturdy warriors. He started toward them, hoping to break their concentration, but as he did, the one with the club raised it and struck at him. Ardon's reactions were swift. He ducked his head so that the club went over it, and when the man grunted with the force of his blow, Ardon struck him a hard blow right where the neck joins the head. With a muted cry, the man sprawled on the ground. Ardon scooped up the club. He held it securely and turned to face the other two. They had separated now and were coming at him from different angles. One of them had drawn a knife.

"Put that knife away," Ardon demanded. He had a hard time keeping his eyes on both men. Suddenly Othniel yelled and threw himself on the one who had not yet drawn his knife. Out of the corner of his eye, Ardon saw the two of them go down kicking and fighting. He knew that Othniel had little experience in this kind of fight, but at least he kept the fellow occupied. Ardon faced the knife bearer and advanced toward him, holding the glittering blade before him like an experienced fighter. He sneered, "You're going to regret this when you wake up in the morning."

The Danite lunged forward, but he was muscular and slow-moving. With one quick swipe of the club, Ardon struck his wrist. The man bellowed with pain, and with another swipe the club hit him in the side of the head and he dropped to the earth like a felled ox. Ardon swung around to see that the third brother had knocked Othniel out, falling down himself in the process. The brother was getting to his feet, but before he could rise, Ardon swung the club again. He did not strike to kill, for he was well aware that Israel needed all of her soldiers, especially tough ones like this. The club made a dull sound like striking a melon, and the third brother rolled his eyes up and sank back to the ground.

The woman named Danzia stared at her brothers, let out a screech, and threw herself at Ardon. She was mindless with rage, and not wanting to hurt her, Ardon simply grasped her by the back of the arm and shoved her hard enough to send her sprawling on the ground. "You do that again and you'll be sorry," he said. He watched for a moment, but as the woman got up, her face pale with fury, he went over and grabbed Othniel, whose eyes were open, staring blankly. Ardon yanked him to his feet and said, "We've had enough fun for one day."

As the two made their way back toward where the tribe of Judah was set up, Othniel walked with his head down. From time to time he would glance at Ardon, but not having words to excuse himself, he kept silent all the way to Caleb's tent.

Ariel was outside stirring some food in a pot over an open fire. She stood right up and stared at the pair. "Well, you found the wandering lamb, I see."

"He's not a lamb." Ardon shook his head. "Lambs have more sense."

"What have you been into, Othniel?" Ariel demanded.

His face flamed and she stared at him hard. "It must be bad if you can't talk about it."

"Go on in. My father's waiting to talk to you," Ardon commanded.

The pair watched as Othniel slunk inside the tent, and soon they heard Caleb's voice, angry and harsh.

"What'd he do, Ardon?" Ariel asked.

"What he always does. Only this time it was even worse. He was in Carphina's tent."

"Why, she's nothing but a harlot!"

"Pretty much so. I'm surprised her husband hasn't beaten her to death before this."

"Father is so hurt by this," Ariel said. "He always loved Othniel's father, and he's poured himself out on Othniel. Why can't that idiot act like a human being?"

"He's got a bad strain in him from somewhere. Maybe from his mother. I don't know. In any case, we had to wrestle with some fighting men to get out of there, and Othniel didn't last ten seconds. He's not going to make much of a soldier. I'm leaving. I don't want to have to look at him anymore."

Ariel watched her brother go, then returned to the pot. She listened to Caleb's angry words to Othniel. When the young man finally stumbled out of the tent, she said, "Well, I hear you had a romance, cousin."

"Don't you start on me, Ariel," Othniel said. His face was pale, and he turned to leave.

But Ariel jumped up and blocked his path, saying, "Tell me about it. I'll bet it was a romantic affair. Did you sing love songs to her? I hear she's a real beauty, that woman is. A woman of virtue."

Othniel didn't move but just ground his teeth while Ariel mocked him. When he could stand it no longer, he turned and ran away. Ariel called after him, loud enough for everyone to hear, "Here he is—the great lover, the seducer of married women."

Laughter followed Othniel, and he heard catcalls and jeers from the women who had stopped their work to watch him.

As soon as Othniel disappeared, Ariel went inside the tent. She found her father seated on a rug, staring at the sword that was before him. He had evidently been sharpening it, and she went and stood over him. "I heard what you said to Othniel. You were pretty hard on him."

"Not as hard as I should have been. We're going into battle very soon. What kind of a soldier will he make? He's a weakling."

Ariel knelt down and put her hand on her father's shoulder. "I know you have a great affection for him."

"I used to, but I'm fast losing it. What a terrible mess he's made of his life." He shook his head sadly. "Why are some men strong and others weak?"

"No one knows the answer to that except God. You're not going to give up on him, are you?"

"I can't do that. Israel needs every soldier she can get. Besides, at times I see some of my brother Kenaz in him. He was a good man, and there's got to be some of that goodness in his son. But I may have to half kill him to bring it out."

Achan saw with one glance that his young friend Othniel was miserable. "You look like you just fell into a well full of scorpions. What's the matter?"

"Nothing."

Achan was eating from a bunch of dried grapes. He stuffed his mouth full and studied Othniel. He had become very fond of this young man, feeling almost like an older brother to him. The two of them liked their pleasure, and though Achan had a family, he still enjoyed the company of the younger man.

Achan's four children swarmed around him. They were very fond of Othniel too and pestered him all at the same time to take them to the river. Another wanted him to play a game with them. Achan watched and said, "You know how to win the hearts of children—" he hesitated—"and women also. Is that the problem?"

"I'm a fool, Achan." Achan listened as Othniel began to talk. The words tumbled from his lips, and his face grew red.

"Why do I do things like that, Achan? She's a married woman and no good. If her husband had caught us, he would have killed me. He may come after me anyway. Everybody knew what was happening."

"He wouldn't dare attack the nephew of our great leader Caleb, but I expect you'd better stay away from him."

"When a man's angry enough and when he's been wronged, he'll do anything."

"Well, the thing to do," Achan said, "is not to let the whole world know what you're doing. If you want a woman, just be sure you don't let anyone know about it. A lot of that goes on in the camp."

"Not with Caleb and Joshua. And Ardon, he's so holy he wouldn't think of touching a woman."

Achan munched on the dried grapes thoughtfully, then shook his head. "Ardon's just like the rest of us. We're all sinners. I am, you are, and Ardon is. He just hasn't found out about it yet."

Othniel laughed bitterly. "You're a scoundrel, Achan."

"Not really. I'm just weak. Nothing wrong with being weak. Even Moses is weak."

Othniel stared at Achan. "What do you mean by that?"

"He isn't a perfect man, and we know a few things he did that were wrong. He admitted it. You've heard it. When he struck the rock instead of speaking to it, he said God didn't like that, so He's not going to let Moses go into the Promised Land. You see? He's weak."

Othniel found something wrong with the reasoning, but he was so depressed he did not care to argue. "We're going across the Jordan pretty soon—as soon as Moses leaves. That's what I hear."

"I can't wait to get there. Just think of all the spoil we'll get. Silver, gold, precious stones." Achan's eyes gleamed, and he winked lewdly. "And, of course, there will be women available."

"You'd better not let Joshua catch you at anything like that."

"Don't worry," Achan said. "He won't catch me. I'm a sly fellow. No one can catch me when I set out to do a thing!"

CHAPTER
7

As Othniel made his way back toward camp after hunting, his attention was caught by a cloud of blackbirds over to his right that wheeled up and away into the distance. He watched them until they became tiny dots, and as he did, he was aware of the song of a bird. He stood very still, searching the desert before him. A tiny bird appeared. It was a color of blue he had never seen before. Othniel thought quietly, *What have you got to be so happy about? You've got enemies all around you, including me. You may not live to see the sunset.* Still, the incantation of the small bird sweetly filled the space that Othniel shared with him.

Othniel laughed aloud at his own foolishness. "Why do I think these things?" he said. "People would think I was crazy if I told them about it." He continued on past the tiny stream that fed the camp. The sunlight was fine and fresh, flashing against the distant mountains, and the smell of woodsmoke and cooking food laced the thin air. He hurried faster, for he was hungry. In one hand he carried a bow, and a quiver of arrows was across his back. In his other hand he bore the carcass of a small deer-like creature whose name he did not know. His luck had been good in his early-morning hunting. As the camp came into sight, he broke into a run. He loved the morning, and he ran as hard as he could, although somewhat awkwardly because of the deer and the bow. But there was a joy in it for him.

He needed some joy in his life, for ever since Ardon had caught him with Carphina, he had been depressed. Caleb's words had seared him, bringing him a sense of shame he had never known before. That had been three days ago, and he had behaved himself marvelously well since then. He knew it would take more than three days, however, to convince Caleb and Ardon, and even Ariel, that he was sorry for his misdeed.

Slowing down, he walked past the outlying tents, speaking occasionally to those who greeted him. He was a popular young fellow, well liked for his good singing voice and for his cheerful disposition. The soldiers had less respect for him, however, for although he was a competent enough archer, he did not give himself to the discipline that was required to make a tough warrior.

Weaving a serpentine path between the tents, he came up behind Caleb's tent, but hearing voices, he stopped before stepping around to the front. He recognized them as Ariel and her suitor, young Zuriel. He hesitated, then peered around the corner of the tent. The pair of them, he saw, were facing each other, and evidently Zuriel was upset. Othniel saw that Ariel was tormenting the young man, as she usually did. He had discovered long ago that she was very good at such things, and he himself had often been the target of her caustic tongue. Zuriel was pleading with her.

"I don't know why you won't become my wife right away, Ariel. I'd be a good husband to you."

"Would you really, Zuriel? What would you do to be so good?"

Othniel grinned at the question, knowing that Zuriel would have no answer for it, and he was right.

"Why, I'd see to it that you had plenty of food, clothes to wear . . ." Zuriel bogged down, unable to add to the list.

"But I have all those things now, Zuriel."

Once again Othniel grinned. *Don't try to match wits with her.*

You don't have the mind for it, Zuriel.

The argument went on for some time, and Othniel was not surprised that Zuriel got the worst of it. As he pleaded more and more pathetically, Ariel took mercy on him and sent him away. "I don't want to talk about it now. I'll talk later," she said with a shrug of her shoulders.

Othniel watched the young man as he trudged away, his shoulders stooped and his head down. Stepping out from behind the tent, he approached silently, leaned forward, and whispered, "You're going to lose your man if you treat him like that."

Startled, Ariel leaped to one side and whirled about. "Don't sneak up on me like that!"

Ignoring her anger, Othniel held up the small deer he was carrying. "I brought you a present."

"Well, why don't you dress it out before you bring it to me?"

Othniel liked fire in a woman, but sometimes he thought Ariel had a bit too much. "I'm sorry, Queen Ariel. I didn't realize I was doing something wrong."

"You didn't bring it to me. You brought it to my father. You're trying to make up to him for making such a fool out of yourself."

Ariel was too close to the truth for comfort. Othniel shook his head and changed the subject back again to Zuriel. "You don't need Zuriel for a husband," he said.

"What do you know about it?"

"He's not romantic, and you are."

"What are you talking about?"

"You know what I'm talking about. You want a fellow who will do daring deeds and will sing love songs for you and tell you how beautiful you are. Zuriel will tell you how many sheep he has, but he'll never do those things."

"And you would, I suppose?"

"Oh, most definitely. As a matter of fact, I'll do it right

now." He dropped the deer, fell on his knees, and spread his hands out. He sang a comical love song he had invented a short time before. As he got up, he saw that she was laughing.

"You're a fool," she said.

"Oh yes, but a romantic fool. You need ..." He leaned forward—so close he could see the tiny golden flecks in her eyes—and whispered, "You need a man who will make you feel like a woman."

"I do feel like a woman!"

"You need a man who will do ... this." He pulled her close and kissed her squarely on the lips.

Ariel was taken off guard. He was strong enough to hold her for a moment, but then she pushed him away and shook her head with disgust. "Go on back to your loose women. I'd more happily marry a lizard than you!"

"You may think so, but you've always been in love with me. I knew it when we were twelve years old."

Ariel could not help laughing. "Well, you certainly have confidence. I like that in a man, but yours is all misplaced. Go find yourself a woman who has nothing to offer but herself."

"What else can a woman give but herself?"

"Go away, Othniel. I'm tired of listening to you." She turned and walked away, and he called after her. "I'll clean the deer for you. You can think about me when you eat it."

For years Moses had worked constantly to write the book that would be the guide for Israel. He was now at the end of his life, but with death at hand, his heart was burdened. He well knew that the people of Israel were prone to doubt the living God who had brought them out of Egypt. And now as he sat writing out the last few words of his testament, God guided his hand with prophetic insight.

Moses' hand trembled as he wrote the words.

... if you do not obey the Lord your God and do not carefully follow all his commands and decrees I am giving you today, all these curses will come upon you and overtake you. . . .

The Lord will cause you to be defeated before your enemies. You will come at them from one direction but flee from them in seven, and you will become a thing of horror to all the kingdoms on earth. . . .

At midday you will grope about like a blind man in the dark. You will be unsuccessful in everything you do; day after day you will be oppressed and robbed, with no one to rescue you.

On and on went the terrible words of the Lord, and Moses' hands kept trembling as he wrote it upon the parchment with a rush dipped in blue fish ink. His whole body was drenched in sweat. He lifted his hands in agony. "I can do no more! I cannot bear the thought of Israel being ground under the feet of God!"

Moses wept and then after a long time he prayed, "God, give me some hope that I may give it to your people."

For a long time it was silent. Then God spoke again. Moses picked up his stylus and began to write to the people.

For you are a people holy to the Lord your God. Out of all the peoples on the face of the earth, the Lord has chosen you to be his treasured possession.

Moses continued writing under the direction of God, but finally he rose up and put away the writing equipment, the ink and the stylus, and the parchment. He put the parchment with others upon which he had let the ink dry, and now he gathered them all together, holding them with trembling hands. These were the records God had given him. Even going back to the story of Adam and Eve and tracing the history of God's dealing with men. This holy book that Moses had written with his own hand would perish, but he had trained the scribes of Israel to make copies of his work and to take monumental efforts to keep the text exactly as God had given it to Moses himself.

"Oh, Israel, your hope must be in this book, for it alone tells us how our God should be worshiped and served."

For a long moment he hesitated, then turned and left the

tent. He found Joshua and Caleb waiting outside and noticed
that both of them were pale. He smiled and handed the book
to Joshua. "Joshua, be strong and anchor Israel to the book. My
time has come, and I must leave you."

Both Joshua and Caleb began to weep. Moses extended his
arms and embraced them both. He was still a powerful, strong
man, though a hundred twenty years old. He held them tightly
and said, "My time is over, but your time is just beginning."

Joshua cried out, "Moses, my master, my teacher, I cannot
bear the thought!"

"Every man serves God in his own generation. As our father
Abraham did and our father Isaac and our father Jacob, so I
have tried to serve the great and almighty Jehovah. Now, know
of the special love I have had for you two." For a long time
Moses stayed with the two men, encouraging them, until he
stopped and said, "I must go."

"Let me go with you, master," Joshua cried.

"You are the new leader of Israel. One day you will join me,
but now it is time for me to go meet with my God."

Moses turned from the two and left. Once he glanced back
at the tabernacle, but he felt very low when he saw it, so he set
his face and turned away.

The entire congregation of Israel had gathered as Moses
made his way, and cries went up from all the people, but Moses
did not stop. He headed straight toward Mount Pisgah, and
there the eye of every man and woman and young person in
Israel watched as he ascended the mountain. The sunlight was
pouring down in golden beams, and Joshua, Caleb, the high
priest, and all the tribes watched as the powerful figure grew
smaller.

Joshua was trembling, for he knew what lay before him, and
he wanted to cry out and run after the man who had been his
master for so many years. But he knew he must not. At last the

figure disappeared in the distance so that even the keenest-eyed Israelite could not see him.

And then Joshua turned to Caleb, tears streaming down his face. "Never again," he whispered, "will we see a man like Moses!"

CHAPTER

8

Achan was running his stubby fingers over a cloth when Ardon appeared. Under his breath he muttered, "How unpleasant Ardon looks."

Othniel, who had just finished eating, was sitting cross-legged, his back against the tent pole. The weather was fine, so the sides of the tent were up, and he had been simply enjoying doing nothing. At Achan's words he straightened up, got to his feet, and nodded. "Hello, Ardon. Good to see you."

Ardon stopped and gave Achan a brief glance, then put his eyes on Othniel. "I'm going to trade with those Amalachites at their village. We're running low on grain. We need more for making bread."

"Do you want me to go with you?"

"No, but I want you to behave yourself while I'm gone. Stay away from women."

Othniel's face flushed and he said nothing, only nodded.

"You'd better be careful," Achan said. "I've done some trading with them—just a week ago, as a matter of fact. They'll steal your eye teeth if you're not careful."

"I'll see to it they don't."

Both Achan and Othniel watched as Ardon turned abruptly and strode away.

"My, he's an unpleasant fellow!" Achan exclaimed.

"He's all right. He's just serious."

"He takes his religion far too seriously if you ask me."

"That's a good thing. I think you and I could learn from him."

"No, he could learn from us. You grew up with him and you know him. He wasn't always like this."

"That's right, he wasn't. He was the best playmate I ever had when we were children—we were just boys together. It was lots of fun. I don't know why he started changing."

"It happens. He got infected with God."

Othniel laughed, his teeth white against his bronze skin. "You make religion sound like a sickness. Something you can catch and suffer from."

"Why, I never thought of it like that, but that's close enough."

"You're a terrible fellow, Achan," Othniel said, turning fondly toward his friend. "I don't know what's going to become of you."

"I'm going to do well enough. I'm a good trader. I know how to do the other fellow before he does me."

"Do you think that's honest?"

"Of course it's honest. Let him watch out for himself. That's what I say when I trade with people. Of course, I don't say that to their faces." Achan grinned broadly, his smooth face beaming. "You and I have got the right idea about religion. Ardon spends too much time with the priests and the scribes."

Something about the conversation made Othniel uneasy. He did not like to hear anybody talk as lightly about God as Achan did. He had a genuine affection for the round little man and his family, but he knew Achan's reputation as a sharp trader, and his word was not always good. He was not terribly dishonest, but he was still not above taking advantage of people.

"I don't agree with you. I think Ardon's a good man. He does a lot better than I do."

"Ah, but he's afraid of God. He's afraid if he commits a sin, God'll send down a lightning bolt and kill him."

"Well, God's done that before. You've heard the history of our people. Remember how the plagues came when we disobeyed God?"

"That was a long time ago. Now me, I have an arrangement with God."

Othniel stared at Achan. "What do you mean, 'an arrangement'? How can you have an arrangement with God?"

"Well, I do the best I can, and that's all any man can do."

"There's something wrong with that kind of thinking. And besides, you don't do the best you can."

"Well, I do fairly well. I'm no worse than others. God won't strike me down. I'm a sinner, but then we all are, Othniel. After all, we're all God has to work with. A man doesn't live very long," he said woefully, "so that's why I say eat all you can, drink all you can, enjoy life today. Have the priest make the sacrifices, and that's it."

"There's got to be more to it than that, Achan."

"No, there's not. There's only a little deal I've been trying to make with that thief over from the tribe of Benjamin. He thinks he's going to do me in, but I'll show him. And I'll show you how to handle life so you get the most out of it!"

Ardon made poor time. The sun was nearly down by the time he got to the Amalachite village. He had brought only a dozen sheep, but that was because sheep were hard to drive. They were prone to wander, and now he kicked one of them with irritation, yelling, "Get on! You're the stupidest sheep I ever saw, and that goes for the rest of you!"

Ardon laughed at himself. "I must be going crazy talking to sheep. Everybody knows they're the stupidest animals in the world."

As he approached the village, he saw a figure coming toward

him, and his eyes narrowed. It was a young woman with jet-black hair and dark, lustrous eyes. She wore the garb of the desert people, which was a simple frock, and he saw that she was wearing rings on all her fingers and one in her nose.

"Greetings, stranger," she said. "You're out late."

"It's been a hard trip. I'm trying to find Abib."

"That's my father. He's the chief of this village. My name is Keli."

"I'm here to trade with your father."

"I'll take you to him. Have you had a long journey?"

The young woman strolled along beside Ardon. The sun was casting its reddish beams down, and Ardon saw that she was well-formed and had a ready smile. He compared all women with his sister Ariel, and he realized what he had not realized before, that this woman, even though she came from a wild tribe, was a rose of the desert. He found himself speaking easily with her. She had a free and easy way about her. When they arrived at the village, she introduced him to her father.

Abib was a tall, rangy man with the same black hair as his daughter and piercing black eyes. "You are welcome, sir," he said. "You will eat with us—a humble meal to be sure, but we welcome you."

Abib was courteous enough, and the meal they sat down to was well done. "Your wife is a good cook."

"I lost my wife two years ago. I haven't taken another yet. My daughter takes care of me. She is a good cook."

"I could fry up leather and you'd think it was good," Keli said, laughing.

"She's too modest," Abib said. "Now, everyone's curious about your people. We've heard that Moses has left you—Moses your great leader is gone."

"That's true enough. Joshua is now our commander."

"We have heard of him. He's a mighty warrior. Do you think you will stay in this country?"

The question was asked cautiously, and Ardon was aware

that Abib, like all the other dwellers in this land, were fearful of the Israelites.

"You're in no danger, Abib. We'll be crossing the Jordan and moving into the land of Canaan very soon."

Abib stared at him. "That's a tall order. There are walled cities over there, and they don't take kindly to strangers."

"God has told us that the land will belong to us."

"What about the people that own it now?" Abib asked.

"They don't own it any longer. God has given it to us."

The young woman had not eaten with the men. That was not customary, but she was bringing a fresh plate of sugared dates, which she set before them. "Will our guest stay the night, Father?"

"Of course!"

"I will fix him a place out in the stable."

"That would be kind of you," Ardon said.

The young woman left, and Abib fired questions one after another. He was a keen-witted man, his wit sharpened by the hard life in this country. At last he said cautiously, "Tell me a little more about your god. They say you believe he is the true god."

"He is the God of all gods," Ardon said firmly. "He delivered our people from slavery, from bondage in Egypt. He promised our father Abraham that He would give us a land flowing with milk and honey, and now we're about to receive it."

Abib listened as Ardon traced the history of the Hebrews. It was a fascinating history, but at last he said, "You're weary, I'm sure, after your journey. We will agree on the terms tomorrow, but your animals are fine and we have plenty of grain, so there will be no problem."

The men got to their feet, and Abib added, "Keli, show our friend to his bed for the night."

"Yes, Father."

The two men bowed to each other, and Ardon followed the

young woman outside. She led him to a spacious outbuilding, and when they stepped inside, she said, "Visitors often sleep here. This will be your bed."

"Thank you, Keli."

"You're welcome, sir." She smiled and waited for him to speak. When he said good night, she bowed low, then left the stables.

Ardon was not tired. He paced back and forth, thinking of what the future held. His mind was filled with the promises of God. He had studied every word that God had given Moses about the land they were to inhabit. But God had made it very clear that it would not be handed to them on a platter. They would have to fight for it. Ardon had devoted a tremendous amount of time studying what little information he could learn about the land. He had spoken with those who had actually been there, and he and his father had plotted, as well as they could, on how the land could be taken.

Eventually he sat down on a bench that was covered with a mat filled with straw. His mind was occupied with the problems that lay ahead for his people when the young woman entered again. She had a finely woven blanket in her hand. "It gets cold at night. I thought you might need this."

"That was thoughtful of you." Ardon took the blanket and smiled at her. To his surprise, she sat down beside him on the bed.

"We don't get many visitors here. Tell me more about what you do, about your people."

"What do you want to know?"

"Oh, anything. Everyone in this country is fascinated by the Hebrews. We heard about how you've won great victories over so many."

"That's true enough."

"Well, what about you? Do you have many wives?" she asked.

"No, I don't have any."

"Not one? A handsome fellow like you?" Keli laughed when she saw the surprise in his eyes at her bold words. "You have to forgive me. We're simple people here. Men marry young and women even younger. I'm surprised you're not married. Do you have a sweetheart?"

"No."

"Why not?"

Ardon was amused by her straightforwardness. She was turned slightly toward him, her lips parted, anticipation in her eyes. "I have been studying a great deal about the history of our people," he said, "and I've been training to be a warrior. It takes all my time."

"Warriors have wives, don't they?"

"Sometimes they do."

"I believe you must be afraid of women."

Ardon's feelings were hurt. "Of course I'm not afraid of women!"

"Don't be angry. I was only teasing." Keli turned to him fully and leaned forward. They were sitting so close he could feel the pressure of her arm against his. It stirred him and he felt a disturbing sense of her beauty.

Keli leaned against him, and the fullness of her figure touched his arm. "You are such a tall, strong fellow. Are all the Hebrews as large as you?"

"Some are—some aren't."

The moment stretched out. Ardon did not know what to make of her. She was almost like a child in her innocence, but there was nothing childlike about the curves of her full figure or the way in which her eyes took him in. He found himself ill at ease, but something else was working in him, and he said, "You are an attractive young woman, Keli. You must have many suitors."

"I've had a few, but I haven't chosen one yet. Most of them are so dull. I like a little excitement in a man."

Ardon's lips broke into a rash grin. He could be a daring

fellow at times, though this usually found its expression in battle or in the games he played with the young men. The young
woman was tempting indeed. She was anointed with some sort
of strong perfume that went right to him. He pulled her close.
"You're an enticing woman, and you shouldn't be tempting
men."

Keli laughed softly. She did not draw away as Ardon had
expected but put her arms around his neck and pulled his head
down. "I like tall men," she whispered, then put her lips on his.
The softness of her lips and the pressure of her body against
him stirred Ardon. He was suddenly aware of his loneliness,
and knowing he was doing the wrong thing, he put his arms
around her and pulled her closer. She did not pull away, and he
felt a rush of indescribable feelings. He knew he should pull
away, but somehow he could not. Ardon, like all young men,
had had his dreams of women. It had disturbed him deeply that
it was such a struggle to forget such dreams, and now as he
kissed the young woman, she clung to him with a willingness
that shocked him. His desire rose like a howling tempest.
Everything in him urged him to take her. He knew that she
would not turn him away. He was on the verge of completely
giving in, but he struggled with his impulses and wrenched himself away and stood up.

"What's the matter?" Keli said, staring up at him, her
mouth soft and her lips parted.

"You'd better go back into your house."

Keli rose to her feet, humiliation on her face. She was being
rejected, and Ardon did not know how to find words to soften
that. It took all the strength he had to say no, and he felt
unclean and filled with sin because of what had happened. "Go
into the house," he said almost harshly.

Keli straightened herself angrily. Her voice was stiff with
suppressed rage. "If you're afraid of a woman, how do you think
you can defeat the enemies of Israel?" She turned and walked
out of the stable without a backward glance.

Ardon was aware that his knees felt weak, and a wave of nausea swept over him. He had come within an inch of committing fornication with this woman. She had been willing, and he recognized in himself that same sort of willingness. He sat down on the bed, aware that his hands were trembling, and he lowered his face into his hands and began to murmur, "Forgive me, God, for thinking such thoughts!"

"... and so you see the sacrifices are not all the same. Some are of grain and some are of oil, but the most important of all is the burnt offering—a living animal killed and consumed on the fire."

Phinehas broke off, for he saw that Ardon's eyes were distant. "Are you listening to me, Ardon?" he asked.

"What? Oh ... yes, of course."

"No you weren't. Your mind was somewhere else."

"I'm sorry. I guess I am a bit woolly-headed today." Desperately Ardon tried to throw himself into the heart of the lesson. "You know," he blurted out, "it must have been wonderful to hear God speak directly. Your grandfather Aaron did, didn't he?"

"Yes, he did. God visited him, but not as often as He visited Moses. My grandfather told me about it many times."

"I wish God would speak to me."

"We all wish that," Phinehas said, smiling, "but that's one thing Moses' book is about. God may not speak to us out of a burning bush, but He's spoken to Moses, and Moses copied His words down, and now we can read in the Book what God demands."

Phinehas, the grandson of the great Aaron, was the high priest from the house of Levi, and he knew the Law. He had actually helped Moses with the Book, going over it and checking it carefully. He and Ardon were very close, and Phinehas had often said, "That young man Ardon is my best student. He will be a true man of God."

Now, however, Phinehas studied the youthful face of Ardon and saw that he was troubled. "What's the matter, friend? You can tell me."

"No I can't."

"Of course you can. You can tell me anything."

Ardon's face was swept by a powerful emotion. His words did not flow easily as they usually did. When he tried to speak he could only stutter. "There was this . . . this young woman . . . don't you see, and I . . . I was . . . interested in her . . ."

Phinehas listened as Ardon described his encounter with the young woman. He had a great affection for Ardon, as he had for his father, Caleb, and for the entire family.

Ardon finished by saying, "I must be the worst sinner in Israel to have such thoughts."

"Of course you're not."

"I tell you I nearly took her, Phinehas. I was that close."

"And you think that makes you the worst sinner in Israel? Don't you think other men have had that kind of temptation?"

"I don't care about other men. I hate myself for what I almost did."

"You've got something wrong in your mind about this thing," Phinehas said quietly. "Listen to me now, friend. You are a man. I am a man. I am the high priest of Israel. Do you not think I have had this feeling, this temptation, to commit fornication?"

Ardon stared openmouthed. "You? You've had trouble with feelings like this?"

"Of course I have. All men do. Don't think you're something unusual. Moses never spoke of it that I know of, but I'm sure he had the same feelings. Why, our fathers Abraham and Isaac and Jacob, they all had to struggle with temptation, many temptations." He smiled and put his hand on Ardon's arm. "And I'm not sure right now that fornication is the worst sin."

"What could be worse than that?"

"Pride. Doubt of God. Things that nobody can see and go on inside your heart. These would be worse."

Phinehas could see that the young man was suffering with his guilt. "You've got to learn to be honest with yourself and with God. You are a man. You're going to be tempted to do wrong. At times you may even give in to that temptation. That doesn't mean you're the worst sinner in Israel, my brother. It simply means that you're on a pilgrimage. On a pilgrimage a man stumbles, he falls, he cuts his knees, he gets scars. But if he loves God, he'll get up, scars and all, and fall forward. Then God has promised to be with him. Now, we will talk about this later, but you must stop beating yourself up."

"I'll try, Phinehas, but it's hard. I want to be a good man."

"No, you want to be a *perfect* man, and that man has not lived since Adam. Determine to be obedient to God and make up your mind when you fail that you won't quit."

Ardon studied the face of the priest and knew that he was right. He always was! "I'll try, Phinehas. I'll do my best."

"I've decided to send some men to spy out the land, Caleb." Joshua had called Caleb into his tent. Now, looking very serious, Joshua abruptly added, "I'm telling you this because I'm going to send Ardon and Othniel to do the job."

Caleb wrinkled his brow. "I understand Ardon. He's a fine soldier, but Othniel—you'd better think twice about him. Why would you choose him? He's never shown any signs of being responsible."

"I've never told you this, but your brother Kenaz saved my life one time."

"I didn't know that. He never spoke of it."

"I'm sure he didn't. He was a modest fellow. We were hunting together and a lion came out. I was caught totally helpless. Kenaz stood his ground and sent an arrow straight into the lion's open mouth. It killed him instantly. That lion would have destroyed me. I tried many times to thank him, but every time he just laughed. You know how he was."

"That sounds like him all right. He was a good man. I wish Othniel were more like him."

"Well, I think I owe Kenaz something. Besides that, I think I see some potential in Othniel. I may be wrong, but I see a good man under that woman-chasing exterior. I want to give him a chance to become a man. So we'll send the two of them out together. It'll be all right. Ardon will keep an eye on him. You talk to him."

"Joshua has given me a mission, and he's chosen you two to carry it out."

Ardon and Othniel stood before Caleb. They had been brought in immediately, and now they listened as Caleb said, "Joshua wants to get some idea about the city of Jericho. It's the most powerful city in our way. We can't conquer the land until Jericho is conquered. Joshua wants to know more about it. How many soldiers are there? What kinds of weapons do they have? Are they good soldiers? The things we need to know that would help us."

Othniel shifted uncomfortably. "Did he really say I was to go, Uncle?"

"Yes."

"I don't see why. I'm not much of a soldier."

"Joshua is the commander in chief, Othniel. You'll go, and you, Ardon, will keep an eye on him. Joshua is putting a lot of trust in you, and so am I."

"I'll do it, Father," Ardon said. He felt a gush of relief that he was able to do something to wipe out the sinful feelings that had been his since he had nearly fallen to the wiles of the Amalachite woman. He said, "Tell us everything you want to know."

The two young men listened. After a while Caleb said,

"You'll leave at dawn tomorrow. Make sure your weapons are ready. Joshua and I are depending on you two, so be faithful."

As the two young men left, Ardon was exultant, but he saw that Othniel was glum. "What's the matter with you, Othniel? This is the chance of a lifetime!"

CHAPTER

9

Ariel closely watched Ardon prepare to leave on his mission. Caleb had told her the sort of mission it was, and she had asked him if it would be dangerous. He had replied brusquely, "Of course it's dangerous. Every mission in a war is dangerous. Now, go away and don't bother your brother."

Ariel ignored Caleb's order, however, and stayed to talk to her brother. "I'm worried about you, Ardon."

Ardon looked up, surprised. "What are you worried about?"

"You could be hurt. It's a dangerous thing you're going to do."

Ardon came over and put his hand under Ariel's chin. The two were very close, and he studied her face with a smile. "It's exactly what I need."

"Something's been bothering you lately. What is it?"

Ardon was not surprised at her ability to read his moods. "Oh, nothing, really."

"I believe you are troubled. You can tell me." She frowned. "It's not a woman, is it?"

"No, not a woman," Ardon said.

Ariel stared at him. "You said that too quickly. I believe it is a woman. Who is she?"

Ardon was uncomfortable with the conversation. "You're too curious. There's nothing wrong with me. It'll be good for me to go on this trip."

Ariel knew she had touched a sore spot, and that made her unhappy. She had long wondered why Ardon had not yet taken a bride. He was twenty-five, and many young men were married and had families by his age. But he had not shown the same interest in women as their cousin Othniel had. Thinking of Othniel made Ariel shake her head. "I don't know why Joshua chose Othniel to go with you. You need a hard, tough soldier so you can protect each other."

"Joshua knows best."

"What good will Othniel be? All he can do is sing songs, eat, and romance loose women."

"Don't be so hard on him."

"You're hard on him yourself. I've heard you lecture him about such things."

Ardon remembered the conversation he had had with Phinehas. The priest had said something very like this. Ardon had been thinking of it ever, since with a troubled mind. He had always been so sure of himself. That he was right and Othniel was wrong. Now the close encounter he had had with the young Amalachite woman was troublesome to him, and he said in defense of Othniel, "He'll grow out of it."

"Grow out of it? He's twenty-one years old, Ardon. He's not growing out of anything. He's getting worse. Why don't you ask Father to let you take somebody else? Take Menaz. He's a fine soldier."

"He would have been my choice, but it's not for a soldier to question his commanding officer. I've got to go."

Leaning over, he kissed her on the cheek and left.

She called out after him, "He'll probably get you killed!"

———

"I never saw anything like that!" Othniel stared at the mas-

sive wall that surrounded Jericho. The two young men had trav-
eled mostly by night to keep themselves hidden. Now dawn was
breaking and the city rose up before them. "How will our army
ever get over those walls?"

"There are ways," Ardon said grimly. His nerves were on
edge, for there were patrols out. They had already encountered
one of them, and there had to be others. Jericho was on its
guard! "I've heard there are ways to knock down walls. Soldiers
build platforms with roofs on them and shove them up against
the walls. The roofs protect them from the enemy's arrows raining down from the top of the wall."

"But we don't know how to do that. Nobody in the whole
camp does."

"God will help us find a way."

Othniel studied the wall despairingly. "That wall is at least
wide enough for two chariots to go around side by side. I saw
one only a moment ago. It so big there are houses built on it,
Ardon."

"I see that, Othniel, but you may as well be quiet."

Othniel fell silent. The two hid in a stand of scrubby trees
and watched as the sun continued to rise. After several hours
Othniel could stand it no longer. "How are we supposed to
judge the army and what it's like? They're on the inside and
we're on the outside. All we'll ever see out here are small
patrols."

"I know it. We've got to get in there."

"There must be a way."

They planned to wait until darkness before making an
attempt to enter, but as the afternoon crept by, they decided to
do some scouting. "Let's circle the wall," Ardon said. "Surely
there is a gate, some way to get through the walls."

Circling the city of Jericho turned out to be a difficult task.
It was a large city and there was little cover. They dared not
move out in the open for long, because they were close enough
that watchmen on the wall could spot them. They had to dart

behind boulders, shrubs, and stunted trees to hide. It was tiring, dirty work, and their water was soon gone. When they came to a creek, Ardon said, "We'd better fill up our water flasks here."

As the two filled their flasks, Othniel said, "You know, this creek runs right through the city."

Ardon blinked with surprise. "You're right. It does. It goes right to the wall."

"We could go into the city through that opening, couldn't we?"

Ardon considered this for a moment, then nodded. "I haven't seen any other place we can try. What we'll have to do—"

A voice cried out, "You two stay right where you are!"

The two leaped to their feet and saw four soldiers headed straight for them. They had appeared out of a clump of stunted trees "It's too late to run." Ardon said. "We'll have to fight them." He cast a quick glance at Othniel. "Draw your sword and do your best."

"Throw down your weapons!" The guard was a burly man, short and thick-armed, and he wore a brass helmet that glittered in the sun. His lips turned up in a cruel smile. "Where are you two from?"

"We're just passing through," Ardon said. His eyes studied the four as he calculated their odds. He wished fervently he had brought a real soldier with him instead of Othniel.

"Put your weapons down. You're coming with us. We have questioners here who will know how to get an answer from you."

Instead of throwing down his sword, Ardon swiftly drew his weapon and charged straight into the four. "Kill them, Othniel!" he shouted.

Othniel drew his own weapon. He had been almost paralyzed with fear, but as he saw Ardon tear into the leader, he forced himself forward. He was yelling as loudly as he could and found himself engaged in a hard-fought battle with one of the guards.

The battle did not last long. Othniel managed to kill one of the men while Ardon swiftly killed the leader with one blow and easily dealt with the other two, and then there was silence.

The Israelite men stood breathing hard. Othniel looked down at the dead man at his feet. Crimson blood spattered across his throat, for Othniel had nearly decapitated him. He felt sick but he had no time for that.

"We've got to get out of here. We can't hide them."

"What should we do?"

"It's almost dark. We'll follow the creek and get through the wall that way."

Othniel saw that Ardon's arm was covered with blood. "You're wounded!" he cried out.

"Yes, but there's nothing we can do about that."

"At least let me bind it up before you bleed to death."

"All right, but be quick. We can't wait here."

Hurriedly Othniel bound up the wounded arm. "That's a bad wound," he said. "It needs to be sewn up."

"Never mind that. We've got to find a good hiding place before they find us."

As they began to walk away, Othniel looked again at the man he had killed and wondered if he had a family. It was the first man he had ever killed, and Othniel felt sick as he followed Ardon into the stream.

———

". . . and so, Your Majesty, the patrol were all killed, all four of them."

"Who killed them?" The king of Jericho glared at the officer who stood before him trembling.

"We're searching for them, but we haven't found them yet."

"Well, I know who they were!" the king screamed. "They were Israelites, mighty warriors and giants."

"No, we saw their footprints. They were not—"

"I tell you the Israelites are here. They are going to kill me like they did Og, king of Bashan. Call out every man. Find them. Kill them or you'll all die!"

The man—whose name Rahab did not even know—came over, put his arm around her, and gave her a kiss with his thick lips. He was dirty and smelled terrible, but she forced herself to smile.

"Here you are, sweetheart. You're an armful for a man." He fished into his purse, handed her a coin, and winked wickedly. "I'll be back again. You can count on that."

Rahab smiled and said something. She had learned the stock phrases that women in her trade had to say to men. She had learned to smile and to pretend feelings that she never had. So, now as the man turned, she had a sudden impulse to fling the coin after him. But instead she held it in her hand, and when he turned and made another crude remark, she simply smiled. As soon as he closed the door, she walked over to the wall, put her arm against it, placed her forehead on her arm, and began to weep. Not wanting the other women to hear her crying, she kept her sobs muted. Women in her position had no right to tears. Most of the other women, perhaps all of them, had chosen the life that had been forced on her. But as the days and weeks and months had gone by, she had found herself considering doing away with herself. Suicide sometimes seemed preferable to enduring this horrible life and the awful men who came to her, but thoughts of her family kept her from actually doing it.

Shalmanezer, of course, took the money from the men, but many of them gave her gifts—some coins, some perfume, some scarves. She turned it all into cash and gave it to her family. She was not able to see them often, but she always found a way to get the money to them.

Wearily she straightened up, went over to a wash basin, and washed as well as she could. After each customer, she always wanted to bathe in warm, clean water, as though the cleansing of her body would purge the terrible stain that rested in her spirit.

When she was clean, she changed her clothes and stepped out into the hall. She was going to the well to get fresh water when she passed by the door of Shalmanezer's room. He had a visitor, a man whose voice she did not know, and she heard the man say, "And so the whole army of Israel is camped out there, just waiting to swallow us up."

Shalmanezer's voice came clearly. "They'll never do that."

"I don't know why you should think so. They haven't been defeated yet."

"They never had to take a walled city before. They have fought all their battles in the open. They're no more than a bunch of wild men, shepherds. What do they know about warfare?" Shalmanezer's voice was filled with contempt. "This wall was built for such a time as this. You know how hard it was to build. It took so many slaves that nothing else in the nation counted, and now it can't be knocked down—at least not by the riffraff out there."

"They say their god will do it for them."

"Their god! We've got gods enough here to stop them."

Rahab listened for a time, and when it appeared that the man was about to leave, she ducked outside. She filled her jar with water and waited until the man had left. When she went back inside, she stopped in front of Shalmanezer. "The monthly time of women is on me," she said. "I need to visit my family until it's over."

Shalmanezer stared at her. He had wanted to break her spirit, but he never had. There was something indomitable in the woman that sometimes caused him to watch her with awe. "Go, then. Be back in three days or I'll send for you and it'll be worse for you."

"I will be back."

Promptly she went into her room and made her preparations. The day was gone now and night had fallen, but she was not afraid of the dark. After all, what could happen to a harlot that was worse than what she was already enduring? She left the house of Shalmanezer wrapped carefully against the cool air. She carried several items she had managed to take from Shalmanezer's kitchen. She had no compunction about taking whatever she could get out with. He was the man who had ruined her life forever, and it gave her pleasure to think that he was paying for it in some very small way.

As she walked quietly, she heard the voices of the soldiers on patrol. One troop of them came running along in order, their officer rapidly calling out commands. The walls were alive with soldiers, and she prayed, *God of the Israelites, destroy this evil place!* The prayer shocked her. She had not prayed like this before. All of her prayers had been for her family, but she knew that somehow the god of the Israelites was different from the gods of Jericho. She knew the gods of that city were futile and helpless, mere fragments of clay or stone or wood.

The moon was still in its quarter stage and cast little moonlight down, barely enough for her to see her way along the wall. The voices of the soldiers echoed from a distance, and she knew they were going all around the wall searching for something. It had to be for an enemy. She had never seen such activity. The man had mentioned that there were spies in the land, yet the thought did not cause her any fear.

She was within a hundred yards of her house when something moving caught her eye. Even in the dark she could see two men, one of them leaning against the other, limping along the street. Narrowing her eyes, she studied them and wished that the moon were brighter.

As she waited quietly, one of the men nearly fell, and the other had to hold him up. She stepped forward cautiously. When she got close enough to hear their whispers, she knew that these men were not from Jericho. Their speech was quite different.

These are the spies from Israel!

Even as that thought came to her, she heard the feet of soldiers approaching from the opposite direction. Without hesitation, she stepped forward, and the man who was holding the other one up drew his sword.

"Stop," he cried in a hoarse voice, "or I'll kill you."

"You must hide. The soldiers are coming," Rahab said. Moving closer to them, she could see that one man had a bandaged arm, and the bandages were soaked with blood. "Quick, this way."

"Who are you?"

"My name is Rahab. You are Israelites."

"How do you know that?" the wounded man gasped.

"Everyone knows there are spies in the area. I know everyone in Jericho, and besides I can tell by your voice and by your dress. The soldiers are coming. My house is right there. I will hide you."

"Who are you?" the wounded man gasped.

"I told you my name is Rahab." She hesitated, then said, "I will not lead you into harm. I am . . . a harlot."

The wounded man laughed weakly. "Wouldn't you know it, Othniel, the only help we have and she's a harlot."

"I don't care what she is," Othniel said. "They're coming. I can hear them."

"We won't go with a harlot!"

"Yes we will. Why would you hide an enemy, Rahab?" he said.

"I have heard of your god. He is a strong god. He's going to destroy this place."

"How did you hear of our God?" Othniel demanded.

"Everyone has heard of him. He is the unseen god, isn't he, the god of Moses?"

"Yes."

"Quickly, come quickly to my house. You must or you will be taken."

"I won't go into the house of a harlot," Ardon said stubbornly.

"Shut up, Ardon, you're dying! You've lost so much blood you can't even walk, and you certainly can't think right." Othniel was frightened but also angry. "This is no time for your self-righteousness." He turned to Rahab and said, "We will be most grateful for your help, Rahab."

"This way," she said. "I will help you. Put your arm across my shoulders."

"I won't touch you," Ardon insisted.

"Don't be stupid, you fool!" Othniel said. "Let her help you."

At this point Ardon was so weak from loss of blood he had little will left. He was just barely aware that the woman was bracing him up on his side and also that she was being careful of his wounded arm.

The three could only move slowly down the street. When they finally arrived at her doorway, she said, "Here, let's go inside." She opened the door and helped the wounded man in. As they closed the door, Ardon slumped to the floor unconscious. Rahab and Othniel stared at each other. The feet of the soldiers pounded by, and the officer's voice said, "Find them. They're here somewhere. Find them!"

"I think you saved our lives, Rahab, and I thank you."

Rahab looked down at the limp figure. "I must take care of his arm or he will bleed to death."

The noise of their entrance stirred the rest of the family. They came in staring, and Rahab cut all questions short. "These men are servants of the god of Israel. We must help them."

CHAPTER

10

"Where is Father?" Rahab demanded. She could still hear the voices and the treads of the soldiers outside, but they were rapidly fading.

"He and Hamath went over to visit with Machiah," Kadir said. His eyes were fixed on the two tall strangers, and apprehension stirred in his eyes. "They've been searching everywhere for these two, don't you know it?"

"I know it," Rahab said. "But we must help them. One of them has been wounded." She turned and stepped closer to Ardon, who was awake again and poised as if he was planning to flee. His face was pale, and she shook her head. "You've lost so much blood. Here, lie down."

Ardon stared at her, then at the rest of the family. "I'm all right," he said, his voice weak.

"Don't pay any attention to him," Othniel said urgently. "Where do you want him?" Stepping forward, he guided Ardon to a low table that Rahab indicated.

"Put him down on this," she said. Without stopping, she turned and picked up a basin and filled it with water from a larger jug. "Get some clean cloths, Romar."

Romar wheeled away and dashed into the other room. By the time Ardon was lying down flat on his back, she had returned.

"Help me get this garment off. It's soaked with blood." She and Romar stripped the garment from Ardon, and Rahab shook her head. "That's going to have to be sewn up. It'll never stop bleeding." She pressed a cloth down on the wound, saying, "Hold this, Romar." She got up smoothly and crossed the room. She took out a needle and flax thread from a small box and threaded the needle. Then she returned and carefully told Ardon. "This is going to hurt, I'm afraid."

When she got no answer, Othniel urged her, "Go ahead. Sew it up."

"I've never done anything like this, but it must be done. Would you prefer to do it, sir?" Rahab said to Othniel.

"You go ahead. I'll help hold the flesh together." Coming forward, he knelt down and held the two edges of the wound together. He watched as Rahab began to work. He knew it must be painful, but when he glanced at Ardon, he saw that his cousin's lips were pressed closely together. He did not utter a word or a groan.

Finally Rahab said in an unsteady voice, "That's the best I can do."

"It's very good," Othniel said. "I don't think anyone could have done it any better."

Skillfully Rahab put a bandage on and tied it, saying, "He's going to need lots of water, and I suppose you're hungry."

"Starved. We haven't had anything since yesterday."

"You sit with him. My sister and I will fix something."

———

There was no privacy in the small room, and Othniel heard every word that was spoken. While Rahab and Romar prepared the food, the girl and boy stared at Ardon curiously. Ardon had drunk plenty of water, and his color was somewhat better.

"We're going to get out of this, Ardon," Othniel said.

"I doubt it." Ardon's voice was weak, and he did not open

his eyes. "They'll be searching everywhere for us. They must have found those bodies."

"What bodies?" The man named Kadir asked. He was sitting on a stool across the room and appeared to be no threat.

"We were trapped outside the city by a patrol. There was a fight and we killed them."

Rahab listened as Othniel spoke. She stole covert glances at the pair, impressed with them. They were both tall, strong men, and the one with the wound, whose name she had heard as Ardon, especially so. Their speech was a little different from those of her city, and she yearned to ask them about their people, but she said nothing.

When the simple meal was ready, Rahab said, "Here is something good to eat."

"Can you sit up long enough to eat, Ardon?"

"I'm not hungry."

"You've got to eat. Here, sit up and lean against the wall."

Othniel helped Ardon to a sitting position leaning back against the wall. Rahab filled two bowls with the stew she had fixed and brought them over. She handed one to Othniel and the other to Ardon.

Othniel tasted the stew and exclaimed, "This is excellent! You're a fine cook, Rahab."

Rahab flushed. "Thank you. It's no more than a simple stew. We'll cook something more substantial a little later."

The boy had overcome his fear of the two men. He came over and stood beside Othniel, watching him eat, then he asked abruptly, "Do you eat children?"

Othniel was startled. He turned and stared at the boy, then laughed. "No, I don't eat children. Why do you ask?"

"He's heard rumors," the girl said. She too had drawn closer. "You're Israelites, aren't you?"

"Yes we are."

"We've heard all about you," Zayna said, nodding. "That you kill everybody in wars."

"Well, not everybody, though we have been in some battles. But," he said, shaking his head, "we don't eat children." He smiled and squeezed Oman's cheek. "Though if I were going to eat a boy, I think you would be a fine one to start with." He saw the alarm and laughed. "Don't be afraid. I'm only teasing."

Rahab introduced her family. "This is my sister Romar, her husband, Kadir, and their son, Oman. This is my younger sister, Zayna."

"Is there anyone else here living with you?"

"My father, but he's gone—and a distant relative named Hamath."

Othniel said, "If word gets out we're here, you'll probably be killed for harboring enemies."

"None of us will tell," Rahab said without hesitating. "Isn't that right? We've got to help these men, for they are the servants of the great god of Israel."

"How did you hear about us?" Othniel asked, finishing the stew and letting Romar refill his bowl.

"Travelers stop here and tell us about everything. Also our relative, Hamath, was living in a city where Og was king."

"That was Bashan. Og was king of Bashan."

"That's what he said, and he told us your people came and there was a battle, and everyone in the city was killed."

"Some of our men were killed too," Othniel said quickly. He continued to answer their questions, then was startled when Ardon spoke.

"Why are you people doing this?"

Everyone turned toward Ardon. The bowl was in his lap, and there was a little color in his cheeks. "Why are you taking us in? We don't know you."

Rahab replied quickly, "We have all heard of the great god that you serve. We don't know his name, but our kinsman told us all about him. What a powerful god he is. Our gods are weak and helpless. I think you've been sent to see what our soldiers and our city are like."

When Ardon didn't answer, Othniel said, "That's right. We're scouts."

"Then your soldiers are going to attack our city, aren't they?" Rahab said.

"Yes, they are."

"I thought so," Rahab said, nodding. "When I saw you it leaped into my heart that if we would help you, then maybe you would ask your god to have mercy on my family."

Othniel waited for Ardon to speak, but he did not say a word. He felt that someone had to say something, and quickly he agreed, "That sounds fair enough. If you help us, we'll help you."

From outside came the sound of soldiers' voices, far away but coming closer. "You can't stay in here," Rahab said. "We've got to get them up on the roof."

"How do you get up there?" Othniel said, quickly getting to his feet.

"Get the ladder, Romar."

Romar disappeared and came back in right away with a short ladder. She put it up to a square hole at the corner that Othniel had not noticed. "I don't know if he can climb or not."

"He'll have to," Othniel said grimly. "Come along, Ardon."

Othniel got Ardon to his feet. When they got to the ladder, however, Ardon whispered, "I don't think I can do it."

"Here, I'll help you." Othniel turned Ardon to face him, stooped over, and picked him up until Ardon was draped over his shoulders. Slowly and carefully he began ascending the ladder. It creaked and groaned under the heavy weight of the two men, and the family watched until Othniel's feet disappeared.

As soon as they were out of sight, Rahab turned to her family and said, "My father and Hamath must not know of this. You understand?"

"Why not?" Oman asked.

"Because this must be a secret, Oman. Nobody must know that these men are here. The soldiers would kill us all if they knew. So you must not breathe a word to anyone."

"I won't," Oman said.

"How are we going to keep it from Father—and Hamath?" Romar asked.

"Here's some money," Rahab said, taking some coins out of a box in the corner. "If Father shows up, give it to him. He'll go out and drink it up. We've got to keep this from him." Quickly she began to fill a jug with water. She put some dry food in a basket and said, "I'm going to take this up to them." She mounted the ladder and emerged under the night sky. The moon was brighter now, and by the light of it, she could see the two Israelites. The roof had a balcony built around it, which would hide them from the view of those in the street. Of course, on the outside of the city wall there was nothing but a sheer drop to the earth far below.

"I brought you some more food and water," Rahab said, drawing near. She knelt down and put the basket and a jug of water beside the wall. "You'll have to be quiet up here."

"Don't worry about that," Othniel said.

"I'll bring some blankets up. It'll get cooler tonight."

"I thank you for what you've done. You've probably saved our lives," Othniel said.

"It won't be safe for you to leave here for a while. The soldiers are everywhere." She hesitated, then said, "My father must not know you're here."

"Why not?"

Rahab shook her head. "He's not an honorable man. He would sell you for the reward I am certain the king has offered to pay for you." She turned to Ardon. "Are you feeling any better?"

"I'm all right," Ardon said gruffly.

"You must eat and drink all you can, and later we'll have to dress the wound." When Ardon did not answer, she nodded and said, "Good night."

As soon as Rahab disappeared, Ardon muttered, "We've got to get out of here."

"Are you crazy! We wouldn't last out there on the streets. You can't even walk. How do you propose to get out?"

"She'll give us up."

"Who?"

"That woman—Rahab."

"Why would you say a thing like that?" Othniel asked with astonishment. "She's saved our lives."

"She's a harlot. She sells herself for money. You think she wouldn't sell us?"

Othniel was disgusted. "I don't know what she is. She may be a harlot, I don't know. But she's not going to give us up. She's an honest woman. Can't you see that in her face?"

"No, I don't believe it."

"Then you're a fool! I know you're smarter than I am, Ardon, but you don't know much about people. If she was going to give us up, she would have done so already."

Ardon did not answer for a long time. At last he lay back and closed his eyes. "You can't trust the word of a harlot," he whispered.

The moon shone brightly on the two men, and Othniel stared down at the face of his friend. He knew that Ardon had many good qualities, but he had long ago noticed that he had an unforgiving, harsh spirit. Once he lost his good opinion of someone, it was lost forever.

Othniel knew a little something about that because he had lost Ardon's goodwill years earlier. He waited until the woman brought the blankets, and he whispered to her, "My friend's asleep, but he's not feeling well. I want to thank you for both of us."

"I'll do all I can to save you," she said.

Othniel stared at the woman and smiled. "I believe you will, Rahab." She went down the ladder, and Othniel turned and quickly covered Ardon with a blanket. Then he sat down and raised his eyes to the stars. He was not much of a praying man, but he knew they were indeed in a bad spot, and he began to pray. "God of Abraham, you'll have to help us with this, for we're helpless. I thank you for this woman. I don't know what she is. Maybe she is a bad woman, but she's been good to us, so I ask you to have mercy on her."

CHAPTER
11

Othniel reached down and ruffled Oman's dark hair. "You're too good for me, Oman," he said. "I never win at this game."

"You just let me win," Oman said. He smiled broadly at the big man who sat on the floor across from him. The two of them had been playing a game that his father had made for him. It involved carved animals and a board.

"You shouldn't let Oman bother you, Othniel."

Othniel turned to look up at Rahab, who had come to look down on the two. "He's no bother," he said. "We're friends, aren't we, Oman?"

"Yes, we are."

"I wish I could take you fishing. Have you ever caught a fish?" Othniel asked.

"No. How do you do that?" He sat still while Othniel began to speak. He spread his hands wide and his eyes sparkled as he described his fishing trip.

"Maybe you'll take me someday."

"That's not very likely," Zayna said. She had been playing with the two but had finally gotten up to help her sister with the work.

"Why would you say that?" Othniel asked.

"Because this whole city is going to be burned and everybody's going to be killed," Zayna said.

"No, that's not so," Oman protested. "You wouldn't let anybody kill us, would you, Othniel?"

"I certainly would not. We're friends, aren't we?"

Rahab looked up from the bread dough she was kneading and said, "Oman, I want you and Zayna to go outside."

"Outside? What for?"

"I want you to find out what people are saying."

"You mean about Othniel and Ardon?" Zayna asked.

"Exactly. Watch carefully, and if the soldiers start for this house, you come in quickly and tell us about it."

"We can do that," Zayna said. "Come on, Oman."

As soon as the two left, Othniel said, "That's a bright boy there."

"Yes, but he's not well. He's always been sickly."

"Well, maybe he'll get stronger as he gets older."

He watched her knead the bread and said, "I remember watching my mother do that."

"What's her name?"

"Her name was Rachel."

"That's a pretty name. Is it common among your people?"

"Fairly common. She was named after a woman who was married to one of the founders of our tribe. His name was Jacob."

"Are there a great many of you?"

"Quite a few, I suppose."

"How do you ever manage to feed so many? You must grow crops."

"We move around so much we don't have time to plant any crops. But we raise animals—sheep and goats and cows. So we have plenty of meat and milk. And we have manna."

"Manna?" Rahab lifted her eyebrows. "What is manna?"

"It's bread that falls from heaven."

Rahab stared at him. "I never heard of such a thing."

"I guess I've gotten used to the miracle," Othniel said with a shrug. "When our God delivered us out of slavery, we were out in the desert with nothing to eat. We would have starved. But our leader Moses prayed and God sent bread from heaven. Every morning when we come out, it's on the ground."

"You just pick up bread from the ground?"

"It's very tiny and it spoils quickly. You have to gather it every morning. I've been doing it all my life."

Rahab was smitten with astonishment. "A god that feeds his people by raining bread from heaven."

"Oh, that's only one of the miracles that God has given to us." Othniel went on to tell about how water flowed from a solid rock in the desert when the people were thirsty and there was no water. He told about how God had miraculously cared for Israel during its long wanderings. "It's been forty years now, and God's taken care of us."

"Tell me about yourself," Rahab said.

"About me? Well, there's nothing much to tell. My parents are dead. Ardon up there on the roof, he's my cousin." He laughed shortly and said, "He's the good one. I'm the bad one."

"Why would you say that?"

"It's true enough. His father's name is Caleb. He's my uncle. He's one of the leaders of our people. He's from a very fine family, but I'm not."

"I don't believe that."

"If you ever visit our camp, just ask about me." He smiled at her.

He was a good-looking fellow, she noted, with an easy manner about him, quite unlike his cousin. "They wouldn't send a man who wasn't reliable on a mission like this," she said.

"You know I haven't figured that out yet. It was a strange choice."

Rahab was quiet for a time, and he studied her. She was one of the most attractive women he had ever seen, much fairer than the women of his people. He noticed her eyes especially were beautiful, well-shaped and of an odd color. "I've never seen anybody with eyes the color of yours," he said.

"They are from my mother, I guess. Almost everyone in Jericho has dark eyes, but my mother was a slave. She used to tell me about her home where she was born. There was ice and snow there. Very cold. Her hair was light and her eyes were blue. She died some time ago."

Othniel could not help but admire the woman's appearance. The lamp was burning, and the yellow light was kind to her, showing the full, soft lines of her body. He noticed also that her face was very expressive. Her feelings showed immediately on her face. She did not smile much, but when she did her whole expression lit up. He wanted to ask her about herself, but it was a delicate situation. Finally he said, "Your father's never home. Does he work?"

"No, he stays drunk most of the time."

"Sorry to hear that. And your brother-in-law, he's crippled. He can't work either."

"Very little."

"Then how do you live?"

Rahab hesitated. She had formed the dough into a solid lump and stood there for a moment. "I have to support them, and I've told you what I am."

The words caught Othniel in a strange way. He had known harlots before, but all of them he had known were hard-eyed, greedy women. Any one of the harlots he knew would have turned him and Ardon in for the reward the king was offering for their capture—a reward that was getting larger every day.

"I'm a harlot," she said, making no excuse for it. "That's why your friend Ardon doesn't like me."

"Well . . ." Desperately Othniel tried to think of some way to tell the woman about what Ardon was like. Finally he shrugged and said, "He's very religious. That's why he's so stiff. Even if you saved our lives."

"I'm glad you're here, Othniel. I know that Ardon would

never ask for mercy from your leaders for a harlot or her family, but I think you would."

"That's right, I will. My uncle Caleb is a hard man but a fair one, and Joshua, our chief, is a wonderful man. When we get back, I'll tell them all that you've done for Ardon and me. You'll be all right. I promise you."

She turned to him and smiled shyly. He was shocked and amazed to find that there was still an innocence about her, despite her profession. He knew what her life involved, but somehow he knew that beneath all of that, down deep, Rahab was a woman of honor.

"I've got to go up on the roof. We do our baking up there."

"I'll stay down here and keep watch."

"Don't go outside," she warned.

"I won't do that."

Rahab climbed the ladder to the roof and walked over to the small stone oven that Kadir had built. She arranged twigs under it, went back down the ladder for some hot coals, and brought them up in a clay jar to start her fire. All the time she was aware that Ardon was sitting with his back to the wall that faced the street, watching her. She had spoken to him when she first came up and he had nodded, but there was no more.

She got the flames going and turned to him. "I'll have to stay here and tend the fire for a while."

"I can do that."

"That would be good of you." She turned to him and studied his face. "I know you're not a man who visits harlots."

"How could you know that?"

"There's something unclean about men who do that. It shows in their eyes."

Ardon stared at her curiously. He was feeling much better physically. His arm was stiff but was healing quickly. He had always been quick to heal. Now he flexed it and said, "I haven't been very gracious, but I want you to know that I'm grateful to you for saving our lives."

"And you're still wondering why I did it, aren't you?"

"It's unusual. I don't think another soul in Jericho would have lifted a finger to save Othniel and me."

Rahab knelt down and fed more twigs into the fire. She was thinking how to answer this man. "As I told you," she said finally, "I did it because of your god. What is his name?"

"He has many names. Jehovah is one of them."

"Jehovah. What does that mean?"

"It's an odd sort of name. It means, more or less, 'one who keeps covenant with His people'."

"And what is a covenant?"

"It's a promise, an agreement. Like if I promised you I would come on a certain day, say next week. That would be a covenant between us."

"And what promises has your god made you?"

"Many," Ardon said. He had studied long at the feet of Phinehas and other members of the priestly tribe and knew the history of his people well. His eyes grew dreamy as he began to speak of how Jehovah had appeared to Abraham. "He promised him a land flowing with milk and honey, and though he was only one man he said, 'One day your descendants will be as many as the stars in the sky.' Abraham was the first Hebrew."

Rahab was fascinated. This was the first time Ardon had spoken to her at any length. "Tell me more about your god."

"Why do you want to know?"

"Surely everyone wants to know about your god."

"I don't think so. Most people want what God will do for them. They don't want God himself."

Rahab exclaimed, "That's exactly what I said! The people in Jericho, they go to the temples to ask for things. Always asking! But I always wanted to know what the god or goddess was like."

"Well, Jehovah is hard to understand. For one thing, nobody's ever seen Him."

"Nobody? Not even Abraham?"

"Not even Moses, really. Moses was our leader who led us out of Egypt. You may have heard about him."

"Yes. Everyone knows about Moses. Did you know him?"

"Yes, of course. He only died a short time ago. He was a hundred twenty years old, but he was as strong as if he were a young man."

Rahab was quiet for a long time. The twigs crackled as they burned, and the smoke began to rise. She put her hand on the oven and found it was growing warm. "The fire will have to be kept going to bake the bread."

"Yes, I know." Ardon got up and came over to stand by the oven. He was hidden behind the banister from the street below, but he could clearly hear voices.

Rahab suddenly asked, "Could I ever be a part of Israel?"

Ardon turned to look at her. She looked at him silently waiting for his answer, and he was not sure what her silence meant. The question intrigued him, but he had only one answer.

"No, you could never be a part of Israel."

"I see." Rahab rose up and left without another word.

Ardon was surprised. He had expected her to argue. He sat there thinking about the strange conversation, and finally Othniel came up and sat down beside him. "The bread smells good," he said.

"The woman just asked me something odd."

"Her name is Rahab," Othniel said with irritation. "You know it well enough."

"Don't bite my head off."

"What did she ask you?"

"She asked me if she could become a woman of Israel."

"And what did you tell her?"

"Why, I told her no, of course." Ardon was surprised at the question. "You know that an idolater and a stranger cannot be a part of Israel."

"You know our history better than that. Moses was married

to an Ethiopian woman. She wasn't born a Hebrew. There are others too. You remember how Moses used to say that the strangers and foreigners could join us if they wanted to worship Jehovah."

Indeed, Ardon did know this, but he had shut it out of his mind. He never understood that and was resentful of strangers who were admitted into the fellowship of the nation of Israel. "But in any case," he said, "she's a prostitute, so that bars her."

"There's something strange about that. She doesn't look like any bad woman I've ever seen. She has very gentle eyes."

"Women are deceitful. You should know that better than anybody."

The two sat there, and Othniel studied his friend. At length he said, "We owe our lives to this woman."

"I know that," Ardon said quickly. "We'll make it up to them."

"Have you told her that?"

"No."

"You should say so."

"All right," Ardon agreed. "I will."

The two were up on the roof dozing. They had eaten heartily of the bread and lamb Rahab had brought them. It was growing darker now, and suddenly there was a sound on the ladder. Both men stiffened, for it could be anyone.

They relaxed, however, as Rahab came up, her eyes wide with apprehension. "The soldiers are searching every house. They'll probably look on the roof too."

"What'll we do?" Othniel asked quickly.

"There's only one place. Get over here. I'll cover you up with these sheaves." The roof was the only place that the family had to store anything, and a great many bundles of flax were there that Kadir used to make into twine.

Ardon grasped his sword and held it, his face tense. "We'll have to fight."

"We wouldn't have a chance," Othniel said. "Come on. Get here in the corner."

Rahab saw the resistance in Ardon, and she shook her head. "There are many of them. Quick, I'll hide you."

Ardon shrugged. "All right, we'll try it," he murmured. The two men sat down, and Rahab began to cover them with the flax.

When they were completely hidden, she said quietly, "Now they won't see you."

"They might poke at us with a sword or a spear," Ardon's voice emerged from the pile.

"I'll try to draw them off. Be very quiet."

The two men huddled there silently.

"I don't think this is going to work," Ardon said.

"Give it a chance, will you?"

They quickly shushed at the heavy clunk of footsteps coming up the ladder and then resounding on the flat roof. A rough voice said, "There's nobody up here."

"See what's under that flax over there," another male voice said.

Both men tensed and gripped their weapons, but then they heard Rahab's voice. "My, what fine men the king has in his army."

There was instant laughter from the two men, and Rahab's voice sounded seductive as she continued. "Come here and give me a kiss."

There was a silence as the two men obviously were taken with Rahab. "I'll come back to see you when I'm off duty."

"We'll both come."

"Come downstairs. I've got some wine that you need to take. I know soldiers get thirsty on their job."

Othniel was holding his breath, and he finally let out a sigh of relief as the voices grew mute and disappeared. "She did it,

Ardon. I thought we were goners for sure."

Ardon threw back the stalks of flax and said, "Yes, I thought so too."

The two waited for some time before Rahab came back up the ladder. "You'll have to leave tonight," she said. "Those two may come back tomorrow or some other day."

She stood looking at them in the falling light, and both of them could see that she was thinking hard. Now Ardon became more aware of her beauty. She was shapely in a way that would tempt any man, and the bones of her face made a strong and pleasant contour. He still was repulsed by the fact that she was a prostitute, but he could not deny what she had done for them. "We'll leave the same way we got in after it gets dark, out through the gate that the stream comes through."

Rahab began to speak. Her voice was quiet but full of insistence. "I know that the Lord has given this land to you and that a great fear of you has fallen on us, so that all who live in this country are melting in fear because of you. We've heard how the Lord dried up the waters of the Red Sea for you . . . and what you did to Sihon and Og, the two kings of the Amorites whom you completely destroyed. When we heard of it our hearts melted . . . for the Lord your God is God in heaven above and on the earth below."

"You are right," Ardon said, astonished by the fervency in her voice.

"Now then," Rahab said, "please swear to me by the Lord that you will show kindness to my family, because I have shown kindness to you. Give me a sure sign that you will spare the lives of my family . . . and that you will save us from death."

Othniel did not think that Ardon would speak, but he did. "Our lives for your lives if you don't tell what we are doing," Ardon said. "We will treat you kindly and faithfully when the Lord gives us the land."

Rahab took a deep breath. "You will never get through the gate. Too many soldiers."

"We'll have to try," Ardon said.

"No. Wait. I have something." She opened a basket she had brought with her and drew something out."

"What's that?" Othniel said.

"Why, it's a rope. I never saw one like it," Ardon said. "It's red, isn't it? It's hard to tell in this light."

"I made it out of spare material from a place where I once worked at a weaver's shop."

"You were a weaver?"

Rahab hesitated. She wanted desperately to tell them her story but did not. "It's long enough to reach the ground. We can tie it here, and you can climb down it after it gets dark."

"We'll go as soon as it's completely dark," Ardon said. "This is a fine rope. It'll hold our weight without any trouble."

The three waited, and finally Ardon said, "We'll go now. There's not much moonlight."

"Go to the mountains," Rahab said. "Hide yourself there for three days."

Othniel felt a warmth in his heart. "After we're gone, pull this rope up. When we come into this land again, it will be as soldiers in a battle, but don't worry, Rahab. When the battle starts, get the rope out again and hang it down from this window. I'll tell Joshua that where we see the scarlet rope lives a friend to Israel."

"That's a good idea, Othniel," Ardon said. "And, Rahab, do not go out of the house when the battle starts. You must stay inside or men will strike you down. I swear to you that we will save your lives."

"You mean," Rahab whispered, "like a covenant?"

"Yes. We have a covenant."

Rahab bowed to them. "According to your words, so be it."

Ardon bound the end of the rope, threw it over the outside of the wall, and said, "You try it first, Othniel."

Othniel grinned. "So if I break my neck, you won't have to

worry about me." He turned then and suddenly put out his hand.

Rahab, surprised, took it and he said warmly, "I'll never forget you or your family, Rahab. Don't worry. Jehovah's going to take care of you." He quickly shinnied down the rope and disappeared into the darkness.

"It will be hard for you with your wounded arm."

"I'll be all right."

"Good-bye, then, and may the God of Israel keep you safe."

Ardon hesitated. He wanted to say something, but old manners die hard and old convictions even harder. All his life he had heard of evil women, harlots, and this woman was one of them. True enough she did not have the appearance of harshness, but still that was what she was. "You have my thanks, Rahab, and you will have the thanks of my father and of Joshua, our commander. Remember to stay in the house when the battle starts. I will come for you."

"It's a covenant, then. I will wait for you, Ardon."

He nodded and awkwardly made his way over the edge. It was difficult with his arm, but he was much stronger now. He lowered himself most of the way, but finally his grasp failed, and he fell a few feet, landed on the ground, and rolled over.

"You should have used the rope," Othniel teased, helping him up.

Ardon got to his feet. He watched as the rope was drawn back up and then said, "Come along. We're not home yet."

"We will be. Rahab has saved us, Ardon."

The two men turned and made their way toward the mountains, groping through the darkness by the pale light of a sliver of moon.

Caleb and Joshua were training a group of younger recruits in the use of the sword. The blades clanged on each other, and the two older men shouted out directions, at times pleased, at times disgusted, with the outcome.

Caleb especially was quick to point out the faults of the younger men. "That's a sword, not a stick to poke at a rabbit with," he said. With one blow he knocked the sword from the hand of an eighteen-year-old, who looked at him in astonishment. "Pick up that sword, boy. I don't think—"

"Master, the spies are back."

Joshua and Caleb both turned to look at the messenger, whose eyes were big. "They just came in. They're waiting for you at your tent."

"Come along, Caleb," Joshua shouted. "Now we'll find out something."

Joshua and Caleb listened silently as the two men outlined what they had found on their journey.

Finally Ardon said, "Man for man we can beat them. They're better trained than we are and our weapons aren't quite as good, but they're frightened to death of us."

"How do you know that?"

"A woman named Rahab told us," Othniel said. "They've heard about what God has done for us, and how we've destroyed our enemies."

"It'll be different this time, though, master," Ardon said. "That wall is unbelievable. It must have taken hundreds of years to build it. It's broad enough to drive two chariots around side by side. Why, there are, as we said, houses on it."

Joshua saw the disbelief on the face of Ardon. "I don't know how God will do it, but He's bigger than any wall."

"Tell us more about this woman and her family," Caleb said.

"Well ..." Ardon began uncertainly, "she's not a good woman. She's a prostitute, as a matter of fact."

"Why did she save your life? Tell us that again," Joshua said. He listened as Ardon spoke of Rahab's fascination with the God of Israel.

"She asked me once if she could ever become a woman of

Israel, and I told her no, of course."

"Why'd you tell her that?" Joshua demanded. "My master Moses always said there would be no difference between a Hebrew and a stranger if their hearts were right."

"I told him that," Othniel interrupted. "She's a good woman deep inside. I don't know what path brought her to what she is now, but she saved our lives."

Joshua listened as Othniel spoke warmly of Rahab; then he nodded, "You have given your word and it shall be kept. When the battle comes, you two will be responsible for bringing this woman Rahab and her family out safely."

"Yes, master." Othniel nodded eagerly. "We'll do it."

Joshua turned and clapped his old friend Caleb on the shoulder. "And now at last we cross the Jordan."

"Yes," Caleb said with feeling in his voice, "we finally come to the land that God promised to Abraham."

CHAPTER

12

For several days after the return of Othniel and Ardon, they spent most of their time relating their adventures. Of course the soldiers all wanted to know about the wall and the strength of the army and the weapons, and the two did their best to describe those.

But Ariel was interested in another part of the story. She caught Ardon alone and said, "Sit down. I want to hear all about the story."

"I'm sick of hearing myself talk about it."

"Well, you're going to have to talk about it one more time. Now sit."

Ardon plumped himself down, and Ariel came to stand before him. "Now, tell me about this woman Rahab."

"I've told you. She pulled us off the street. I had been wounded and was bleeding to death."

"Why did she do that?"

"She said she had heard about Israel and how we were defeating all our enemies. She wanted us to have mercy on her and her family."

"But she was a bad woman?"

"Yes, she was."

"How do you know that, Ardon?"

"She told us," Ardon said, throwing his hands wide. "She came right out and said it. She's a harlot."

Suddenly Ariel laughed. "That's amusing."

Ardon was offended. "Why is it amusing?"

"Because you're so pure and stainless you'd cross the street to keep from walking close to one of those women, and now God chooses one of them to save your life."

"I don't think of it like that. As a matter of fact, maybe we made a mistake. I felt we were doing wrong just by being in her house."

"From what you said there wasn't any other choice."

"I should have found a better way."

Ariel shook her head. "You're a stubborn man, brother. One of these days you're going to have to learn how to change your mind. Well, I can get a better story from Othniel than from you."

As she left, Ardon called out, "Don't pay any attention to him. He's taken with the woman."

"Well, to be truthful, I liked her a lot, Ariel."

Ariel had drawn Othniel aside, and the two were sitting down on a bench side by side. She had demanded the whole story by saying, "I've heard what my brother said. Now I want to hear it from you. Don't leave out any details. What about the woman?"

Othniel was silent for a while, and she asked, "Well, what about her? She was a prostitute, wasn't she?"

"She said she was, but she didn't look like one, Ariel."

"What did she look like?"

"Why are you so curious?"

"She saved my brother's life. Naturally I'm interested."

"But not because she saved mine?"

"Never mind that. Just tell me the whole story. Don't leave out anything."

Othniel began to talk, and as he related the tale, he was surprised to think of many details he had left out earlier. Perhaps it was because Ariel kept prompting him for more information, and finally he ended by saying, "... and so we slid down the rope and made our way back here."

Ariel had listened intently. "I'm not surprised that you wound up in the house of a harlot, but I am surprised about my brother."

"Ardon's worse than you are, but I wish you wouldn't be so judgmental."

"I didn't mean to be. Tell me. What did she look like?"

"She's a very nice-looking young woman."

"Was she as pretty as me?"

"I didn't know it was a beauty contest," Othniel said with a grin. "She's quite different from you."

"Tell me. What did she look like?"

"Well, she had the most unusual eyes. They were violet, purple like the sunset looks at times. Never saw anything like it. She told me her mother was a slave from up north with fair hair and blue eyes. I guess that's where she got them."

"Did she offer to make love to you?"

"Of course not!"

"Why are you so surprised? That's what she does for money."

"I don't want to talk about this anymore. Your brother would be dead if it weren't for her, and so would I."

Suddenly Ariel was filled with compunction. "I'm sorry, Othniel. I don't mean to be mean. I'm just so glad you and Ardon are safe. If I ever meet the woman, I'll tell her so, no matter what she is."

"You'll meet her, all right. When the battle starts, I'll be right there with Ardon, I hope. She'll have the scarlet rope hanging out the window, and it'll be our job to get her and her family out alive."

"It would make a nice story if you would fall in love with

her and marry her, wouldn't it, Othniel?"

"Oh, I couldn't do that."

"Why not?"

"Because I have been in love with you since I was twelve years old. No, eleven, I think."

Ariel laughed. Othniel had often thrown this up to her and she had never believed a word of it. "Get away with you, now. I don't want to hear any more of your stories. But if you do bring the woman back, I want to thank her."

Othniel started to leave, but first turned to say, "Tomorrow we're crossing the Jordan. That'll be something to see. It took us forty years to get from Egypt to this point. Should have taken no more than a month at the most."

"What'll happen when we cross the Jordan?"

"We'll be in the land of milk and honey. That's what Moses always called it. I could use a little milk and honey."

Joshua had prepared the priests by telling them to sanctify themselves, and now the morning had come. The Lord had awakened Joshua early and given him a message. *"Today I will begin to exalt you in the eyes of all Israel, so they may know that I am with you as I was with Moses."* He had also given careful instructions about the crossing of the Jordan, and now the sun shone brightly down on all the people, who had gathered themselves together, every man, woman, child, and young person.

And Joshua had stood on a high rock and cried out loudly, "This is how you will know that the living God is among you, and that He will certainly drive out before you the inhabitants of the land. See, the ark of the covenant of the Lord of all the earth will go into the Jordan ahead of you."

Then Joshua commanded that twelve men be chosen, one from each tribe of Israel, and that as the priests bore the ark into the water, the Jordan would be cut off. "As He dried up the Red Sea, so will He dry up the Jordan."

And so it was on that day. As the people prepared to pass over the Jordan, the priests bearing the ark of the covenant moved forward. As their feet touched the water of the Jordan, the waters that ran from upstream began to pile up. It was as though a huge dam had been built and the waters could go no farther. The people grew silent, and Caleb, who stood beside Joshua, said, "It reminds me of when God made a path through the Red Sea."

"That was a miracle in its day, but this is a miracle for us now."

And so the people watched until the bed of the Jordan was dry and they were all able to pass over. It took a long time for all of them to cross with their flocks and herds. About forty thousand men armed for battle also crossed over to the plains of Jericho. Finally, when everyone was on the far side, Joshua said to the twelve men he had selected from each tribe, "Go into the Jordan where the priests are standing and each take up a stone."

He waited until the twelve men had brought out their stones, and he commanded them to take them to where they set up their camp, piling them up for a memorial to what God had done for them this day at the Jordan River. Then he stood and cried out with a ringing voice, "In the future, when your children ask you, 'What do these stones mean?' tell them that the flow of the Jordan was cut off before the ark of the covenant of the Lord. When it crossed the Jordan, the waters of the Jordan were cut off. These stones are to be a memorial to the people of Israel forever."

When Joshua stopped speaking, a mighty cry of victory went up from Israel. Othniel was standing beside his friend Achan. "If God can dry up the waters of the Red Sea and the Jordan River, then He can do something about the walls of Jericho too, I expect."

Ardon stood beside his father, Caleb, and found that he was thinking not of the massive wall of Jericho but of the woman who had saved his life. He tried to put her out of his mind, and now with an effort, he shook his head, determined to concentrate on what lay before them. Still, he could think of little besides the woman with the violet eyes whose name was Rahab.

PART THREE

THE WALLS OF
JERICHO

CHAPTER

13

King Jokab of Jericho stroked the silken skin of the woman who lay close to him. She was a sloe-eyed woman with black hair and a wide, sensuous mouth. There was a lewdness about her that pleased King Jokab well.

Suddenly voices rose outside the door, and the king sat up, not releasing his hold on the woman. When he saw the commander of his army enter, he scowled. "What do you mean bursting in like this, Zanoah? I could have your head for this."

Zanoah was a stocky man with bulging muscles and a scar pulling the right side of his face down. He was a fighter not a diplomat, and even though he knew it might be at the cost of his own life, he ignored the king's angry shouts. "Sire," he said, "I have evil tidings."

King Jokab glared at his commander. "We'll talk about it at the council meeting."

"I think it's something you should know now, Your Majesty."

Roughly Jokab shoved the woman aside and got out of bed. He put on a silken robe and then turned to face the stocky commander. "Well, what is it, then?"

"It's the Hebrews, sire. We have bad news."

"Are they coming to attack?"

"Yes, sire."

"I'm sure they are, but we have some time. Out with it, man, what have they done?"

Zanoah swallowed hard and was obviously trying to think of some way to put the news in a more palatable form. "It's the River Jordan," he said. "They ... they dried it up."

"Have you lost your mind, Zanoah! What do you mean they dried up the river? It's still there, isn't it?"

"It's still there, but our spies reported what happened. We've been keeping track of them. The whole nation gathered on the far side of the Jordan, and then their priests headed for the river. It was a flood tide. It's the time of year, sire."

"I know what time of year it is! What happened?"

"As their priests' feet came to the water, the river ... well, it backed up. It was like an invisible dam was built upstream, and it held the waters back until all the people were across. Then, I suppose, their magicians took the spell off so the waters came rushing back into the river's channel."

"The spies were drunk!"

"No, they were reliable, King Jokab. They all agreed on what happened. Sire, these are mighty men, and more than that, they have a powerful god. I'm not a diplomat, but let me counsel you. Make peace with these people."

"Peace with them! You know what they'd do? They would take my crown, they'd cut off your head, they would take over the city of Jericho."

"They may do that anyway, sire."

"Get out—get out—get out!" King Jokab screamed. "You're the commander in chief of my armies. I want every man given a sword. Every man or boy who can walk. We have the strongest city in the world. No army can breach our walls. Now, do your job, Zanoah, or I'll have your head for it."

Zanoah stared at the king, then nodded and started to speak, but seeing the insane rage on King Jokab's face, he shrugged his burly shoulders, turned, and walked out of the door.

King Jokab turned back to the woman who was watching him carefully. She smiled and held out her arms seductively. "Come back to bed, my love. Don't worry yourself about those desert rats."

King Jokab was a rather stupid man. He was able to put problems out of his mind instantly, and with a smile he walked across the room toward the dark-skinned woman.

———

"We would have been in poor shape if any enemy attacked us, Joshua."

Joshua looked over at Caleb, who had come into his tent and now sat on the floor across from him. Caleb's face was drawn tight, and Joshua at once asked, "What's the matter?"

"I think you know."

"You mean the matter of circumcising all the males?"

"I know you thought it was the right thing to do, but if anybody would've attacked us, we'd have been annihilated." The expression on Caleb's face was gloomy, but it brightened as he said, "I know the Lord told you to do it."

"That's right. He told me that the old generation of men that had been circumcised, the ones who came out of Egypt, were dead. But those born in the wilderness had not been circumcised. The Lord said it was something we had to do. It's the mark, Caleb, that identifies us as Hebrews and the servants of the most high God."

"Well, there was a lot of complaining about it, but the men are well now. So we can talk about strategy."

Joshua laughed shortly and shook his head. "Strategy? I don't have any strategy."

Caleb stared. "You must have, Joshua. We can't just go aimlessly wandering around the country. You know how strong some of the enemies are."

"I know that well, but I have no idea what we are to do—except that our first target will be Jericho."

"Well, that's going to be difficult. I haven't seen that wall, but from what my son and nephew report, it is tremendous."

Joshua moved his shoulders restlessly. He changed the subject by saying, "We've got to do something about food now that the manna has ceased."

Caleb's eyebrows went up and he shook his head in a gesture of astonishment. "That was a great miracle, the manna. It came from the hand of God when our people needed it, but now that we've crossed the Jordan and we're in the land that God promised our fathers, it has just stopped. The people are wondering about that too."

"They've taken God for granted," Joshua said shortly. "Now they'll have to plant seed and harvest grain to make their bread."

The two men talked for a while, and finally Joshua got up and said, "I'm going out to think. If you can come up with a way to breach the walls of Jericho, I wish you'd let me know." Without another word he turned and left the tent rapidly. He walked through the camp, ignoring those who spoke to him, for his mind had leaped far ahead to the city of Jericho.

The sun was high in the sky and beat down on Joshua, but he ignored the heat. Finally he was out of sight of the camp and walked aimlessly along the rocky pathway. He had come to a slight rise when suddenly he looked up and there stood a man, a stranger, with his sword drawn.

In a flash Joshua drew his own sword. His first thought was that the man was a spy from Jericho. As he approached, he studied the man's features and saw strength and fearlessness. *If they're all like this,* he thought, *we're in trouble.* Aloud he said, "Are you for us or for our enemies?"

The stranger was tall and well built and wore a simple garment with a belt about his waist. His eyes were clear, and Joshua could not make out the color. They seemed gray at times or blue, but they were deep-set and were fixed intensely on Joshua. When he spoke, the voice was quiet and yet struck Joshua with a force almost like the blow from a sword.

"As the commander of the army of the Lord I have now come."

Instantly Joshua knew he was standing in the presence of one of the servants of the most high God, an angel, perhaps, and a high-ranking one at that! Dropping his sword, Joshua fell on his face and struggled to speak, for great fear had come over him. "What message does my Lord have for His servant?"

"Take off your sandals, for the place where you are standing is holy."

The man waited until Joshua had taken off his sandals and then began to speak, and Joshua did not raise his head as he listened to the word of the Lord. *"See, I have delivered Jericho into your hands along with its king and its fighting men. March around the city once with all the armed men. Do this for six days. Have seven priests carry trumpets of rams' horns in front of the ark. On the seventh day, march around the city seven times, with the priests blowing the trumpets. When you hear them sound a long blast on the trumpets, have all the people give a loud shout; then the wall of the city will collapse and the people will go up, every man straight in."*

Joshua waited for the man to go on, but there was a silence almost as thick as rock. Fearfully he lifted his eyes and saw no one. "It was the Lord or one of His angels," Joshua whispered, as he put on his sandals. Scrambling to his feet, he grabbed his sword, shoved it into his sheath, and turned. He headed for the camp at a dead run, and as soon as he was within hearing distance, he began to shout, "Caleb—Caleb! Where are you?"

He found Caleb rushing to meet him, and Joshua's eyes were glowing with excitement. "You asked for strategy for defeating Jericho. Well, I have it!"

"Tell me," Caleb demanded, his eyes blazing with excitement. He listened as Joshua related what he had heard from the man with the sword.

Finally Caleb said, "Was that all?"

"Was that all? What else could it be?"

"Let me get this straight," Caleb said. "All we do is march around the city once a day for six days, and on the seventh day we march around the city seven times, and then the priests blow the trumpets, the people shout, and the walls fall down."

"Yes, isn't it wonderful?"

Caleb reached up and scratched his gray hair. "It doesn't sound like any battle I've ever heard of. You're going to have trouble explaining it to the people."

"It's the word of the Lord, Caleb, and God has given us the victory. Come, we have plans to make. When those walls fall down, the city must be taken."

———

"Well, it looks silly to me," Achan grumbled. He was walking alongside Othniel. The two of them were part of the mass of people who were circling the walls of Jericho. Achan and Othniel had listened as Joshua had given one simple command: "Walk around the walls of Jericho. Do not make a sound."

Achan glanced up at the walls and shook his head. "Does Joshua think we're going to frighten them?"

"I don't know what he thinks," Othniel said shortly, trying to keep his voice down. It disturbed him that Joshua had not shared his plan except that they were to walk around the wall. He glanced up at the wall and saw that the walls were lined with archers. The flash of weapons reflecting the light of the sun was brilliant, and he shook his head. "There's a lot of them in there and we're out here. I think we ought to just let them alone and occupy the rest of the land."

Achan laughed curtly. "You don't think they'd let us do that, do you? The city has to be taken. Even I can see that."

Othniel looked ahead where the priests bearing the ark were marching in a stately fashion. Behind them Joshua and Caleb walked slowly. There was not a sound of a single voice raised, for Joshua's commands had been strict. "No talking," he had said. "No whispering. Absolute silence. The man or woman who makes a noise will answer to me."

His orders were not kept, of course. There was whispering. "People don't like not knowing what's going to happen," Achan complained.

"We just have to believe that Joshua does."

Achan glanced up the wall. "I'll wager that's a rich city inside there. Full of gold and silver and treasure of all kinds. Once we get in, we're going to grab all the stuff we can."

"I don't think that's the object, Achan." Othniel grinned slightly. "It's to conquer them."

"We can do both, can't we? When they're all dead, I'm going to get my family, and I'm going to haul off all the gold and silver I can lay my hands on."

"You can't do that."

"Why not?"

"You heard what Joshua said. He said that all the gold and silver in Jericho are for the Lord."

"Oh, Joshua always talks like that."

"He means it, Achan. He said that anyone who takes any spoil from the city for himself will be cursed, and a curse will fall on the whole nation."

"That's just scare talk," Achan said. His round face was coated with perspiration, and he grinned slyly. "You just watch. Everybody will be taking things. If you've got any sense, you'll take some yourself."

"Not me," Othniel said, "and I'm going to see to it that you don't take anything either." He reached over and put his arm around the short man. "I couldn't let anything happen to you, old friend."

———

When the seventh day came, everyone somehow understood that this was going to be different from the other days. The air of mystery that surrounded the tactics had caused much talk, but as the days passed by, there was something impressive about the silence of the nation as they encircled Jericho. Othniel knew that the silence troubled the dwellers in the city. They had shouted insults and curses, and when not a single voice was raised, they had finally fallen silent themselves. Othniel had heard Joshua say, "They don't know what to make of it. They'll know even less on the seventh day."

Joshua was now standing on a little rise. It was just before dawn, and he was preparing the people. He spoke again of the power of God and reminded them of how God had delivered them over and over since their fathers had left Egypt, and he encouraged them to be courageous and true.

After the speech he motioned to Othniel and Ardon. They came straightaway to stand before him, and he said, "Go in and bring the woman who saved you when I sent you as spies. Bring out her family and take special care of her. She has been a great blessing to Israel."

"Yes, Joshua," Othniel said, brightening up at once.

The two turned, and then Joshua lifted his voice to the people: "Now we will march around the city seven times."

It took a long time to march around the city, and the nation of Israel remained solemnly silent on each circuit. Finally, on the seventh time around, Joshua shouted to the priests, "Now sound the trumpets and let all the people shout!"

The trumpets blared out with their brazen voices, and at the same time every soul in Israel shouted at the top of their lungs. It made an awesome din, and even as the voices were on the air, Othniel was shocked to see a crack develop right in front of his eyes. It ran from the ground all the way up to the top of the wall. Other cracks began springing up, and the shouting increased.

"The wall, it's falling!" one of the soldiers shouted.

The wall was indeed falling. Down it came with a thunderous crash, the roar of it almost drowning out the screams of the archers on the wall as they fell and were crushed by the huge blocks. The houses that were on the wall fell too, and Othniel grasped Ardon's arm. "God is destroying the walls!" he cried.

"But not that part. Look!"

Othniel saw that part of the wall was still standing and that from one of the houses the scarlet rope on which they had escaped from Jericho was dangling. "Come on. We'll get them out."

Othniel drew his sword along with the other soldiers. They were all screaming and running straight for the wall. The cries of the dying who had been crushed by the wall were soon joined by the shouts of the remaining soldiers who were met by the flashing swords of Joshua's army.

Joshua led one wing of the army in and Caleb the other. Joshua saw a man running out of a fine house.

"I'm Shalmanezer! I have much wealth," the man cried.

Joshua ran straight at him. "A curse on you and your wealth," he said. He struck one mighty blow, and the head of Shalmanezer, who had ruined so many women and men fell on the street. Joshua did not even pause.

Othniel and Ardon scrambled up the stairway that was left in the part of the wall still standing. They reached the top and saw a few of the soldiers left cowering there, staring at the battle that was raging below them.

"At them!" Ardon cried, and at once he and Othniel ran straight at the soldiers. Ardon killed two instantly, and Othniel engaged in a furious duel with one rather fat soldier. He finally managed to kill the man, and then he ran toward Rahab's house.

He beat on the door and cried out, "Rahab, open the door!"

The door opened, and Rahab came out, her face pale but radiant. "God has destroyed the wall," she whispered. "He is the great God."

Ardon heard this and stared at her. He could not understand how a heathen woman, a harlot and an idolatress, could
feel so strongly about a God who could never be her own—no
matter what Joshua claimed.

"Come," he said. "Our commander has told us to bring you
and all of your family and all that you have."

"We are ready," Rahab said. She ran inside, and soon the
whole family was carrying out those things they held most precious. Othniel helped carry part of the burden, and they went
down the stairs. The battle was still raging and death was everywhere. Othniel saw Achan lifting a bloody sword and grinning
at him. "Come on, Othniel."

"No, I cannot. You be careful, Achan."

"I'll be careful. Is that the woman that saved you?"

"This is the one."

Achan grinned and shouted, "Well, woman, you saved a
good man! Take care of him." He turned then and plunged back
into the fray that was going on in the heart of the city.

"Come, Rahab," Othniel said, "you must get away from
here."

Ardon said, "You take care of her. I'm going to join the
fight."

Othniel knew that Ardon had little opinion of his soldier-
ing ability, and he nodded, "Come along, Rahab. You are safe."

"It's the God of Israel. He has done it," she said simply, and
she and her family followed Othniel out of the city of Jericho,
which had become a place of death.

As they moved away and the sounds of battle faded, Rahab
turned and looked back. Surprised, Othniel stopped also.
"What is it?" he asked.

"He hates me, doesn't he?"

"Who?"

"Ardon."

Othniel was embarrassed. "No, he's just a strange fellow.
You have to get used to him." Othniel knew his cousin's ways

well and how straightlaced he was with all women. He thought of trying to explain this to Rahab but knew that it was useless. "Come along," he said. "I'll take you to my cousin. She'll take care of you until we can find you a permanent place."

———

Ariel had been waiting along with the other women in the camp. When she saw Othniel walking along carrying a bundle and leading what appeared to be refugees, she at once knew that this was the woman she had heard of—Rahab the harlot.

"Ariel, this is Rahab and her family," Othniel said. He named them off and then nodded. "This is my cousin Ariel. She's the daughter of Caleb, one of the leaders of Israel."

"Is the battle still going on, Othniel?" Ariel demanded after nodding briefly to Rahab and the others.

"Yes, and really I ought to get back. Will you take care of my friends?"

"Of course."

Othniel turned and said, "Rahab, my cousin will take care of you. Joshua has given special instructions that you're to be well cared for. When the battle's over, I'll be back and we will make more permanent arrangements."

"Was Ardon all right when you left him?"

"He was fine. He went back to join in the battle after we got Rahab out."

Ariel's lips curled with disdain. "I might have known you'd find a way to romance a woman and leave the battle."

At that moment Rahab knew that Ardon's sister was no friend of hers. She could not think of a word to say, but she watched as Othniel trudged away. Feeling lonely now, she wished that he had left her and her family in the care of someone else.

"Come along," Ariel said to Rahab's family. "You all must be hungry."

"I sure am," Oman piped up.

"Well, we have some stew ready."

Rahab offered to help, but Ariel said curtly, "No, I'll fix it." So Rahab sat down between her sister and brother-in-law and waited until the food was served.

As they began to eat, Ariel said, "I've heard all about you. Rahab. You did a great service in saving my brother and my cousin."

"I'm glad that I was able to help," Rahab said. She studied the woman covertly and was impressed at her beauty. She saw that some of Ardon's characteristics were in Ariel as well, for she was as tall as he was, with a fair complexion and the same black hair and gray-green eyes.

"Tell me about the battle," Ariel commanded.

Rahab began haltingly telling how the walls had fallen down, and finally she said, "We would be dead by now if it hadn't been for your brother and your cousin."

Ariel kept pressing for details, but Rahab was depressed. She had lost her home, the only one she had ever known, she was living amid strangers, and she knew that her reputation had been brought back to Israel by Ardon and Othniel. Everyone knew she had been a prostitute, and there was no way to get around that. She had a sudden impulse to weep, which was strange, for she had endured great humiliation and shame and hardship in her life, but now she felt so alone she wanted to cry out. But there was no one to cry to.

CHAPTER

14

By the time Othniel made his way back to the city, the battle was basically finished. He could hear the sound of triumphant cries as he approached, and as he made his way over the rubble that had once been the proud wall of Jericho, the sight that met his eyes was astounding. He saw his fellow Israelites waving bloody swords and knives, and the streets were littered with the bodies of the dwellers of Jericho. The slaughter was not completely over, however, for down some of the streets he could see men and women and children trying to escape. Their cries of terror were cut short as the keen weapons of the Israelites cut down the terrified inhabitants of Jericho.

As he picked his way forward and arrived on the flat surface just inside the wall, Othniel heard a faint cry. Turning quickly, he saw the upper body of a soldier of Jericho who had been crushed when the walls fell. He was obviously dying, and Othniel heard him plead, "Kill me! Kill me!"

Othniel drew his sword and approached, but the soldier was no more than seventeen or eighteen and blood ran down his mouth and had pooled under his head. One of his arms was trapped. It was broken and set at an oblique angle, and the shadow of death was on him. Once again he cried out, "Please—kill me!"

Othniel reluctantly advanced and raised his sword, but somehow he could not bring it down.

At a sudden yell from behind him, he jumped back, thinking an enemy soldier might be at his back. It was, however, a man he knew—a young fellow from the tribe of Dan. His hands were bloodied up to the elbow, and his eyes were wild. He swung his sword and severed the throat of the man. "What's the matter with you, Othniel?" he yelled. "We're to kill them all!"

Sickened, Othniel shook his head and turned away. He had steeled himself to take part in the battle, but now nothing remained as he roamed the streets but executions. He saw a small girl no more than seven or eight running, her arms outstretched, her eyes wild with terror. She did not get far, for a burly Israelite cut her down with a wild swipe of his sword.

Othniel turned away from the sight and continued to search. He was determined to fight, but there was no one to fight except helpless people. The soldiers, for the most part, were dead, and at the orders of Joshua, the army was slaughtering every human that breathed in the city of Jericho.

Many of the soldiers had turned from the work of slaughter to pillaging the city. They came out bearing all sorts of treasures—golden statues, silver chains, jewelry with precious stones of red and green and blue. Finally Othniel saw Achan. He called out to him, "Achan!" and ran toward him.

Achan had his arms full of plunder. His eyes were shining, and he yelled, "Where have you been? Go in there. We won the battle!"

"I know. I wish—"

When Othniel broke off his speech, Achan stared at him. "What's the matter?"

"I don't like all this killing."

"They're the enemy."

"Some of them are women and children. They're not much of an enemy."

Achan shook his head. "Come on. We're filling up that wagon over there with treasure. Joshua is going to burn the city, but first we're taking out all the gold and silver, everything valuable."

Othniel found it easier to help with this task than with the task of mopping up survivors. He worked with the others to load up several wagons, which were then towed off by oxen.

Finally Joshua appeared with Caleb at his side. He was shouting orders, "Get those wagons out of here! All the rest of you start firing the city. Burn it to the ground, everything that will burn."

Othniel never forgot the sight that followed. The city was set on fire in a thousand places. The victorious warriors yelled with delight as the flames rose higher and higher. Finally the heat grew intense, and all the soldiers withdrew at Joshua's command.

Ardon had fought hard, for he had thrown himself into the first wave when there were still enemy soldiers to battle. Now, as he backed up from the heat of the blaze, he heard his name called. "Ardon!"

Turning, he saw Joshua. He went to him at once. "Yes, master."

"Did you get the woman out safe?"

"Oh, yes. She's all right."

"What was her name again?"

"Rahab, but she's only a harlot," he said slightingly.

Joshua struck Ardon across the chest with his forearm. The blow drove Ardon backward. He stared at Joshua in disbelief.

"Don't you speak like that of her! She was used of Jehovah to bring victory to our people."

"I didn't mean—"

"You've got a hard heart, boy, but I'm going to help you. I'm putting you in charge of the woman and her family. I'll expect a good report. See that they're well taken care of. You hear me?"

Ardon had always been the favorite of Joshua, but now he saw the anger blazing from the commander's eyes, and he could only swallow and say, "Yes, sir. I'll see to it."

———————

Rahab and her family were seated outside of the tents that housed Caleb's family. Ariel had seen to it that they had food but had shown no further interest in them.

"Look. There comes Ardon." Being crippled, Kadir had a hard time of it, and now he was leaning against one of the tent poles. He pointed, and Rahab turned quickly to see Ardon striding toward her. His face was stern, and she recoiled from fear of him.

Stopping in front of Rahab, Ardon looked down at her. "The battle's over," he said. "Is your family all right?"

"Yes. Thank you, Ardon. We're all well."

Ardon looked over at Kadir. "I'm afraid you had a hard time of it, Kadir," he said. "But it's over now."

Makon had shrunk back behind Romar. He had been terrified the whole time, convinced that they were all going to be slaughtered.

"Please, master, don't hurt us," his voice quivered.

Ardon stared at the old man in disgust. "Nobody's going to hurt you," he said. "Come along. I'm going to see that you have a place. We'll be staying here for a while."

"We don't want to be any trouble, sir," Romar said, her voice not quite steady. The sight of this fierce-looking warrior frightened her.

"Don't worry. You'll be all right. What happened to your other relative, the one who was living with you?"

"He ran away when he saw your army."

Rahab and the family followed Ardon, and they all took heart, for he commandeered two tents for them to share, neither one of them overly large but both in good shape. He also saw to it that they were supplied with the necessary tools for keeping house—pots, pans, cups, and various pottery vessels. He borrowed these from different families, and by nightfall they were all set up.

He helped get a fire started, and Romar began cooking a late meal with the food he had allotted to them.

"You'll be all right here," Ardon said.

He moved away, but he heard Rahab calling after him. He turned and saw that she was trembling. "Don't be afraid," he said crossly. "Nobody's going to hurt you."

"Are . . . are they all dead, everyone in Jericho?"

"Yes. All dead," he said, watching her face. He saw shadows and shapes of odd things come and vanish, and though she was afraid, there was a certain courage in her.

"I'm sorry, but your family's all right."

"Yes. God has delivered us all. Jehovah is a great God."

He could not think of what to say, but at that moment Joshua and Caleb were passing by. They were both weary with battle, but Joshua's eyes took in the pair. He came over at once and said, "This is Rahab, I take it?"

"Yes, sir."

"We owe you a great debt, young woman," Joshua said warmly. "Have you been taken care of?"

Rahab was warmed by the man's thoughtful air. He was rough-looking and his voice was rather gruff, but he had kind eyes. "Yes. Ardon has seen to it that we have a place to live and food to eat."

"Is there anything I can do for you in return for your service to our people?"

Rahab hesitated, and then she gathered her courage and said, "I want to worship your God, sir."

Joshua was tremendously pleased with her answer. "Why, of course. Ardon, take her to Phinehas. Tell him that I want him to teach her the ways of Jehovah."

"But—" Ardon almost blurted out that the woman was a harlot and an idolatress, but Joshua's eyes met his, and he stopped at once. "Yes, sir," he said.

"Moses said many times that there would be no difference between our people and the stranger. He was very stern as he spoke these words. Now, you see that my orders are carried out. And Rahab," he said turning to her, "you will always have a place in Israel."

"I thank you so much—for me and my family."

When Joshua and Caleb continued on, Caleb remarked, "Ardon doesn't like that woman because she's a harlot."

"She saved many lives. Maybe all of our lives. Your son is too hard and proud."

"I know," Caleb said quietly. "He's a strong man, but he hasn't yet learned what it's like to suffer rejection."

"He will someday—and when he has experienced such pain, perhaps he will be kinder to others who have suffered," Joshua said grimly. "Now. We've got to think about other things."

Ardon had been silent as he took Rahab to the tents of the Levites. He found Phinehas, introduced the two, and said, "Our commander requests that you teach this woman the ways of God."

Phinehas was a small young man with bright black eyes and a black curly beard. He studied Ardon, then turned with a smile. "It will be my joy, my sister. We will start tomorrow. It's late tonight and I know you're tired."

"Thank you, master," Rahab said. She waited until the two men had made the arrangements, and then as they headed back, she said, "How can I thank you for all your kindness?"

"It's my duty," Ardon said, his tone brittle. He resented being assigned this job, and he could not hide it. "Come along. I'll take you back to your tents."

For two days after the battle the camp was in a state of rejoicing. God had delivered them from their enemy and given them a tremendous victory. Ariel had joined in all this but noticed that Othniel never smiled. She wondered about him until finally late one evening she found him sitting on the outskirts of the camp, staring out into the sunset. The air was cooling, the earth itself growing cooler, and the wind made a musical sound as she sat down beside him. "What's wrong with you, Othniel?" she said. "Are you sick?"

"No."

"You look sick. Did you get hurt in the battle?"

"No."

Ariel said with exasperation, "Come, now. You can't fool me. I know something's wrong. Tell me what it is."

"It's what I saw at the battle."

"What do you mean?"

"It was a slaughter. By the time I got there, the battle was really over. The soldiers of Jericho were mostly dead already, but the women and children and old people were being cut down. I couldn't stand the sight of it."

"But they were our enemies. It was Jehovah's command that everyone be killed."

Othniel did not answer. He sat there looking down at his feet, his hands locked around his knees. Finally he turned to her and said, "I saw a little girl there. . . . She was killed by one of our soldiers. She . . . she reminded me of you, Ariel, when you were a little girl."

"Of me?"

"Yes. She was like you. What if it had been you? Her mother loved her. Perhaps her father. She had a life before her, and the soldier didn't think twice about killing her. I couldn't help being angry and grieving for her."

Ariel reached out and put her hand on Othniel's arm. "You were always tenderhearted, even when you were a boy. You couldn't even stand to see an animal hurt. I remember," she said, "when an animal had to be butchered for meat. You couldn't stand to watch."

"I suppose so, but this was no animal. This was a little girl."

Ariel was subdued by Othniel's words. "I remember once when I was very young," she said quietly. "I think no more than six. I fell and cut my knee on a stone, and you were the one who came and carried me in. You washed it off and put a bandage on it. I think you were hurt by it worse than I was."

"I remember that. It was a long time ago."

The two fell quiet for a while, then Othniel sighed and turned to face her. "You know, I really did fall in love with you when we were children."

"Not really, Othniel."

"Yes, really. You were always so pretty. I hated all the boys who chased you."

"I know you did. I made them chase me sometimes just to irritate you. You remember how you fought with Ezra when you caught him kissing me?"

"I remember. I jumped in and he whipped me."

"Well, he was two years older than you and almost twice your size."

"He gave me a bloody nose and a black eye, and you laughed at me."

"Wasn't I awful?"

"I didn't think so."

The silence of the evening had descended upon the camp. There were still the sounds of voices and the lowing of the cattle and the bleating of the sheep. Othniel had been shaken by the slaughter of the battle. He felt lonely and afraid, and now he turned and studied Ariel. It was true that he had loved Ariel with a boyish ardor. As he had grown older, he had learned to hide this, for she was scornful of him, but now he asked, "Could you ever love a fellow like me, Ariel?"

Ariel was shocked. She turned to see if he was joking. "Why, Othniel, you've chased every woman in our tribe. You've been in love so many times you've lost count."

"I know it. I'm ashamed. I've been foolish. But I've always thought deep down that if you could love me, I'd be a better man."

Ariel was absolutely stunned. "I don't think we're suited. We're too different."

"I know, and I know you despise me."

"No I don't," Ariel said. "We can still be friends." She reached out her hand and put it on his shoulder.

He covered it with his own and said, "You think I'm a foolish fellow, don't you?"

"You always were, but a sweet one at times. I really liked it when you fought Ezra for me, but I was afraid to show it. Then when you grew up and started chasing other girls, it hurt me."

"All that didn't mean anything."

Ariel was very much aware of his hand on hers. It disturbed her, and she got up abruptly. "Come along. You didn't eat anything, did you? I'll fix you something."

"I'm not hungry."

"Well, I am. You can watch me eat." She pulled at him, and he came to his feet. "What about that woman you and Ardon brought back? Rahab. Ardon doesn't like her."

"You know Ardon. He's not going to like a prostitute."

"Well, you'd better stay away from her too."

"But she's different now, Ariel. She's taking instruction from Phinehas. She wants to be a worshiper of Jehovah."

"And you believe that?"

"Yes I do. She took care of her family under terrible circumstances. I think she's a woman of great courage."

"She's attractive too. You stay away from her. You don't need to get mixed up with a woman like that."

"No problem there. We'll be off fighting more battles."

Ariel took his arm and pulled at him. "Come on. No more talk like that. I have some dates covered with sugar. You always like those."

The two headed back toward the camp, and Ariel found herself wondering what kind of man Othniel really was. She had known him all her life and knew that he had a gentleness and a sensitivity that most men of Israel lacked. It intrigued her, but it also seemed like a weakness in a man. Or so she thought.

CHAPTER
15

The battle of Jericho didn't come without a price for Israel. They had lost men in battle, not a great many, but the cries of grief had filled the air as the families who had lost loved ones mourned. Many others were wounded, and the healers among the people were kept busy.

During this period Rahab was also very busy. She had to see to it that her family was cared for, and it was Ardon who saw to it that they had food to eat and were not bothered. There were some in Israel who despised her, as they despised all who were not what they called true Hebrews, that is, the descendants of Abraham through blood. She and her family had received many dark looks, but Joshua's protection was upon them and no one dared violate the wishes of the commander.

Rahab was also suffering through other kinds of attention she did not welcome. Word had gotten out that she had been a prostitute, and she had learned to read the eyes of men only too well. They were sly about it, but they made their offers very plain. Rahab wasted no time on them. She either ignored them, or if they persisted, she reminded them that she was now part of Israel and would have nothing to do with such things. This did not make her popular with the men she rejected.

She mentioned this once to Phinehas while he was instructing her in the history of the Hebrews. He listened as she haltingly explained her problem and finally ended by saying, "I want nothing to do with anything like that. I was forced into prostitution to save my family. They would have been sold into slavery if I hadn't."

"I did not know that."

"I've not told anyone. My family knows it. No one else."

"Didn't you tell Ardon?"

"No. He didn't seem interested."

Phinehas knew his friend well. "He's a very straight-edged sort of man. He studies the law of Moses all the time. I think that's good, but he's too strict. He has a tender side, but it's as if he's afraid to show it to anyone."

"He hasn't shown it to me."

"As I say, it's as if he's afraid for anyone to see that side. Be patient with him, Rahab. About this other matter. You are doing the right thing. If any man persists, come and tell me. I'll see to it."

Rahab hesitated, then said, "I heard what you did when the plague was among the people, how you killed the two who had shamed Israel with their adultery."

"It happened so fast. I knew that people were dying everywhere," Phinehas said, his eyes cloudy. "And then the voice of God came and told me to kill them. If I had time to think about it, I might not have been able to. I had never hurt anyone before."

"I know so little about God, sir. I'm so ignorant."

"You have a hungry heart, Rahab, and that's all that God requires. I'm very proud of the progress you've made."

"Moses left so many laws. I'll never learn them all."

"Oh, yes you will, because you're eager to learn. True, there are many laws. Laws about what we can eat. Laws about the family. God is protecting us by giving us these laws. So you must be patient and study and ask God to help you."

"I will do that, sir, and I thank you for your help."

"Were you ever married, Rahab?"

"No. I never was."

"Likely you will be someday. Men are drawn to your beauty now, but as you grow to know more about the ways of God, they will be drawn to the inner woman."

"I hope so, sir, but I don't think I'll ever marry. Men could never forget what I was."

"A good man could forget. We're all flawed vessels. Every one of us. We have to learn to forgive each other."

The two spoke for a while, and after Rahab left, Phinehas went to find Ardon. When he did, he said, "I wanted to give you a report on Rahab. She's doing very well. She has a good heart."

"You think that about everyone, Phinehas."

"I wish I could, but I'm afraid I don't." He hesitated, then went on, "Why are you so hard on her, Ardon?"

"You know what she is."

"No. I know what she *was*. You've got to understand people better."

"I understand well enough what a harlot is."

"If you hate everybody who has ever sinned, you're going to have a narrow circle of friends," Phinehas said wryly.

"I don't understand you, Phinehas. You're too easy."

"God is merciful. We know that. You remember what He told Moses on the mount? How He was a God full of mercy and that He was tenderhearted?"

Ardon was silent, for he could not argue that. Moses had told the people that often enough.

"But Moses could be hard too. And God can be hard."

"Oh yes. God is good and just. He chastises us as we would chastise a child, for our own good."

Ardon listened, but it was clear to Phinehas that he had shut his heart. "One of these days," he said, "you're going to grow up. Until you do, you're just a spoiled boy."

Ardon was angry at his friend's words, but he did not argue, for he respected Phinehas, as did everyone.

"You may be the one who's surprised," he said. "She'll go back to her old ways. There are men looking at her."

"No question about that. She's a beautiful woman. But is she looking at them?"

In all honesty Ardon could not answer yes, for he had watched Rahab closely and had seen nothing like this. "She'll fall. You'll see." He turned and left Phinehas standing there.

Phinehas called out after him, "Grow up, Ardon. Learn to be a man with a heart."

Ardon did not answer, but the conversation troubled him. He went about his work that day until finally he went home. He found Ariel waiting for him.

She greeted him affectionately, as she always did, for the two were very close. "Well, how's the mighty warrior today?"

"I don't feel much like a warrior. I am having a hard time putting the destruction of Jericho behind me, Ariel."

"It just about sickened Othniel. He told me about it."

"He's not much of a soldier. Too tenderhearted."

"He's different from most men. I don't really understand him." She waited until Ardon was seated, then brought him some meat she had just cooked. "Eat a little of this. I found some greens. They'll be good when they've simmered awhile."

She sat down at his feet and studied him. "Othniel told me about watching a soldier killing a little girl. It made him sick."

"Nobody likes that, but it was God's commandment."

"So I told him." She hesitated, then went on, "You know, Othniel likes me. He told me he's cared for me since we were children."

Instantly Ardon shook his head. "Don't let him romance you, Ariel. He's good with women. You know that. But he's a weak man."

"Maybe he could change."

Upset, Ardon put the meat aside. "Listen to me, Ariel. People don't change. He's a weak man and he always will be."

"I think you're too hard sometimes."

"That's not hardness, Ariel. That's strength."

Ariel was disturbed by this attitude. She studied her brother's face and then said quietly, "Someday, Ardon, you're going to make a mistake. When you do, you'll find out what it's like to be weak."

"I hope God strikes me dead before I turn against Him and disobey Him."

Ariel suddenly felt a love for her brother. "You're so odd," she said. "You're such a strong man and yet that strength is a weakness that could hurt you badly. Try to be more understanding." She got up and left him, and Ardon watched her go. He did not like to see her disturbed, for he loved her greatly, but he knew he was right.

"You'll see, Ariel. Rahab will fall, and poor Othniel is no man. He'll fall too. Then you'll see."

"Well, you two fellows did so well working together I'm going to give you a chance to do it again."

Joshua was smiling as Othniel and Ardon stood before him. He was in very good spirits. The victory of Jericho had given him hope that he had never dreamed he would have. Joshua had been convinced he could never take over leadership for Moses, but now God had spoken in the victory of Jericho. "There's a little city called Ai. It's beside Beth Aven to the east of Bethel. I sent some scouts to view it, and they've brought me back word that it will be easily taken. I'm sending just three thousand men up, not the whole army. I want you two to go."

"Of course, sir," Ardon said at once. "So you don't think it will be a hard battle?"

"Not at all. After Jericho," he said somberly, "anything else will seem easy."

"When do we leave, sir?" Othniel asked. He was not at all excited about going, for he still had some doubt about his capabilities as a soldier. He felt the eyes of both men on him, as if he had asked an inappropriate question.

But Joshua only said, "You'll leave tomorrow morning. It shouldn't take long. Remember, I'm very proud of both of you."

As the two young men left the tent, Ardon said, "Well, here's a chance to get out of here and do something. I'm bored stiff, aren't you?"

"I'm not the soldier you are, Ardon."

"You could be if you tried. You're a good swordsman and you're strong. You've just got a bad attitude when it comes to battles."

"That's a nice way of saying I get scared, isn't it?"

The admission startled Ardon. He himself was fearless in battle. "Why should you be afraid?"

"Because I might get killed."

"Well, of course—every soldier risks that. If you sit around and think about it, it'll drive you crazy. Just put it out of your mind and go at the enemy with all you've got."

"Doesn't it ever occur to you that you might get killed, Ardon?"

"If the thought comes to me, I push it away and fight all the harder." Ardon was disturbed by his friend's admission. "Just stick close to me in the battle. We'll make a soldier out of you yet. Like Joshua said, this one should be easy."

"All right, but these things don't always turn out like people plan."

———

The battle, indeed, did not turn out as anyone in Israel had planned. There was a carefree sort of attitude in the soldiers as they had approached the city. It was as if they were going to a banquet. They were laughing and joking—all except Othniel.

"This is a pretty cocky bunch," Othniel said.

"What's wrong with that? It shows they're good soldiers, doesn't it?"

"These fellows we're attacking might be tougher than Joshua thinks. That was a rumor I heard."

"If you listen to rumors, you'll never get anything done." Ardon was in high spirits. He reached over and punched Othniel on the arm, then seized his hair and gave it a tug. "You're going to be a hero. We all are. When we go back, there'll be dancing and singing and feasting, and this time I think Joshua will let us keep some of the spoils for ourselves. Why, we might be rich enough to take wives."

Othniel managed a smile, but he was worried. "Don't you think we should circle around and try to catch them by surprise? Attack from different angles?"

"No. We should just go right at them," Ardon said, his eyes glittering with excitement. "Come on. It's time to attack."

Othniel ran forward to keep up with the line that was headed toward Ai. They had to go through a valley, and they were exactly in the middle of it when a cry of agony split the air. Both Ardon and Othniel turned to see one of their better soldiers with an arrow driven through his neck. He had fallen to the earth clawing and kicking, his blood pooling beneath him.

"It's an ambush!" Ardon yelled. "Protect yourselves!"

But there was no way to protect themselves from the excellent archers of Ai. They had hidden themselves in the rocks at the top of both sides of the valley, and the men of Israel were trapped below.

Ardon yelled, "Come. We'll charge up that hill and take them!"

"We won't have any chance!" Othniel protested. "We'll be in the open, and those archers are hidden."

"We'll overrun them," Ardon yelled. "Come on."

Othniel thought it was foolhardy, but he and the others

followed Ardon up one side while another soldier led an attack on the far side.

Both attacks were failures. The arrows came whizzing down, men started falling, and before they had reached half the height of the summit, even Ardon saw the hopelessness of it. "Retreat!" he yelled. "Get out of here!"

That began the rout. The survivors made their way back down into the valley and were attacked by infantry that came charging out of hiding. There seemed to be thousands of them, and Othniel cried out, "We've got to get away from here! We don't have a chance!"

Ardon wanted to fight, but he saw the foolishness of putting up a struggle. "Retreat!" he yelled. "Every man retreat back to the camp!"

They made their way back to the camp, fighting a rearguard action. When the men of Ai broke off the attack, the Israelite soldiers staggered back into the camp, where Ardon took a count.

When Joshua met them and listened to the report, he asked, "How many men did we lose?"

"Over thirty."

"How did this happen?" Caleb asked, astounded.

"We were beaten," Ardon said, his head down.

"It should have been easy," Joshua said. "Something is wrong." He turned and walked away. The victory of Jericho had lifted his spirits. Now he fell on his face and rent his clothes before the ark of the Lord. He stayed there until evening, and the elders of Israel put dust on their heads. Cries of mourning and grief for the slain filled the camp.

Othniel went back to his tent and found Ariel there.

"Where's Ardon?" she asked anxiously.

"I don't know. We were beaten. We lost a lot of good men."

"How did it happen?"

Othniel shook his head. "I don't know, Ariel, but it could

have been worse. They could have killed all of us. I think we were overconfident."

Ariel was upset. "So you have no idea where Ardon is?" she demanded again. "Is he wounded?"

"No. I think he's helping to tend to some of the wounded."

"I'm going to him."

"He probably won't be too glad to see you. He's angry with himself, and he doesn't like to lose."

"He never did," Ariel said bitterly, "but I'm thankful you're both back, Othniel."

"Even Joshua was shaken by it. I've never seen him like this," Othniel said. "He's in front of the ark now, tearing his clothes and throwing dust into the air. He's crying out for God. Well," he said bitterly, "we needed God then and I think we need Him now."

CHAPTER

16

The dirt on Joshua's face was creased by the tears that had made tracks down his cheeks. He had torn his clothes and was still crying out in agony. "Ah, Sovereign Lord, why did you ever bring this people across the Jordan to deliver us into the hands of the Amorites to destroy us? If only we had been content to stay on the other side of the Jordan!"

Joshua did not care that many of his soldiers were close enough to hear his voice. His heart was broken, and he continued to cry out, "O Lord, what can I say, now that Israel has been routed by its enemies? The Canaanites and the other people of the country will hear about this and they will surround us and wipe out our name from the earth. What then will you do for your own great name?"

Joshua had prayed like this for many hours and the heavens seemed to be made of brass. There was no answer from God.

Finally, totally exhausted, Joshua lay on his face. He had cried out to God with all of his heart, and now he had completely run out of anything to say. A silence had fallen upon the camp, at least the part where Joshua lay before the ark. Then the voice of the Lord came to him. Joshua lay very still, afraid to move.

"Stand up! What are you doing down on your face? Israel has sinned;

they have violated my covenant, which I commanded them to keep. They have taken some of the devoted things; they have stolen, they have lied, they have put them with their own possessions. That is why the Israelites cannot stand against their enemies; they turn their backs and run because they have been made liable to destruction. I will not be with you anymore unless you destroy whatever among you is devoted to destruction.

"Go, consecrate the people. Tell them, 'Consecrate yourselves in preparation for tomorrow; for this is what the Lord, the God of Israel, says: That which is devoted is among you, O Israel. You cannot stand against your enemies until you remove it.

"'In the morning, present yourselves tribe by tribe. The tribe that the Lord takes shall come forward clan by clan; the clan that the Lord takes shall come forward family by family; and the family that the Lord takes shall come forward man by man. He who is caught with the devoted things shall be destroyed by fire, along with all that belongs to him. He has violated the covenant of the Lord and has done a disgraceful thing in Israel!'"

As always, when Joshua heard the voice of the Lord, he was stunned and could not move for a long time. Finally he got to his feet. Caleb had been standing at some distance, and now he came forward and studied Joshua's face. "What is it, my lord?" he asked quietly.

"The Lord has spoken, Caleb."

"And what has the Lord God said?"

"Someone in Israel has sinned and has taken part of the spoils of Jericho for his own use."

"Who would do such a shameful thing!" Caleb exclaimed.

"We shall know in the morrow. In the morning we will call all the people together, and God will show us who has brought disgrace and shame upon Israel."

Rahab was mystified at what had happened. She had listened to the reports of the soldiers who had returned and finally had sought out Othniel. She listened as he told the story of defeat, and when he had finished, Othniel spread his hands.

"I don't know what's going to happen, Rahab, but something is. Joshua has commanded that the whole nation be assembled this morning."

"What about the strangers, like myself?"

"He didn't say anything about that, and I don't understand what's happening."

Ariel and Ardon approached then, and Othniel asked at once, "Did your father say what's going to happen?"

"He didn't say a word," Ardon replied. "Joshua just told him to have all the people ready."

"Somehow I'm afraid," Ariel said, "but I don't know why."

"No need to be afraid," Ardon assured her. He turned to Rahab and asked, "Are all your needs being met?"

"Yes. Thank you so much."

"I understand you're studying with Phinehas about the things of God," Ariel said.

"Oh yes." Rahab's face was radiant, and all three of the Israelites wondered at it. It was strange to see someone grow so excited about the worship of Jehovah—especially one of the strangers in Israel. "The God of Israel is so wonderful," Rahab said. "He's full of mercy and love. That's what Phinehas tells me."

"Well, he's right. He's always right," Ardon said.

Suddenly Ariel turned. "Look. There's Joshua and Father."

Joshua and Caleb had mounted a small hill, and Caleb cried out with a loud voice. "Let all the tribes separate themselves one from another!"

There was some shifting around while those who had wandered from their place reassembled with others. All of the tribes were separated then, with Joshua, Caleb, and the high priest in the center.

Joshua began to pray, and Othniel asked, "What's he doing, Ardon?"

"I have no idea, but something is happening."

"Look. He's coming toward our tribe, the tribe of Judah."

Joshua came and stood before the assembled tribe of Judah. Caleb was beside him, and Joshua turned and said, "Caleb, the offender is in your tribe."

"Death be to him!" Caleb exclaimed, his face pale. "Woe that a man of my own tribe would defy the God of Israel."

"Separate them by families," Joshua commanded. This took some time, but finally each household was separated. Joshua prayed again and stood silently, and finally he lifted his head and everyone knew that God had spoken to him. "Let the family of the Zerahites come forward, for within them is the guilty man."

The other members of Judah drew aside, their faces pale. The other tribes kept their distance, for they knew that something terrible was happening.

Othniel stood beside Ariel and whispered, "This is bad, cousin."

"Yes it is. What's going to happen?"

"I don't know."

Joshua prayed again, and the family of Zimri was taken.

When Joshua announced that the household of Zimri contained the guilty party, Othniel felt a wave of fear go through him. He stared at all the members of that tribe and saw his friend Achan standing. Something in the man's posture warned Othniel. He began to pray, *God, don't let it be Achan!*

But after Joshua had prayed again, he came and stood directly before Achan and said loudly, "My son, give glory to the Lord, the God of Israel, and give Him the praise. Tell me what you have done; do not hide it from me."

Achan was trembling then from head to foot. His face was ashen, and he lifted his hands, which were shaking violently. "It is true!" he cried out. "I have sinned against the Lord, the God of Israel."

"What have you done, my son?" Joshua asked. His voice was quiet, but there was a deadly quality in it.

Othniel wanted to run and pull Achan away, but there was no hope of that now.

Achan could barely speak. Finally he cried out, "This is what I have done: When I saw in the plunder a beautiful robe from Babylonia, two hundred shekels of silver and a wedge of gold weighing fifty shekels, I coveted them and took them. They are hidden in the ground inside my tent, with the silver underneath."

Joshua pointed to some of his officers. "Go see."

The men left immediately, and whispers ran throughout all of the camp. But Achan fell on his face, weeping and crying. His wife and children were with him.

"It looks bad for your friend Achan, Othniel," Ardon whispered.

Othniel could not even answer. He had been afraid when charging into the line of battle, but it was nothing like this. His legs felt so weak he thought he might collapse. Finally the officers came back. "The things are there, my lord," they reported. One of them held out the exquisite garment and said, "The silver and gold are there too."

"Bring all those things to the Valley of Achor," Joshua said sternly.

Joshua led the way, and soldiers had to pick up Achan, who was crying and could not seem to walk. His family was brought too, and others went to get all of his livestock.

"Surely they aren't going to kill them!" Othniel cried out to Ariel, who was walking beside him.

Ariel could not say a word. She knew a great deal of the history of the Hebrews, and she knew that men had been executed for lesser offenses than this. "I don't think you ought to watch this, Othniel," she said.

But Othniel paid no attention. He walked along stiff-legged, as if unable to hear. His eyes were fixed on the pitiful form of his friend Achan, and he kept muttering, "They can't kill him—they can't."

Finally they reached the Valley of Achor, a small valley between two small hills where refuse had been thrown. Now Joshua turned, his face stern. "Why have you brought this trouble on us?" he cried. "The Lord will bring trouble on you today." Then he moved away and said, "Carry out the commandments of Jehovah."

Othniel wanted to tear his gaze away, but he seemed to be frozen, turned to stone. He saw men and women pick up stones, and he heard the cry of Achan and his family as the stones hit them. He saw a large stone strike Achan on the forehead, opening up an awful wound, and he fell with a cry that Othniel knew he would never forget if he lived to be an old man.

Caleb then came and held out a stone. "You must take part, Othniel."

Othniel stared at him and said, "No. I will never do such a thing!" He turned and fled, his eyes blinded with tears.

Ardon and Ariel were standing near their father. They watched Othniel as he ran, and Ariel said, "I think this is wrong, Father."

"No, it is right. The God of Israel never does anything wrong." He turned to his daughter and stared at her. "It is hard, but the judgment of God is hard."

"I was right about Othniel. He is too soft to be a soldier."

Ariel had turned away from the execution. The victims were silent now. She was thinking of the boy who could never stand to see an animal slaughtered, and now to see his best friend and the family he loved dearly battered into bloody corpses . . . it was no wonder he ran.

"I don't know if Othniel will ever get over this," she said.

"He'll have to," Caleb said grimly. "If he's going to be a man and follow God, he's got to learn to do as God commands."

CHAPTER

17

After the execution, the bodies were burned and a great heap of stones was raised over them while Joshua wept for Israel. But the Lord spoke to him and comforted his heart. *"Do not be afraid,"* He said. *"Do not be discouraged. Take the whole army with you, and go up and attack Ai. For I have delivered into your hands the king of Ai, his people, his city and his land. You shall do to Ai and its king as you did to Jericho and its king, except that you may carry off their plunder and livestock for yourselves. Set an ambush behind the city."*

Joshua was encouraged. He began to give orders, but he saw that Caleb looked sad.

"What's wrong? God will surely give us the victory, brother."

"It's Othniel."

"What's wrong with him?"

"He hasn't gotten over the execution of Achan and his family. He loved them, especially Achan. It was hard for him. I have tried to get him to take part, but he will not."

"Where is he now?"

"He's drunk. You know that band of wanderers that lives out north of the camp?"

"They're a rough bunch. Mostly harlots and thieves."

"That's where he is. They've got plenty of wine. I had him

followed. I even tried to get him to come back, but he wouldn't even talk to me, he was so drunk."

Joshua laid his hand on Caleb's shoulder. "I know this is grievous to you, my brother, but we must go on. We have Israel to think about."

"I know, Joshua. It is grievous. I loved his father dearly and promised to do my best for his son, but it seems nothing will touch Othniel. He's a weak man."

Ariel looked up and saw that Rahab was waiting to speak to her. The woman was very modest, she had to admit, not like she had always thought a harlot would be. Now she said, "What is it, Rahab?"

"I came to ask about Othniel."

"What do you want to know?" Ariel said sharply. She was ashamed of Othniel and didn't particularly want to talk about him.

"I came to ask you if you would go and try to talk to him," Rahab said.

"I'm not going over to that camp," Ariel snapped. "It's full of thieves and robbers and evil women."

"I will go with you, mistress. And surely your brother will go."

"No he won't. We're all disgusted with Othniel. He's no good."

"I think he loves you," Rahab said.

Ariel was startled. "That's foolishness!"

"I don't think it is. I've watched his eyes always go to you."

"He's fond of me—we were children together. But now he's ruined his life, and he's blamed his family. He's the nephew of Caleb. My father is the second in command in Israel, the head of the tribe of Judah. And now his own nephew is pouting and crying like a child."

"Have you ever lost a dear one to death, Ariel?"

"My mother, when I was very young . . . but . . . no."

"I didn't think so."

"That's neither here nor there. Othniel is a bad man. He's no good."

Rahab was silent for a moment; then she faced Ariel. Her eyes were clear, and she held her head high. "There's good in all of us," she said quietly, "and there's bad in all of us too."

Ariel could not face the young woman. "I'm not going to argue about this. Othniel has got to grow up. Now, don't come to me anymore about this matter."

"I won't," Rahab said. She turned abruptly and went away, leaving Ariel to stare after her.

Who does she think she is? Ariel thought. *She's not a member of our family. It's none of her business.* The thought came to her then, *Unless he's been sleeping with her. She's pretty enough.* That thought troubled her even more, and she could not shake it out of her head as she went about her work that day.

———

Phinehas had listened to Rahab as she made her case. She had come to him and asked him in a straightforward fashion to help Othniel. She had not begged outwardly, but there had been a pleading in her eyes.

Phinehas listened until she fell silent; then he said at once, "I love Othniel. I think he has great potential."

"Will you help him?"

"I'm not sure that I can."

"Surely, sir, if anyone can, it's you. He respects you greatly."

"Sometimes a man reaches a point when he won't listen to anyone. I think Othniel is there. It's as if he's on the edge of a narrow wall. If he falls one way, he'll be saved and make a life for himself. If he falls the other way, he'll be ruined." Phinehas considered the young woman. He had come to know her better than most. Despite her past, he sensed goodness in her, and her hunger for God warmed his heart.

"When someone we love falls, our first impulse, Rahab, is to rush in to save them. To fix whatever situation that they're in so that they'll be all right."

"Isn't that a good thing?"

"It can be," Phinehas said, nodding. "But sometimes it doesn't succeed. People have to be ready to accept help. If they're not, there's no helping them."

"But is there nothing you can do?"

"Yes, there is, and you can help me."

"How can I do that?"

"We can pray together that God will watch over this young man until he finds himself."

"I am but a stranger in Israel. You are the high priest."

"Do you think God hears only priests? No, no, my sister. You must learn that our God is everywhere and He's always listening. He is searching for a humble and a contrite heart, and when He finds it, I promise you, He listens."

"I will pray, then."

"Let's pray together right now."

The two prayed silently, and finally Phinehas said aloud in a firm voice, "God, put your hand upon Othniel. Let him not come to harm. If he must be hurt, so be it. But we pray together that you will redeem him."

Rahab smiled shyly at the priest. He was almost angelic to her, so holy and good and righteous, while she had had a terrible life. She could not understand how he could be so kind and loving and others could be so judgmental. Still, she said, "Thank you, sir."

"Will you believe that Jehovah will help our friend?"

"I will believe."

After her visits with Phinehas and Ariel, Rahab tried to do as Phinehas had said. She tried to believe that all would be well for Othniel. Finally, however, after two days, she found herself more anxious than ever. She determined to speak with Ardon on his next visit. He always came two or three times a week under the orders of Joshua to be sure that all was well with her and her family. When he came next, she did not hesitate. "Ardon, have you thought about going to see Othniel?"

"For what purpose?"

"Tell him that he's ruining his life."

"He knows that."

"You could tell him that you love him."

Ardon snorted and shook his head. "That's woman talk. No, I won't go. He knows I'd be ready to help him, but he doesn't want help. He wants to stay drunk and live with those evil men and women." As soon as he had said those last words, Ardon could have bitten his tongue off. "I didn't mean to say that."

"It's what you think, though, isn't it?"

"I think he's given up. I don't think he'll ever amount to anything."

"But will you go to him and try to help him?"

"No, I won't. It would be foolish."

"One day you'll have a problem and you'll fall, Ardon. And when you fall, who will pick you up? Who will love you?"

Ardon was stunned. It was almost exactly what Ariel had said to him. But then he dismissed it as merely weak, womanish thought and answered roughly, "He knows where his family is. He knows we'll take him back if he comes. Until he does, there's nothing I can do." He turned and walked away, but the words of the woman stayed with him. *"When you fall, who will pick you up? Who will love you?"* He could not get away from it, and it disturbed him so greatly that he threw himself into the activity of getting ready for the battle to take Ai.

———

Rahab found her way to the tents of the Amorites, who sometimes traded with the Israelites. They were a rowdy, sinful people, a type she knew well. When she approached the camp, several men tried to approach her, leering at her, but she cut them off sharply. "Where's Othniel?"

"You need a real man. Not that drunk." A big, burly man approached her and put his hand on her arm. Swiftly she drew her knife and raked the blade of it down his arm.

"Hey—ow," the man said. "Why, you vixen, you cut me!"

"I'll cut your throat if you put your hands on me again."

The man grinned. "Well now, you've got some temper. Come on. I'll take you to Othniel. He's drunk, though. I doubt if you can get any sense out of him. What's the matter with him, anyway?"

"He's had troubles."

"So what? Who hasn't?"

The burly Amorite led her into a tent. She found Othniel sitting up but obviously drunk. He had a bottle of wine in his hand, and a sluttish-looking woman stared at her.

"What do you want?" the woman said.

"Get out," Rahab demanded. "I need to talk to this man."

The woman started for her, but at the sight of Rahab's knife she changed directions, and with a curse she left the tent. Replacing the knife in her clothing, Rahab went over and stood before Othniel. "You must leave this place, Othniel."

"Why?"

"This place is not for you. These are not good people."

"I'm not going back."

That was the beginning of a conversation that went on for a long time. Othniel drank steadily, and finally in desperation, Rahab cried, "God still loves you. He understands."

Othniel drank the last of the wine and threw the leather flask away. He turned to face her. "Don't talk to me about God."

"Don't say that, Othniel. Jehovah is the God of love."

"Then why did He let my friend Achan get killed?"

That was the essence of Rahab's visit. No matter how she

pleaded, Othniel stubbornly refused to go. Finally she rose and went over to him. She laid her hand on his head and prayed, "God of Abraham, Isaac, and Jacob, this is one of your children. Do not let him perish." She looked long and hard at Othniel, then turned and left the tent.

Othniel stared angrily at the entrance of the tent, trembling. Then he fell forward, and great sobs racked his body.

PART FOUR

OTHNIEL

CHAPTER

18

Dawn was just breaking, and as always, Zayna was pleased with the world. As she walked along with Oman beside her, she lifted her eyes to where high in the sky a flight of birds made their way steadily toward the south. Their V-shaped formation pleased her and made her wonder, *How do they know to make that kind of shape?* The thought stayed with her as she glanced at Oman, who had stopped to poke a frog with a stick.

"Leave that frog alone, Oman!" Zayna said. "We've got to hurry and get the water and get back."

"I wonder if anyone eats frogs?"

Zayna laughed. "I don't think so. I wouldn't want to eat one."

The two hurried along toward the stream, invigorated by the fresh morning air and the pink glowing light. Just a few minutes ago it had been quite dark, and the stars had been clear in the sky. Now as Zayna watched with delight, the eastern horizon was pulled apart, and long waves of light rolled out of the east. It was her favorite time of day.

When they reached the stream, Zayna dipped her pot into the water and let it fill. She set it down on the bank and smiled as Oman splashed noisily in the shallows. His health had improved greatly since they had left Jericho, much to the delight of his family.

Glancing back toward the camp, Zayna thought about the weeks that had passed since she had been taken away by the two Hebrew soldiers. She remembered her fear when she and her family had been thrust into the life of a people they did not know. Zayna had been terrified of them, for she had seen their soldiers kill without mercy, and at times she would curl up at night and have bad dreams of men with swords and spears coming to kill them.

Now, however, as the fresh sunlight flooded the earth, she thought of how different it had been from what she had expected. The man called Ardon had seen to it that they had a large tent to share, and he had also made certain that they had plenty of food. The food was different from what Zayna and the others were accustomed to; nevertheless, both Rahab and Romar were excellent cooks, so they had actually fared better than they had in the city.

"Come on, Oman. It's time to get back."

As the two made their way back to their tent, they suddenly noticed two boys who were evidently on their way to the stream. One of them was a heavyset individual with blunt features and piggish eyes. The other was just the opposite, skinny and with the face of a fox. The foxy one said, "Hey, look. There's the harlot's sister."

The pig-eyed boy laughed crudely. "Yeah," he said, "let's make her tell us some stories of what it's like to be a harlot."

The fox-faced boy laughed and the two came at once to stand before Oman and Zayna. "Hey, girl, my name's Ezibal. This is my friend Kon."

Kon was the brutal-faced one, large and hulking. He grinned rudely and grabbed Zayna's arm.

"Let me go!"

"Don't be that way," Kon said with an unfriendly grin. "We're going to show you a good time, aren't we, Ezibal?"

"Sure. We heard about you and your sister." He took her other arm, and they began pulling Zayna toward a clump of underbrush. "Come on. We've got something to show you."

Zayna cried out, and Oman ran quickly and threw himself against the smaller of the two. Ezibal knocked the boy flat on his back. "Stay out of this. You better go on back," he warned.

Zayna was fighting, but the brute strength of the large boy was painful. She could not pull away, and as she continued to cry, he laughed. "Go on. Nobody's out here to hear you."

"What's going on?"

Both Kon and Ezibal turned quickly to see who had spoken. Zayna turned her head also and saw a boy no more than two years older than herself come out of the brush. He had evidently been hunting, for he had a bow in his left hand and a quiver of arrows on his back. In his free hand he held a brace of rabbits. His clear gray eyes watched the two carefully. "Better let her go, Kon."

"None of your business, Elam," Kon growled.

Elam dropped the rabbits and with a quick movement pulled an arrow from his quiver, nocked it, and drew the string. "You know I didn't have much luck today, just two rabbits. I need a little practice. Maybe I'll have better luck with you."

"Watch out what you're doing with that thing!"

"You two just get on your way."

For a moment Zayna was afraid that the two bullies would challenge Elam, but his hands were steady, and he was smiling as if he hoped they would do exactly that.

"Aw, come on, Kon. Let's go get those fish."

The burly Kon stared at Elam. "I'll see you later, Elam."

"Always glad to see you, Kon. A real pleasure."

Kon released Zayna, and she rubbed her arm and watched as the two stalked off toward the river. She turned and whispered, "I'm so glad you came."

"Well, they're not very mannerly. My name's Elam. What's yours?"

"I'm Zayna, and this is my nephew, Oman."

"Don't know you, do I?"

"No, I don't think so." Zayna hated to let the young man know about her family, for he might feel the same way as the other boys felt. "We lived in Jericho, but we live with your people now."

"So you're the family that helped the scouts."

"Yes," Zayna said quickly. "That was my sister Rahab."

"I heard about that. That was a great thing you did." He looked down and said, "Oh, you broke your pot. You'll have to go get another one. Come on. I'll go with you."

Zayna fell into step with the young man, and Oman came and cast glances at him. "Are you a soldier, Elam?" he asked.

"I will be one day. Maybe you will be too."

"I'm too little."

Elam laughed. "Well, you won't always be little. You'll be big and tall and strong like me." He winked at Zayna, and she smiled back at him. "How do you like it here with our people?"

"We like it fine, but some people don't like us—like those two."

"Don't judge all our tribes by them. They just need to have their heads soaked. I like you fine." He turned and winked at Oman. "Say, I found some good berry bushes. Do you like berries?"

"Yes!"

"Come on. We'll go fill up on 'em. And then we'll pick some. Maybe they'll make good cakes. Can you cook?" he asked Zayna.

"A little."

"Well, we'll pick the berries, and you can bake a cake, and I'll eat it. How does that sound?"

Zayna felt much better now. "That sounds wonderful."

———————

As the three youngsters approached the tent, Rahab glanced up and said, "Look, Romar, it appears that Zayna and Oman have found a new friend."

Romar had been grinding some grain in a rounded-out stone with a rounded rock. She stopped and looked up and her eyes narrowed. "I don't think I've been him before."

"Fine-looking boy," Rahab observed.

"I broke your pot," Zayna said as they approached. "I'll have to go back for more water."

"Who is your friend, Zayna?" Rahab smiled.

"This is Elam. Two boys were bothering us, but Elam ran them off."

"That was very nice of you, Elam." Rahab smiled.

Elam shrugged his shoulders. "Oh, it was nothing," he said. "They aren't really all that bad."

"They are too," Oman said. "I wish you would have shot 'em with an arrow."

"Couldn't do that. They'll grow up to be good soldiers one day." Elam was studying Rahab. He had heard the story and, of course, there were the usual ribald tales about the woman being a harlot. But as he studied Rahab, she seemed to be very nice. He admired the smoothness of her complexion and her large lustrous eyes, and she had a very nice smile. "I've heard about you," he said. "It was wonderful what you did helping us take Jericho."

Rahab shook her head. "It was a hard thing for us to lose all of our people, but your God took care of my family."

"We brought some berries," Zayna said, holding up a cloth bulging with the juicy fruit. "Look."

Romar came over and looked down at the berries. "Those are just right," she said. "Did you eat many?"

"I did," Oman said. His face gave credence to his words, for he was smeared with the red juice. "They were good!"

"Could we make some cakes with them?" Zayna asked. "I promised Elam we would."

"I don't see why not. It'll take a while, though."

"We'll go back and get some more water," Elam said. "If those two come back, I'll put an arrow right where it hurts."

"Good!" Oman said. "Do both of them, Elam."

"We have plenty of water now," Rahab said. "You can go later. Why don't you sit down and tell us about yourself?"

Elam felt very much at ease. He sat down and watched the women as they began to bake the cakes. One of them stirred up the fire, and another made dough. He watched as Zayna helped put the juicy berries in the dough, and soon the air was fragrant with the smell of baking.

"What do you think will happen now?" Rahab asked.

"Oh, there's going to be another battle."

"What makes you say that?"

"I heard my father talking about it. He's a great soldier. We are preparing to return to Ai. I'm going to be in it too."

"Will your father let you?" Rahab asked gently. The boy seemed to be no more than fourteen, far too young to be a seasoned soldier.

"I'm not going to tell him. I'm from the tribe of Benjamin, but I have a friend who is of the tribe of Judah. His name is Ziza. He's two years older than I am, and he said I could go with him when the battle starts."

Rahab picked up a small twig and began poking the cakes. "These are about ready," she said. "Be careful now. They're hot."

Her warning did no good, for Oman began to pick one up, bit into it, and immediately dropped it in the dirt. "Ow," he yelled. "That's hot!"

"That's what I told you. Now pick that up and dust it off."

The youngsters were eating the cakes with great satisfaction, but Rahab was thinking of what the boy had said. "I don't think that would be a very good idea for you to sneak into battle."

"What's that?"

"I think you ought to tell your father. He would be very sad if anything happened to you."

Elam shifted uncomfortably. "Why, I'll be all right."

"Nobody knows what will happen to them in a battle."

Rahab was gentle, and she kept feeding the boy the small cakes, and finally she said in a kindly tone, "It'd be a very good idea for you to talk to him first. You wouldn't want to make him unhappy."

"No, I wouldn't. All right," he said. "I doubt he'll let me go, but I can try."

Even as the boy spoke, Ardon came along and stopped, sniffing the aroma of fresh-baked cakes.

Rahab smiled at him. "Here. Try one of these."

Ardon reached for a cake and sank his teeth into it. "Hmmm . . . good," he said.

"The berries are fresh. The young people found them."

"Hello, Ardon," Elam said. "Are you getting ready for the battle?"

"Oh, Elam. I'm surprised to see you. What are you doing over here?"

"Eating cakes. What about the battle?"

"That's for grown-ups."

"I'm practically grown up."

Ardon smiled. "I thought I was too when I was your age. You'll just have to wait."

"Sit down and rest yourself, Ardon," Rahab said.

"No. I came to speak with you privately."

"Oh, all right." Rahab left with Ardon, and the two walked away from the tent. The camp was busy with women doing their work and the men mostly talking.

"Have you seen Othniel?"

"Not recently. Why?"

Ardon frowned. "I've got to find him."

"Is it something about the battle?"

"Yes. Joshua and my father have told me to bring him. He's to have a part in it."

"You don't like that idea, do you?"

"No, I don't. He's been drunk ever since Achan was stoned."

"Yes. It grieved him a great deal, Ardon."

"That's weak. Achan got what he deserved. He disobeyed God's command."

"I know, but Othniel has a tender heart, and it's never easy losing a friend."

"He needs to pick his friends better, and besides that, you don't know everything about our people, Rahab."

"Oh, I know—I'm just learning. I know very little, really."

"You've been listening to Phinehas. He's a good man and a good friend, but he's soft too."

"He seems very wise to me."

"Well, he's not very wise about the enemies of Israel."

"What do you mean?"

"We've got to conquer this whole land, Rahab. There's no time to be merciful."

"But Phinehas said that God told Moses that He was merciful."

"That may be true, but He has also told us to kill everybody in the land as we move into it."

Rahab's temper flared at how matter-of-factly Ardon said this. "I think you're being very unfair," she said impatiently, "and I think you're wrong."

"You see? You don't know anything, Rahab. God has told us that the land is ours, and Achan broke one of His commandments."

"We all do that, don't we?"

"Yes, I'm pretty sure *you* have broken the commandments."

His words hurt Rahab terribly. Tears burned her eyes, and she turned away, angry and bitter, unable to speak a word.

CHAPTER

19

"Wake up, Othniel!"

Ariel had diligently searched for Othniel and finally located him in the tent of one of his married friends. The tent was empty—except for her worthless cousin—and Ariel, kneeling down beside the still form, shook him and said angrily, "Wake up!" She continued to pull at Othniel until his eyes began to flutter and he groaned, "Leave me alone!"

"Get up! You can't sleep anymore."

Ariel watched as Othniel almost painfully sat up. He leaned back against one of the tent poles and stared at her without comprehension.

"What are you doing here?"

"I've come to find you."

Othniel licked his lips. "Thirsty," he muttered and began to grope around for a jug of water. He found it and lifted it to his lips. He drank thirstily and spilled the water down over his chest. Lowering the jug, he stared at her. "How'd you find me?"

"It wasn't easy," Ariel said. "You've got to hurry."

"Hurry and do what?"

Ariel leaned forward and whispered, even though there was no one to hear. "You can't afford to miss the battle to take Ai."

"What are you talking about?"

"My father was talking to my brother, and I heard them speak of the battle that's coming. Joshua's sending a force up to take Ai. My father wants you to be there in the battle. I don't know why. A lot of good you'd be."

Shakily Othniel got to his feet. He grasped the tent pole, for he had a splitting headache that felt a great deal like a spear was being thrust clear through his skull. "I'm not going to any battle," he said sullenly.

"What are you going to do?" Ariel demanded, her eyes flashing. "Stay here in this tent and pout and act like a spoiled child?"

"Get out of here, Ariel!"

"I'm not going. Not until you wake up to what's happening."

"I know what's happening. My friend Achan's dead."

"Are you going to spend the rest of your life grieving over him?"

"It wasn't right!"

"It *was* right."

"How can you say that, Ariel! He was a good man. He just made a mistake."

"I know it's right," Ariel said, "because God gave the commandment that he be stoned. If God says it, it has to be right."

Othniel opened his lips to answer angrily but suddenly knew that he could not. He was well aware that God had commanded Achan to be executed, but it had been a bitter pill for him to swallow, and now he reached up and ran his hands through his greasy, uncombed hair. "I don't want to hear any of this, Ariel."

"Well, you're going to hear it!" Ariel suddenly grabbed his hair with both hands. She shook his head, saying, "Wake up, Othniel, you're ruining your life!"

"That hurts!"

"That's too bad! Listen to me. You've got a chance to redeem yourself."

"No I don't."

"So you plan to be a drunk all your life? Are you a coward?"

Othniel forcibly removed Ariel's hands from his hair, holding on to her wrists. "Stop yanking my head around. I've got a splitting headache. Why do you care, anyway?"

Ariel did not answer for a moment, and thoughts ran rapidly through her mind. Why did she care?

"Because you're my kin," she said. "And my father loves you."

Othniel had no answer for this, for he knew it was true. He was still holding her wrists and realized he was squeezing them too hard. "I'm sorry," he mumbled, letting go of her. "I didn't mean to hurt you."

"That doesn't matter. What matters is that you've got a chance to be a man."

"All right. I'll be there. When are they leaving?"

"I don't know, but it won't be long." She put her hands on his chest. "You have so much potential, Othniel, and you're wasting it all." Then she turned and left without another word.

Othniel stood staring after her. His jaw tightened, and with a new determination, he began to prepare himself for the battle.

———

Caleb and Joshua had thoroughly gone over the battle plan. As the senior officers in the army of Israel, they each recognized what a monumental task lay before them.

Joshua stared at Caleb and smiled. "Well, this will be a good training exercise for the men. We've got some hard battles coming up, and they need to be tested."

Caleb rubbed his chin thoughtfully. His voice was somewhat doubtful as he spoke. "Well, let's go over the plan one more time. I think I've got it in my mind, but before we give the orders, let's be sure we know what we're doing."

"The people are feeling confident now. Winning the battle in Jericho was all God's doing, not ours."

"That's right. To God be the glory." Caleb nodded assent. "But this new battle will be different. There're no walls."

"That's right, so it ought to be easy."

Caleb said, "You know, Joshua, if God is not with us, no matter how easy it looks, we're going to lose. That's how we lost the first battle at Ai."

"That was because there was sin in the camp, but that's gone now," Joshua said grimly. "I don't think anyone else will make the mistake Achan made."

"His death really hurt Othniel."

"I know it did, but it was God's command. Now, here's what we're going to do. I want you to take thirty thousand men and swing wide around the city. Be sure that you're not seen. Then get as close as you can on the other side of the city."

Joshua spoke clearly, and his eyes gleamed as he weighed out the attack. "I'll take five thousand men and make a frontal attack. I'll make a lot of noise about it so they'll be looking at us."

"And so they'll come out of the city in full force to attack you."

"That's what I hope. They'll be overconfident. As soon as they leave the city and we've engaged them, you take the city and set it on fire."

"And we'll have them caught between our two forces. It ought to work, Joshua."

"It will work. Now, let's get started."

———————

Ardon was standing beside Caleb looking over the men when he spotted Othniel. "Look, Father, here comes Othniel. He looks terrible."

The two men waited until Othniel came up to them. His eyes were red and his hands were unsteady. "Well, I'm ready," he said.

"You look it," Ardon said grimly. "You might as well go

home. You're no good to us drunk."

"No, I won't do that," Othniel said stubbornly. "I've come to fight."

"You two stick close together," Caleb said. He went forward and laid his hands on Othniel's shoulder. "I wish your father were here, my boy. I know you want to make him proud of you."

Othniel could not meet Caleb's eyes. He was thoroughly ashamed of himself and knew that he was in no shape for a battle, but he muttered, "I'll do the best I can."

"Good. Now, look. We'll leave right now and take our position. . . ."

Othniel lay flat on his back. Caleb's force had made the journey around the city of Ai in complete and utter silence. They had not been spotted by any sentinel, and now they were lying in wait behind a series of low hills. Othniel was feeling terrible and wished he were anywhere but here.

"You look rotten, Othniel."

Othniel looked up to see his friend Ezra, from the tribe of Dan. Ezra threw himself down and grunted, "We may be here for a long time. Here. Have a drink." He unslung a leather flask that dangled from his neck and offered it to Othniel.

"No, I don't need it."

"Sure you do. We all do." Ezra took a healthy drink from the flask, then urged Othniel, "Just one little drink won't hurt."

"All right. One little drink."

But that one little drink was followed by another—and then another, and before Othniel knew what he was doing, he was drinking deeply. He fell into a drunken stupor, and as the sun grew hotter, he crawled up under the shade of the bushes. He did not hear the sound of Caleb's voice crying out, "Attack! Attack!" but slept on as the attack was made.

The attack worked perfectly. The king of Ai saw the small body of men and cried out, "Come! They're in our hands!" His men rushed out of the city against Joshua. Joshua commanded his men to keep backing up as if they were in a panic.

The men of Ai were exulted and cried out with voices of victory.

But in the midst of the battle, as soon as all of the men of Ai had joined in to annihilate Joshua's small force, the Lord said to Joshua, *"Hold out toward Ai the javelin that is in your hand, for into your hand I will deliver the city."*

Joshua stretched out his spear, and as soon as he did, he saw movement beyond the city. Caleb was attacking!

The men of Ai had been pressing the attack against Joshua when a loud a cry went up. The soldiers turned, and the king himself turned and saw smoke.

"The city's on fire, sire!" a courier cried out.

At that moment the king of Ai understood that he had been tricked. His face grew pale, but there was no escape.

Caleb's force flooded out of the city, and Joshua's men were reinforced. They caught the army of Ai as if in a nutcracker and crushed it. They annihilated the army and then did as they had with Jericho. They killed the inhabitants of Ai, but Joshua had counseled them, "This time God has said we may keep the cattle for our spoils."

Joshua gave commands for an altar, and quickly the soldiers built one of uncut stone, simply a pile of rocks. As soon as it was ready, Phinehas the priest offered a sacrifice to the Lord. And Joshua gave commands that a copy of the Law of Moses be placed on these stones. Joshua stood up on a large promontory and began to read the Law of Moses. The soldiers stood rank upon rank listening, knowing that God had given them another victory.

Finally Joshua finished and gave commands that the cattle should be taken back to the camp. "There'll be feasting this night," he cried.

———

When Othniel woke up, he could not remember where he was for a moment. The sun was low in the sky, so it was mid-afternoon. With a start he realized that the army was gone!

Crawling out from under the bush, he stared about wildly. He climbed the crest of the hill and saw Ai was a smoking ruin.

"The battle's over," he whispered hoarsely, "and I missed it."

Othniel cringed with shame. He wanted to run away, but there was no place for him to go. Slowly he walked past the city of Ai, trying not to look at the bodies of the slain, for it reminded him of the slaughter at Jericho. As he came close to the Hebrew camp, he heard the sound of laughter and singing and could soon smell burning meat. He tried to sneak around and get to his own tent, but he was spotted and his fellow soldiers began mocking him.

"Look. There's mighty warrior Othniel! Are you awake at last?"

Others took up the cry, making Othniel want to slink away and die.

Suddenly he was face-to-face with Ariel, whose eyes were fixed on him. Othniel started to speak, then discovered he had nothing to say as he read the bitter disappointment in the woman's eyes.

"I'm nothing, Ariel—and there's no need of my trying to be anything."

With these bitter words he turned and moved quickly away, not bearing to face the scorn that he had seen in Ariel's eyes.

CHAPTER

20

Nothing gave Rahab more pleasure than to view the tabernacle, the spot where Jehovah met to speak to His people. She was not permitted, of course, to go inside the tabernacle itself. No one could do that except the priests, who were all of the tribe of Levi. But she found herself going again and again to view the tabernacle and the fence that surrounded it.

It was late in the afternoon, after her work was done, that she made her way to a rise, and from the crest of it she turned to look down on the tabernacle. The sun was brilliant, and the tabernacle was dyed in resplendent colors, primarily of crimson. In the front were five huge pillars made of gold. Phinehas had told her that the entire structure was ten cubits wide, thirty cubits in length, and ten cubits high. Gold-covered pillars were settled into sockets of silver. The walls were fastened to each other by golden bolts, and a curtain surrounded the entire structure made of linen of blue, purple, and scarlet thread.

From where she stood she could hear the pleasant sound of voices singing and laughing, the voices of children and of older people as well. The camp surrounded the tabernacle so that the tabernacle was the center of the heart of Israel. Now she studied the courtyard encircling the tabernacle. Twenty pillars on each long side and ten pillars on each short side surrounded the entire structure, forming an outer court. She admired the hangings of fine linen work, blue and purple and vermilion, that caught the falling sun. Suddenly it seemed to her that the sanctuary had glowing walls that seemed to rise out of a sea of molten silver.

Rahab had become enamored by the God of Israel. True, she knew very little about Jehovah, but much of her waking moments were spent meditating on the stories she had heard of the Hebrew people from Phinehas. The gods of her people, which included Ashtaroth and Baal, were utterly crude and vile to her now, and she could not bear to think of the terrible things that were done in their names.

But Jehovah—He was a God to be worshiped and adored. He had spoken to Moses, and she recalled how Phinehas had told her that Jehovah had said He was a God of tender mercies and infinite love. A God of love! She had never heard of such a thing from her own people in her own land. From her own experience of life in Jericho, she knew the gods of Canaan to be only fierce and cruel and bloody. The people who worshiped them became every bit as cruel as their gods. She often wondered at what seemed like cruelty on the part of Jehovah in demanding that the Canaanites be completely wiped out, but when she saw the goodness of the Hebrew way of life—their devotion to God and their kindness to those who loved their God—she began to understand a little more. From Phinehas she had learned that God was all wise, and knowing that helped her trust Him more, regardless of whether His ways all made sense to her or not.

"Well, again I find you here admiring the tent of meeting."

Startled out of her reverie, Rahab turned and saw two men standing there. One was Phinehas, the high priest, the grandson of the great Aaron. The other man she did not recognize.

She bowed low and greeted them with reverence. "Good afternoon, masters."

Phinehas turned and looked down on the tabernacle. "I

never get tired of looking at that."

"It is beautiful. It seems not to be made with human hands but by angels," Rahab whispered.

To her surprise the other man laughed. "Well, there were times when I wished angels would have come, but in all truth it is the handiwork of men, not of angels."

"You have not met Bezalel, Rahab?"

"No, sir. I have not."

"Then let me make him known to you. You will find him interesting. Bezalel, this is Rahab. You have heard the story of how she preserved the lives of our scouts Ardon and Othniel of the family of Caleb."

"I have heard much, but it is an honor to meet you," Bezalel said. He was a tall, well-formed man with silver in his hair and a few lines on his face, but he had obviously been a strong, active man all his life.

"If you want to know about the tabernacle, this is the man to ask," Phinehas said. "He is the man God selected to build it."

Startled, Rahab's lips flew open. She stared at Bezalel as if he were a visitor from a foreign land. "I cannot believe it. You built that?"

Bezalel seemed embarrassed. "It was Moses' doing, all of it. God spoke to him when he was on Mount Sinai and gave him specific instructions on how to build the tabernacle and all of the furniture."

"I was not there when that was done," Phinehas said, "but it must have been a wonderful time."

Bezalel seemed lost in a reverie. "It was. No one was more shocked than I when Moses told me that God had commanded Him to choose me to be the builder. Me and my friend Oholiab were both shocked."

"It must have been wonderful," Rahab said.

"There is no way to describe it," Bezalel said. He began to speak freely, and it was obvious that he was remembering the high point of his life. "I had no idea where we would find the materials to build such a thing. You remember we were in the desert. There was not a shop to go buy what we needed, but God provided. Moses commanded that the people bring in the materials. I must admit I was doubtful, yet it happened. Every day the people brought in all that was required. Why, there were piles of materials. Jewels, metals of all kinds, wool for the walls. Everything! Finally Moses had to command them to stop."

"But where did they all come from, all those rich things?" Rahab asked.

"Has the high priest not told you how when we left Egypt, delivered by the hand of our God, the Egyptians loaded us down with precious things? I thought it only just, for we had built Egypt with the sweat of our brow. It was little enough pay for four hundred years of hard labor."

Rahab listened as Bezalel continued to speak. "Everyone worked in those days. We were free from slavery and working for our own God now. No one held back. The spinners and the weavers, the workers in metal. Look at the tabernacle. It was a tremendous job to put it together. It's not just one covering but several all joined together, for everything has to be moveable."

Indeed, Rahab had once witnessed the tabernacle's dismantling when the camp had been moved at Jehovah's command. She had seen the entire tabernacle stripped down, packed, loaded, and moved.

"And does no one ever go inside the tabernacle, except the priests of Levi?"

"Only the priests, according to the Law of God," Phinehas said.

"It must be beautiful on the inside."

"It is indeed beautiful," Bezalel said. "I remember after all this time how I labored over the golden ornaments for the interior of the tabernacle. I made the roof of pure gold, and two cherubim are woven into the curtains that separate the Most Holy Place."

"The Most Holy Place?"

"Yes. That is where the ark of God is. Only the high priest can enter that and then only one time a year. He must take blood inside and make an offering for the sins of the people."

"That must be wonderful. May I ask what it looks like on the inside of the Most Holy Place?"

Phinehas shifted uneasily. "I do not like to speak of that. It is frightening."

"The ark was the most difficult of all to make." Bezalel spoke for some time, his face glowing as he remembered those days when the tabernacle was being constructed.

Finally he said, "I must go now. But first I would like to show you something else very special that might help you understand a little of how God's hand is on the Hebrew people." Bezalel carefully pulled a beautiful gold medallion out from under his tunic, which hung about his neck on a leather strap, and showed it to Rahab.

"Why, it's lovely," she whispered, gently fingering the raised figure of a lion on the medallion. Bezalel turned it over to show her a lamb on the opposite side. "Did you make this too?" she asked.

"No," Bezalel said. "This medallion was given to me. It has been passed down through the people since the time of Noah, and I was given instruction to pass it on to whoever God tells me to before I die. So I will await His instructions."

"What is it for?" Rahab wondered.

"It is some kind of sign," Bezalel replied. "But its total meaning is a mystery . . . much like our God is to us, Rahab. I believe it points to a day in the future when a Redeemer will come into our midst and save us all. Perhaps then we will understand the full significance of the lion and the lamb. But for now we can rest in the peace that God has a future and a hope for each one of us."

Rahab looked up at him with wonder in her eyes.

"It has been good to meet you, Rahab," Bezalel said. "I am so glad that you now serve the true God."

"Thank you, master," Rahab whispered. She watched as the tall man tucked the medallion back into his tunic, nodded, and left them. She turned to look at Phinehas. "What a wonderful man!"

"Yes, indeed. He could tell some stories. He was barely twenty when God's judgment fell on Israel when they refused to enter the Land of Promise. But I get him to tell the stories as often as I can so they will not be forgotten."

Rahab suddenly asked a question that had been on her heart ever since the destruction of Jericho. This man, the high priest of Israel, surely must know the answer!

"Sir, I have often wondered why it is that the people in Jericho and Ai had to be killed. Some of them were only children, some of them very old people. I do not understand it. You have said that Moses discovered that God was the God of love, but is that love to kill a whole people?"

"I gave up a long time ago trying to understand God," Phinehas said. "He is not a God who can be apprehended by a finite man or woman. But I have prayed much, and I talk often with my father, who was intimate with Moses. The two of them wondered about the same thing. What I have now come to believe is what they taught me. The people of this country," he said, waving his hand around at the darkening landscape, "are altogether given over to idolatry. Moses told my father that Israel would fall into that same error if the land were not cleansed. God knew that there had to be a new beginning for Israel."

"But I cannot help but feel sorry for those who died."

"I feel that too, Rahab," Phinehas said.

"Doesn't God care about the Canaanites?"

Phinehas' face grew sober, and he stroked his beard. "I think He cares for all people."

"I never heard of Jehovah, and I don't think anyone else ever did among my people."

"I can't answer your question, Rahab. In my own heart I have settled it that God speaks to every man. To every idolater there comes some moment in his life—or in her life—when God makes himself known. It may not be a very dramatic moment, but I believe it to be true. I have told you the story of Noah and the flood that covered the earth?"

"Yes, I remember it well."

"I do not have the word of God on this for God has not revealed it, but I think there may well have been many on the earth who were righteous people. Surely Noah, his wife, and his sons and their wives were righteous, but the people were spread out over all the earth. I cannot help but believe that there were some in that day who were in far-off lands who were also believers in God, even though they did not know His name was Jehovah. And I have come to think that if they did believe, even though they may have drowned in the flood, God has not forsaken them. For all who believed, their souls are with the great Jehovah."

"May I ask you something about myself?"

"Of course. What is it, Rahab?"

"You know about my life. I told you how I was forced into prostitution, but still it was a sin. I was a sinful woman. I can never get that out of my mind."

"You have seen the sacrifices that we make on the brazen altar outside the tent of meetings?"

"Yes. I don't quite understand it, though."

"You have seen us kill an innocent lamb, then sprinkle the blood on the altar."

"Yes. What does it mean, master?"

"I am not at all sure that I understand it. But somehow that innocent lamb means something to Jehovah. The blood of a lamb could never take away sins, but God has spoken to me and there have been prophets such as Moses that have said that one day there will come the great Messiah."

"The Messiah. What is that?"

"He is the Redeemer Bezalel spoke of, the one who will come and who will deliver all people from their sin. I do not know when He will come or what He will be like, but every time I sacrifice a lamb, I pray, 'Let the real lamb of God come soon.'"

"And what can I do about my sin?"

"You have done it, my daughter," Phinehas said kindly. "You have come to the God of Israel. You have bowed yourself and confessed your sin. God has forgiven you."

A great joy rose up in Rahab at that moment. She did not know how it was, but the doubts and the fears and the guilt that had enveloped her were suddenly gone. "I believe you," she cried with a glad joy. "He is the God of forgiveness!"

"Yes. And He never comes again after you're forgiven to remind you of the past. You are as pure as any woman in Israel."

The words sank down in Rahab, and she began to weep. "Thank you, master," she cried.

"It is not me you should thank but God, who has made a way for His people to be free from sins."

Everyone noticed the difference in Rahab. She was entirely changed and went about singing, filled with joy. The burden of her sins in Jericho had bowed her down, but now she stood straight and tall, and her dark eyes glowed with a fierce joy. The praise of Jehovah was on her lips constantly so that many were made to ask, "What has happened to Rahab?" Those bold enough to ask her got the same answer. "I am happy because I serve the great God Jehovah, the God of Israel, who forgives sins."

It was three weeks after this new joy came into Rahab's life that she was on her way back to her tent. She had been out gathering berries and now carried a basket almost full. She had learned to use the berries of the desert for cooking, and she was mentally planning the meal she would fix when suddenly a man stepped in front of her. It was in an isolated place and shielded from the camp by underbrush that rose sometimes as high as five feet.

"Rahab," the man said. He blocked her way, and she stopped for a moment and waited for him to speak again.

"My name is Jehu."

Suddenly Rahab remembered the man. She had seen him a few times, and someone had told her that he was a very wealthy man who owned immense herds and flocks. He was tall and lean as a skeleton. His full beard was shot with gray, and he had small eyes that seemed too close together. When he smiled he exposed yellow teeth, several of them missing. "I greet you, Rahab of Jericho."

Rahab was on her guard. She was alone and this was a man. Her past had been enough to tell her that she must be careful. "Good afternoon, sir. I must hurry back."

Rahab would have gone on, but Jehu reached out and took her arm. "Just a moment. I would like to talk with you."

"Let me go, sir."

Jehu laughed. "You need not be shy with me. Everyone knows your past. It is not as though you are a pure maiden."

At that instant Rahab remembered the words of Phinehas. *"You're as pure as any maiden in Israel."* She tried to pull her arm away, but Jehu's strength was greater than would seem possible in such a thin man. "Listen to me, woman. I know you're a harlot. I have money. Come and lie with me. I will pay you well."

"No. I will do no such thing. My past is gone. I am now a worshiper of Jehovah."

Jehu sneered. "Don't be ridiculous. You're not even a Hebrew. How could you be a worshiper of Jehovah?"

"Jehovah loves all people."

But Jehu did not come to talk about Jehovah. His eyes were

glittering with lust, and he reached out and tried to embrace her. Rahab dropped the basket and pushed him away. She was a strong young woman, and Jehu went reeling backward.

"Leave me alone!" she cried. She snatched up the basket and, turning quickly, made for camp.

"I will have you, woman!" Jehu screamed after her, his face red with lust and anger. "You may be sure of that! I will have you!"

Rahab was breathing hard, not from effort nor from fear. She had turned her back on her old life, but now she thought of the man with loathing—not his advances, for she could fight him off, but that he would disturb her life in Israel.

When she reached the camp, she found Ardon standing beside some food he had brought and given to her brother-in-law Kadir. Kadir turned to her and, seeing something in her face, asked, "What is it? Is something wrong, Rahab?"

"No, not at all. I've been out picking berries. I suppose I may have gotten too warm." She walked by the two men and sat down to sort out the berries.

For a time the two men spoke briefly; then she was aware that Ardon had come to stand beside her. "You do look troubled," he said. "What is it?"

Rahab looked up, surprised that Ardon would comment on such a thing. He never seemed to care one way or another about her, and now she hesitated. "It was nothing really."

"Must be something. I've never seen you this upset before." He moved to get a better look at her face, and his eyes narrowed. "Something's wrong. Are you sick?"

"No. It's . . . well, I just had an unpleasant meeting."

"Unpleasant how?"

"It was a . . . a man. He troubled me."

Ardon studied her carefully. "I've noticed that men are drawn to you, Rahab."

"Let them leave me alone."

"You're a beautiful woman. They can't."

It was the first compliment of any sort Ardon had ever paid to her, and it brought a flush to Rahab's face. "I don't want anything like that in my life, Ardon."

"Who was it?"

Before Rahab could think, she had called out the man's name. "It was the man called Jehu."

"Jehu! Why, he's a member of the council."

"I don't know anything about him, but I want him to leave me alone."

Ardon was staring at her. "He's a prominent man in Israel. He wouldn't do such a thing—unless he were enticed."

Rahab jumped to her feet and threw her head back, her eyes flashing. "You think I enticed him?"

"It wouldn't be the first time, would it?"

"Yes."

"You never enticed men when you lived in Jericho?"

"No. I hated what I was doing."

"Why did you do it, then?"

"Because I was forced to."

"No one can force a woman to be a harlot."

"You don't know much of anything, Ardon. My family was going to be sold into slavery. My little sister, my father, if I didn't give in to the man who had trapped us. Should I have let them die?"

Ardon was shocked at the woman's anger. He had long known that there was a fire in this woman, and once he had thought that she was the kind of woman who could, if she had to, stab a man through the heart and then go about her business. He studied her now with fresh interest. "You're never going to be happy here. You'd be better off with your own people."

"My people are all dead except for my family. Would you have me go back to the ashes of Jericho?"

Ardon felt he had gotten in over his head. "I think you were mistaken about Jehu."

"No, I wasn't mistaken. He made no secret of what he wanted. He said he would have me no matter what I did."

Ardon was at a loss for words. He had a respect for the hierarchy of the tribe and a suspicion of this woman. "I think you'd better stay close in, always be with somebody. Men are drawn to you. Sooner or later you're going to give in to them," he said bluntly.

"You don't ever forgive or forget, do you, Ardon?" she said.

"As I said, you'd be happier in another place. I can take you to any village you say so you can be with your own people."

Rahab faced him squarely, her lips firm. "These are my people," she said. "I am a daughter of Israel no matter what you think, Ardon!"

Later that day her father came to her and said, "I hear Jehu is interested in you."

"Who told you that?"

"He did. He admires you. He might make a good husband. He's rich."

"He's not looking for a wife. He's looking for a loose woman, and I'm not that anymore."

Romar overheard the conversation and approached her father. She grasped his garment and shook him like a child. "Shut your mouth, old man! You were the reason for what happened to Rahab. I never want to hear you refer to it again."

Makon had rarely been challenged by his own family. He opened his mouth to shout at Romar, but something in her face stopped him. He grumbled, "I didn't mean anything," and fled at once.

Romar put her arm around Rahab. "You mustn't pay any attention to Father. He has no sense at all. He never did have."

"No, he didn't."

"Tell me about this man Jehu." Romar listened as Rahab told of Jehu's assault.

And then Rahab spoke of Ardon's attitude. She finished her story saying, "He hates me."

"But you don't hate him, do you?"

Startled, Rahab said, "I don't want to hate anyone."

"I think you care for Ardon."

Rahab was even more startled. "How could I?" she laughed shortly. "He despises me."

"Put him out of your mind, then. I've seen you watch him," Romar said. "He's not for you."

"I know that," Rahab said, then turned and walked away.

Compassion filled Romar's heart as she watched her sister. "She's headed for a bad time, and there's nothing I can do about it."

CHAPTER
21

Ariel stared at Ardon, eyes wide with surprise. "Are you telling me," she said, "that Jehu tried to force himself on Rahab?"

"Yes. At least that's what she says," Ardon said, troubled in spirit over the incident. He rubbed his chin and said doubtfully, "I don't know how much truth there is in it."

"Well, personally I don't doubt it. That man has evil in his eyes."

"You can't tell if a man's evil by his eyes."

"Of course you can. The eyes are the mirror of the soul."

Ardon laughed. "There's your romantic side, sister. You were always that way. What's in a man's heart is secret—in a woman's too, I suppose."

Ariel doubled her fist and struck Ardon in the chest, not playfully but angrily. "I can't believe you would just decide that what Rahab says is a lie and everything that man Jehu says is the truth."

"But he's a member of the council."

"And all the council members are angels? I suppose they came straight down from heaven without a single sin among the lot of them!"

"Now, wait a minute—"

"No, you wait! You have a tendency, Ardon, to judge people too severely. From what I can tell, Rahab has behaved in a perfectly respectable way since she came from Jericho."

"You can't change what you are, Ariel. She can never be innocent again."

"Of course she can."

"No, she can't," Ardon said firmly. "No one can recapture innocence."

"You don't know the history of our people very well, do you?"

"What are you talking about?"

"I'm talking about Aaron—haven't you ever heard of the time when he made the golden calf?"

"Yes, of course, but that's different."

"When Moses came down from the mountain," Ariel said, her eyes narrowing, "and found that Aaron had helped our people become idolaters, Moses killed him right there, didn't he, because he could never be innocent again."

"You know that's not the way it happened."

"I know it, but I don't think you do. Aaron did a terrible thing, but he was still a man of God, and God honored him. God forgave him for his idolatrous act. If He can forgive Aaron, He can forgive Rahab."

"I just don't believe that." Ardon was no match for his sister in a debate. She had a quick, sharp mind and was able to look at all sides of a matter. He himself had a tendency to cling stubbornly to an idea. Finally he shrugged. "Aaron was a Hebrew."

"So? Only Hebrews can find forgiveness?"

"I didn't say that."

"It's what you meant, though. Ardon, you need to broaden your mind. Now, get out of here and leave me alone, and don't come to me with any more of your foolishness."

"Women are all alike," Ardon cried and left the tent abruptly.

As soon as he was gone, Ariel shook her head fiercely. "Brother, you are such a wonderful man in so many ways, but at times you're as blind as a rock."

She turned to her work but could not concentrate. The story that Ardon had told her was troubling. She could not get out of her mind what she had seen in Rahab. During her brief time in the Hebrew camp, from all Ariel could observe, it appeared she was a good woman, meek and cheerful.

"I don't believe it," she said. Being a straightforward young woman, she left her tent and made her way to the tent Ardon had put up for Rahab and her family. She found Rahab outside cleaning the carcass of a sheep. Her hands were bloody and Ariel smiled. "That's a messy business, isn't it?"

"It's the only way there is to fix meat, though," Rahab answered with a smile. She had developed a great respect for Ariel. As the daughter of Caleb, Ariel enjoyed a high position in the camp, but besides that, she had shown a courtesy and kindness toward Rahab and her family that her brother obviously lacked.

"I need to talk to you, Rahab," Ariel said directly.

"Of course. What is it?"

"You may think this is none of my business, but my brother told me about Jehu and what happened."

Rahab waited for Ariel to say more, but when she saw that Ariel was finished, she said, "Perhaps I shouldn't have told Ardon, but I was so disturbed by it, I had to tell someone."

"You can tell me about it."

Rahab briefly repeated the details of the incident and then said, "I wish it hadn't happened."

"What are you going to do about him?"

"I'm going to try to stay away from him."

Ariel hesitated. "That's a good idea," she said, "but it may be impossible. Don't go anywhere alone."

"That will be difficult too."

Rahab could see that Ariel had something on her mind.

"What is it, Ariel? Is there something else?"

"I don't want to insult you, but everyone knows that you had a . . . a bad life in Jericho."

"Yes I did. I worked in a brothel."

The words seemed harsh to Ariel, and she winced. "That must have been a terrible life."

"It was death," Rahab said flatly, and her face grew still as memories flooded through her. "I would have killed myself, except I had to help my family."

"How did you get into such a life?"

"There was a man who got power over my father and led him into gambling. My father gambled us away, the whole family, into slavery. The man agreed to let my family remain free if I would do what he asked."

"It must have been terrible."

"As I say, it was worse than death." Tears glittered in Rahab's eyes. "I was as innocent as you are, Ariel, before that man trapped us."

"I don't think I could have done it."

"Not even if it meant saving your family? What if it were a choice between prostitution or having your whole family made into slaves to be beaten and tortured?" Rahab's voice grew low. "I cried out to our gods, but they didn't help me. So I chose to save my family in the only way I could."

Ariel melted with compassion for this young woman. They were approximately the same age, and she said finally, "I'm sorry. I shouldn't have pried."

"I'm glad I told you. Maybe it'll help you understand me a little bit better."

Ariel moved forward and embraced Rahab. "You're a courageous woman. May Jehovah bless you in all your ways." She turned and walked away, and as she left, she was thinking, *That woman has more courage than I have.*

———

The abortive encounter with Rahab had left Jehu filled with venomous anger. He became impossible to live with, and his family and servants fled from him whenever they could safely do so. For three days he was sullen or shouting with anger at nothing. Finally he could stand it no longer. "That woman thinks she can get the best of me, but she won't."

Jehu had studied Rahab's habits, and he had to wait another two days before he finally found her going down toward the stream where many of the Hebrews got their fresh water. Usually one of her family members came with her, but this time she was alone.

Jehu had concealed himself behind a towering group of shrubs by the path, and as Rahab came bearing her water pitcher, he fell on her and dragged her to the ground. He began tearing at her clothes and laughed as she cried out with anger.

"You might as well be quiet. No one's going to hear you. Nothing's going to happen to you that hasn't happened before."

Jehu was not an especially strong man, and Rahab had been an active young woman. She threw him to one side, and before he could move, he felt a cold blade at his throat.

"Wait—don't kill me!" he pleaded.

Rahab got to her knees, keeping the blade on Jehu's throat. "You're a beast! I ought to slit your throat right now."

Jehu begged her not to, and Rahab knew at that moment she could not kill him. "You lie still or I will kill you." She moved the blade down the side of his face. It was razor sharp, and his thick beard fell away.

"What are you doing?" Jehu asked and reached out to grab her wrist. Rahab turned the blade so that he grabbed it. He let out a yell of pain. "You cut my hand!"

"I'll cut your throat if you move again." She began to rake the side of his face again, and the keen blade cut through half of his beard. With one side of his face scraped raw, she got to her feet, scooped up the fallen hair, and held it in one hand. "If you don't leave me alone," she said, still holding the blade, "I'll show them what I've taken from you. That'll show all of Israel what a feeble man you are, that a woman has taken your pride and joy."

Jehu sat up and felt his face, which was now half bearded and half bare. She had nicked him several times and his cheek was bleeding. He felt naked and defenseless. Getting to his feet, he knew he could not appear like this before Israel. He made his way back to the camp, cursing Rahab under his breath, and when he finally got into his tent, he called for his servant Jehaza.

Jehaza appeared at once. He was a thickset, burly man with blunt features and dull eyes. "What happened to your face, master?" he cried out.

"Shut your mouth! Get a razor and shave the rest of my beard off."

Jehaza had little imagination, but he knew something unusual had taken place.

Jehu told his servant nothing, but as he suffered the rest of his beard being removed, he made a vow. *That woman has defiled a master of Israel,* he thought grimly. *I'll have my revenge if it's the last thing I ever do.*

Aloud he said, "I have a job for you, Jehaza. It'll pay you well."

"What is it, Master?" Jehaza asked and grinned. "I always need money."

"Here's what I want you to do. . . ."

CHAPTER

22

The sunlight glittered on the water, the tiny waves making flecks of brilliant light. Oman was watching his line carefully when the slender sapling that composed his fishing pole was drawn almost double. He let out a shrill cry. "Rahab—I've got one!"

Rahab had been sitting beside Oman for some time, enjoying the sibilant murmur of the water at her feet and the warmth of the sun. She turned quickly and laughed as Oman tugged at the pole. "Hold on to him, Oman. Don't let him get away."

"It's big!" Oman cried, his eyes wide with excitement. "It's the biggest one I ever caught."

"You want me to help you?"

"No, I can do it myself."

Oman struggled with the fish until the fish tired. Rahab reached out over the water and grabbed the line and pulled it in. "Oh, that's a nice one!" she cried. With a tug she threw the fish back on the bank, where it flopped around wildly.

"He'll be good for supper, won't he, Rahab?"

"Yes, he will. With what we've got, we can feed the whole family. You're a good fisherman, Oman."

"Let's catch another one."

"No, it's time to go back. Come along."

The two gathered up all the fish they had caught, mostly small ones, into a sack. Oman insisted on carrying the largest one himself, and as they passed through the village of tents, he would hold it up and cry out, "Look at what I caught!" Several admiring young people came to comment on it, and Oman was happy.

Rahab was happy also, for it had been a good day. She was pleased with Oman's health. He had improved greatly, and though she could not be certain of the reason, she privately thought it was the doing of Jehovah, for she had prayed often for her nephew. Whatever it was, she felt content with his progress.

"Look! There are some men in our tent!" Oman said.

Quickly Rahab glanced up and saw that, indeed, there were a collection of serious-looking men with beards. For some reason a stab of fear touched her, and as she drew closer, one of the men stepped forward. She had seen him before but did not know his name. His face was stern as he said, "You are Rahab?"

"Yes, master. That's my name."

"You must come with us."

"Come where, sir?" Rahab said. She saw the other men forming a semicircle, their faces all very stern. Quickly she looked between them to see her family watching with fearful eyes. "What is it?" she said. "What's happened?"

"You have been accused of breaking the Law of Moses," the leader said. "You must come with us to appear before the council of elders."

"Which law have I broken?" Rahab asked, looking from face to face. She knew she had seen several of them but could not think of any of their names.

"A man has confessed that you have sold your body to him."

"It's a lie!" she cried.

"You must come with us."

Rahab had no choice. The elders formed a group around her, and she cast one look at her family and saw that Zayna's eyes were pale. Romar had put her hands to her lips in a gesture of despair. Makon had gone back into the tent, trying to avoid trouble wherever possible.

They passed through the camp, and Rahab heard the whispers and saw the curious glances on the faces of her neighbors. One voice called out, "Harlot! Stone her!" and her heart seemed to grow cold.

————————

"It is going to be a hard task to conquer this land," Ardon said. He was eating a bit of mutton with Ariel, and the two had been speaking of the future. Ardon was thinking mostly of the battles, and he started talking about the various difficulties that lay ahead of the army. They both looked up when Caleb came in with an odd look on his face.

Ariel got up at once. "What is it, Father?"

"Something's happened to Rahab."

Ardon got to his feet quickly. "What's the matter?"

"She's been accused of selling herself to a Hebrew."

Both Ardon and Ariel were shocked by the news. Ariel demanded at once, "What will happen to her?"

"If she is found guilty, she will be stoned."

Ariel stared at her father. "Who was the man?" she demanded.

"That hasn't been revealed yet."

Her father's answer infuriated Ariel. "What do you mean it hasn't been revealed? Someone had to accuse her."

"She has been accused, but the name has been kept secret."

"What kind of justice is that?" Ariel demanded, her face flush and her eyes glinting. She was not a woman who concealed her emotions particularly well, and both Caleb and Ardon saw that she was fiercely angered.

"It's the way things are," Caleb said.

"Well, it's wrong! Can any woman be killed if a man goes to the council and accuses her?"

"You have to understand how important it is that a man be protected."

"Well, what about a woman being protected?"

Ardon and Caleb glanced at each other helplessly as Ariel's voice rose. While Ariel accused the council of being a group of unjust men, Caleb finally said, "You mustn't talk like that, daughter. They're the Council of Israel."

"They're men, aren't they? Well, I'm going with you to this council meeting!"

"A woman can't do that!" Ardon exclaimed. "Women aren't permitted at the council meetings."

Ariel threw her head back and stared directly into Ardon's eyes. "Well, one woman is going this time!" she declared. "Come on if you intend to go with me."

Rahab had been put in a tent, and she knew that there were guards outside. She was pacing back and forth now, fighting the fear of what was to happen next. She had been left alone, and the councilmen who had brought her had refused to answer her questions. Finally she sat down, bowed her head, and began to pray. Strangely enough, despite her fears, she found herself drifting off into a strange dreamlike state. She was not asleep, yet she was not awake either. She had been simply praying for God to deliver her, and now she had the strange experience of feeling herself out of her own body. It was as if she could look down and see herself kneeling with her head bowed and her face to the earth. She had never experienced anything like this in her life, and she waited in a silence that was almost palpable.

A voice came to her—and yet it was not a voice. It was more like one of those faint memories that come brushing against the mind when one is asleep at night. She knew she was dreaming, and yet the voice, though soft, was clear. Suddenly Rahab knew she was in the presence of the Lord. "What is it, Master?" she whispered, her lips barely moving.

The voice came again, this time soft and gentle, yet some-how strong and powerful as well. *"Do not be afraid, my daughter. You must have faith in me."*

"Who are you?" Rahab asked quietly, fearful of the answer.

"I think you know who I am. I am the one who saved you from Jericho, and I will save you from this trouble also. Can you believe that?"

Faith flooded Rahab, and she cried out, "Yes, O Lord God, I believe you!"

"Have faith in me, even to the last second of your life, my daughter."

The voice fell silent, and slowly Rahab returned to full con-sciousness. It was like swimming from the depths of a deep pool up to the surface, and when she broke through, she began to weep. She was overwhelmed, for she had the utmost confi-dence that God had spoken to her—a woman who had been a terrible sinner. She knelt there weeping and praising God, and when she got up and wiped her face, she looked up. Though she could see only the inner canopy of the tent, she lifted her hands and cried out, "I will believe you, O God, even unto death!"

The tent used for council meetings was the largest and longest tent in the camp. It was now packed with men, most of them in their early forties or fifties. They were of the new gen-eration of Hebrews, the old men having died off in the wilder-ness wandering. Now there was an air of strength about them. The leader, Remkiah, was in his midforties. He was a strong-looking individual with keen, dark eyes and a short-clipped beard.

"Bring the woman in," Remkiah called, and whispering filled the tent as one man left.

He soon appeared with Rahab. She was wearing a simple Hebrew garment, a scarf covering her hair, and she was silent, but her head was held high as she was brought into the center of the council.

"My name is Remkiah. I am the head of the council. You are Rahab?"

"Yes, sir. That is my name."

"You have been accused of—" Remkiah broke off and turned, as did everyone else, for three newcomers had entered. Remkiah addressed them. "You are welcome, Caleb, and you also, Ardon—but women are not permitted at the council meetings."

Ariel stood straight and faced the head of the council. "Does the council believe in justice?" Her voice was clear, and there was no trace of fear on her features. She stood boldly before them, waiting for an answer. She ignored the murmur of displeasure going around among the council members. "I know you are men of honor," she said, her voice clear and strong. "The accused is my friend. I will stand beside her."

Rahab's eyes filled with tears, and she wiped them away furtively. She said nothing, but her eyes went to the head of the council.

"I'm afraid I cannot permit such a thing," Remkiah said.

And then the strong voice of Caleb filled the tent. "She will stay!"

Every eye turned to Caleb. Next to Joshua he was the most powerful man in Israel. He was not only the head of the tribe of Judah, the most powerful tribe, but he was a man who had walked beside Moses. He and Joshua had served as the right arm of Moses, and now Remkiah dropped his eyes, unable to meet Caleb's gaze. "Very well. If you insist."

"I do insist," Caleb said coldly. "Now, get on with this thing."

Remkiah turned to Rahab and said in a subdued voice, casting glances at Caleb and Ariel, "You have been accused of selling your body to a member of the nation. Such offense brings death by stoning. What have you to say for yourself?"

Ardon was watching carefully, and when Rahab lifted her head, he felt a shock of astonishment. He had always thought her face was beautifully fashioned, but now he also saw the strong will and pride in her eyes and in the set of her lips. *How can a woman who looks like this be guilty?* he thought. To his surprise she turned and met his eyes. Normally, her face in repose had a quality he could not name. It was something like the gravity that comes from someone seeing too much. It was, in fact, a mirror of sadness. She looked at him silently, and Ardon wondered what her silence meant. It pulled at him like a mystery, and he found his own thinking confused, but it was as if he were seeing the woman in a new light. He was stunned to note that there was an enormous certainty in her, a will like iron, and he could not but admire her as she courageously stood there.

"I am innocent," she said. Her voice carried throughout the tent, and then she added, "God has told me that I am to put my trust in Him."

The men of the council were shocked. "God does not speak to a woman," a voice came.

Ariel spoke up. "And how can you know that? Are you Jehovah?"

The sharpness of Ariel's reply was enough to send shock waves throughout the group.

Ariel ignored them. "I insist that this woman's accuser be brought in. Let him face her and make his accusation."

"I do not think—" Remkiah stammered.

"Bring the man in," Caleb said. "It's only just. The law of Moses clearly says there must be witnesses to a wrong."

Remkiah shrugged his shoulders. "Very well." He lifted his voice and said, "Bring the man in."

Every eye was turned toward the doorway, and when a man entered, Caleb said with a snort, "This is the accuser?"

"Yes. His name is Jehaza," Remkiah said.

"I know his name. I think everyone knows about him."

"I know about him," Ariel said. She moved to where she faced Jehaza squarely. "You are a coward and a liar."

Jehaza seemed to shrink. He had not been informed that this would happen. He had been told by Jehu that he would simply have to make the accusation and he would be kept out of it. "Let's hear your claim," Ariel demanded.

Jehaza looked wildly around the room, but there was no help. "I was going to the river, and this woman came out and offered herself to me if I would give her money."

Ariel listened as the man told his sordid tale; then she said, "When did this take place?"

"Why . . . I can't remember exactly."

Caleb's voice boomed. "Answer the question. If you made the charge, you must remember when you claim it happened."

"It was . . . it was two days ago at the river."

"At what time of day?" Ariel said.

Jehaza twisted and turned and looked as if he were about to flee. "It was at midday."

Phinehas stepped forward. "I would like to know one thing. How is it possible that this woman Rahab could have been at the river tempting this man and at the same time sitting with me in the shade of my tent? For that is exactly where she was two days ago at high noon."

A mutter went around the council, and a strong voice said, "This man is a liar. He's the one who should be stoned."

Caleb moved to stand before Jehaza. "You should die for planning the death of an innocent woman!"

Ardon drew his knife and held it up before the eyes of the trembling Jehaza. "Stoning is too good. I'll slit his throat right now."

"I couldn't help it," Jehaza screamed. "It wasn't me. It was my master Jehu. He made me do it."

At that moment there was a scuffling activity in the back of the crowd. Two of the members of the council pushed their way through. They were dragging Jehu with them. "Here he is," one of them growled. "Now let him stand trial."

Remkiah swallowed hard. "Joshua, our master, will judge

the liar." He turned to Rahab and said, "You are free to go, with the apologies of the council." Then he turned to Ariel, and despite himself, a smile turned the corners of his lips upward. "No woman has ever attended a meeting of the council. You are the first, but I am glad you came, my daughter."

"Thank you, master. Maybe you will be more ready to listen to a woman's truth next time. Come, Rahab, let us go."

Rahab cast one look at Jehu, who was ashen and trembling. She walked outside, and she and Ariel were followed by Ardon. Ardon said almost at once, "You were very fortunate, Rahab, to have a friend like Ariel."

Rahab turned and asked, "Would you really have cut his throat, Ardon?"

"We'll never know, will we? But I do hate a liar." He stopped, took her arm, and turned her around. "I'm glad it turned out well for you."

At that moment, when the two faced each other, Ardon felt the power of Rahab's beauty and it disturbed him. He broke off what he was going to say and, without another word, walked away.

"Why is he angry?" Rahab whispered.

"He's never been good with women. I think he's afraid of them." She put her arm around Rahab and hugged her. "I think he's afraid of you."

"Because of what I was?"

"No. Because you're a woman he finds attractive and he doesn't want to admit it. I've seen it in his eyes as he watches you."

"He doesn't need to be afraid of me," Rahab said. She watched Ardon as he made his way back through the camp and then faced Ariel. "You saved my life, Ariel. I thank you."

Ariel laughed. "We couldn't let those men have their way. Come along. Your family will want to know how all this has turned out. And I want to hear about how God talked to you."

CHAPTER

23

"Master, could you spare a little time?"

Ardon had been striding toward the northern part of the camp, where his father and Joshua were meeting with the many officers to plan the next battle. He was brought up short by the voice and turned to see his father's chief herdsman, a short, wiry man named Ezra.

"What is it, Ezra?" he asked. "I'm in a hurry."

"This won't take a minute, sir." Ezra was the best herdsman in all of Israel, as far as Ardon and Caleb could discover. No matter how many cattle or sheep or goats Caleb owned, Ezra seemed to know every one of them by name. He was up at dawn and the last to leave the flocks, and he got along well with the other shepherds, who respected him greatly.

"Well, it's like this, sir. You know I lost my wife two years ago."

"Yes. A fine woman she was too."

"She was indeed. The very best. And I have two children, you know, a boy and a girl."

Ardon could not imagine what Ezra was getting at. "Yes. They are fine children."

"But you know, sir, it's hard on a man to raise children alone."

"Oh, I assume, then, you're thinking of taking another wife. I hope she's from the tribe of Judah."

Ezra was a slow-speaking man and seemed to think over each word carefully before he let it escape his lips. He was handsome in a rough fashion, a plain, simple man, quiet, who did his duty, but a man who could fight if called upon. Ardon and his father both respected him greatly. "No, sir, not exactly," Ezra said carefully.

"Not exactly? She either is or she isn't. Who is it?"

Ezra was holding his shepherd staff in his hand, and now he fingered it nervously, poking a hole in the ground with it as he considered his next words. Finally he looked up, his honest brown eyes steady. "It's the woman that you and Othniel helped out of Jericho. The woman named Rahab."

Ardon was so surprised he could not speak. He had not really given a thought to Rahab's future, and now the matter was thrown into his hands. He opened his mouth to speak, but his mind was blank. For once he was a slower speaker than Ezra himself!

"I'm not much of a man with words," Ezra went on, "but I thought if you would speak to the woman for me, it would be a kindness."

"Why, you can speak to her yourself. She has a father. You could talk to him. But, Ezra, have you thought this over?"

Ezra again was slow in answering. He was studying Ardon's face. "You don't want me to marry, sir?"

"Oh, I have no opinion on that," Ardon said hastily. "But—" He tried desperately to think of some way to put the matter. Finally he said, "Well, if you feel it would help, I'll be glad to speak to her."

"Thank you, sir. That would be a favor indeed."

Ardon watched as Ezra headed back toward the herds. Lately he had thought much about Rahab. Since the trial, the entire tribe had thought about the woman. The villain Jehu had been severely chastised by Joshua. Part of his punishment had been that a large number of his animals were forfeited to Rahab, so that she was now a woman of some substance. He had also been ostracized by a large part of the population.

Making up his mind abruptly, Ardon threaded his way between the tents. When he came to Rahab's tent, he found her father sitting outside doing nothing, as usual. "I need to speak to Rahab, Makon."

"She went out to see some of our sheep."

Our sheep indeed, Ardon thought with contempt. He nodded and headed out of the camp. It took him some time to reach Rahab, for the herds were enormous by this time. He finally located her talking with a young man named Birum, whom she had hired to watch her livestock. She turned at the sound of footsteps, and when she saw him, her face lit up with a smile. "Ardon, come and see my sheep and cattle."

Ardon stopped and nodded. "Nice-looking animals. So you've become a shepherd."

"Oh, I know little about them, but Birum here, he knows. Don't you, Birum?"

"Yes. I know a lot about sheep and cattle." Birum was no more than fifteen, but he had been around animals all of his life and was smiling broadly. He had a gap between his teeth, and his eyes were sharp and piercing.

"Walk with me, Rahab," Ardon said.

"Why, of course."

As soon as they were out of hearing distance of the shepherd, Ardon stopped and turned to face Rahab. She was wearing a light blue garment that was loose and flowing and outlined her form well. Her eyes were brilliant this morning. She was happy with her new occupation. "I have a request from our chief shepherd, Ezra."

"Yes? What does it have to do with me?"

"He wants to marry you."

Rahab's eyes flew open. "Marry me? But I don't even know him."

"You have probably seen him. He's been with us a long time. In any case, he's seen you." Hastily, he added, "His wife died two years ago. He has a boy and a girl about twelve or thirteen, something like that. He's a good man. I can vouch for him."

Rahab shook her head vigorously. "I've not thought of marrying anyone, Ardon."

"Most women think of that."

Rahab laughed. "I haven't had time to think much of anything lately. It's been a difficult time, and I believe more difficult times lie ahead. Isn't there going to be another battle?"

"Not just one but many. The whole land has to be conquered."

"Well then, I don't think it's time for people to be marrying."

Ardon was puzzled. "Most women think of that first. Don't you want a husband and a family?"

"I always thought I did, but . . ." She could not explain her feelings to Ardon. Her life felt too complicated right now to contemplate marriage. She simply smiled and said, "Thank the man for me, and tell him I'm not thinking of marrying at the present time."

"I'll tell him. But he'll be disappointed, I'm sure. He's not a rich man, but he's a good fellow."

Rahab's eyes had gone back to the sheep. Ardon watched her as she walked away and said under his breath, "Well, Ezra will just have to take her answer whether he likes it or not."

He hurried on then to the meeting and found that it was well under way. Joshua had drawn a primitive map in the dust and was pointing out the various strongholds of the tribes. "And over here," Joshua said, "are the Hittites—over here are the Amorites." He continued to name off the different kingdoms that had to be conquered, and when he was finished, Caleb said, "It's going to cost something to take this land."

"Yes." Joshua nodded, looking around at his captains. "It's

the Land of Promise, but it's not going to be easy to make it ours. God will have to be with us, as He has been all the way."

Ardon stood at the back. He was not one of the major captains and he just listened. Finally, the discussion was interrupted when a scout came running in and announced to Joshua, "Sir, a group have come!"

"Who are they?"

"They are from Gibeon, sir. They insist on seeing you."

"Are they soldiers?"

The scout laughed, his white teeth flashing against his bronze skin. "They look more like tramps to me."

"Well, bring them on, then."

Ardon agreed with the scout. The five men who came all looked much the worse for wear. Their animals were worn, and the wine bottles on their backs were torn and bound up with leather strings. Their sandals were practically falling to pieces, and their old tattered garments were in a pitiful condition.

"Who are you and what do you want?" Joshua demanded.

The leader, a tall man with a narrow face scored by a thousand wrinkles, bowed low. "Sir, we be the men of Gibeon. We come from a far country just to see you."

"What do you want?" Joshua repeated.

"We have heard," the old man said, "of all that you and your soldiers have done to the Amorites beyond Jordan. We have heard of how you annihilated Sihon, king of Heshbon, and Og, king of Bashan. Our leaders know that we cannot stand against you. They have sent us to make a peace treaty with you."

"How far away is your land?"

The leader waved at the sorry animals and said, "This bread was warm on the day we started. Now, as you can see, it's dry and moldy, and these wineskins? You see how cracked they are? And our sandals are worn out because of our long journey."

Joshua studied the men and said, "And you come seeking peace?"

"Yes. At all costs."

Joshua said, "We will speak of it." He turned to one of his aides and said, "See that they have food and drink, and we will meet and talk terms."

The visitors from Gibeon stayed for three days, during which time the whole camp came to see them. After much discussion, an agreement was made, and Joshua said to his leaders and to all the people, "We have given them our oath by the Lord, the God of Israel, and we cannot touch them now. We will let them live according to our agreement."

That seemed to end it, but almost at once two scouts came back and gave a report to Joshua. "The cities of these men are not far. They have deceived you, sir."

A cry went up from the captains, and Joshua called for the Gibeonites and said sternly to them, "Why have you lied to us?"

"Because," the old man said, confident now that he was safe since the agreement had been made, "we have indeed heard how you conquer all who stand before you. Let us be your servants. We ask no more."

Joshua was angry at the deceit, but he agreed to their request. "You will have what you ask. Now, therefore, none of you will be freed from your bondage. You will be woodcutters and water carriers for the community and for the altar of the Lord."

This did not seem hard to the men of Gibeon, for they only smiled and said, "We will serve you, for now we know that we will live and not die."

The five kings who met together were usually enemies of one another. They were from Jerusalem, Hebron, Jarmuth, Lachish, and Eglon.

The king of Jerusalem, Adoni-Zedek, had called them

together, and now he told them for what purpose. "We have all been concerned about the Hebrews that are coming to fight against us. I have news now that one of our number, the king of Gibeon, has made an alliance with the Hebrews."

Angry words arose among them, and Adoni-Zedek said, "Come up and help me attack Gibeon because it has made peace with Joshua and the Israelites."

The king of Eglon was a burly man with tiny, glittering eyes. "We will kill them all," he said with evident pleasure.

———————

The tall Gibeonite who had negotiated the peace came scrambling into Joshua's presence. They had been gone now for two weeks, and his face was sallow and his hands were shaking. "Sir, you must help us. Amorite kings that dwell in the mountains are gathered together against us."

Joshua listened as the trembling man spoke of the armies of the five kings that were headed toward Gibeon.

"I will ask God's guidance," Joshua said.

"Sir, there is no time."

"There's always time to seek Jehovah." Joshua went at once to his tent and prayed for a brief time.

The Lord said, *"Do not be afraid of them; I have given them into your hand. Not one of them will be able to withstand you."*

Joshua jumped up and ran out of his tent, shouting, "Captains, get your men together! We will fight at once!"

———————

Othniel was shaken out of sleep by a rough hand. He looked up to see Ardon standing over him. "What is it?" he asked, sitting up abruptly. He rubbed his eyes and tried to focus them, for he had been as drunk the previous night as he had ever been.

"There's a battle and you're going. I don't know why, but

my father still has hope for you. Now, get your weapons and come on."

Othniel opened his mouth to speak, but there was no denying the hard look on Ardon's face. He scrambled to his feet, gathered up his weapons, and left. "Where are we going?" he asked.

"We're going to fight five armies."

"Five! That's insane! We can't whip five armies."

Ardon shook his head. "This is your chance to redeem yourself, Othniel. I want you to fight by my side. I'll be watching you and so will everyone else. You've proven yourself a drunk and a coward. Now Israel needs every man."

Othniel did not answer. His head was splitting, and his knees were unsteady. He could not help but think about his failure at the battle of Ai and knew that Ardon was speaking the truth. It was his one chance to make up for that disaster.

The battle turned out to be furious. The five kings had united their armies into one force, and the army of Israel had fought them with a fury they had never seen.

But the Lord threw them into confusion before Israel, and the battle went well for a time. Othniel was on the right flank while the main force of the enemy was in the center of the line. He did little more than keep up with Ardon, and now Ardon yelled, "Look! They need help in the center. Every man, come on!"

At that exact moment, however, a large enemy force appeared on their own flank. Othniel's heart went cold as he saw the soldiers headed his way. He looked around frantically, and seeing how few Hebrews there were, he yelled, "Ardon, we'll be surrounded!"

"Fight! Fight to the death!" Ardon was already engaged in the battle.

Othniel did not run forward but fell back as the attack was made. He managed to fight off several of the attackers, slaying one, and then his sword was struck from his hand. He looked up to see a huge soldier grinning at him. "Now I've got you, Hebrew dog!" the soldier yelled. He leaped forward and Othniel threw himself backward. He felt the tip of the sword graze his chest and he scrambled to get up. The soldier was joined by others, all intent on killing him.

There was no hope, Othniel thought, and he turned and ran away. He could hear the yells of the enemy all about him and the cries of the dying. His only thought was to get away, and he did not even hear Ardon's cry, "Don't run away, Othniel!"

He ran until he could run no more, and the sound of the battle faded behind him. Then he fell on his face, gasping for breath. He gripped the earth, and all he wanted was to get away from the battle.

The Hebrews were outnumbered, but God came to their aid. He hurled large hailstones down from the sky, killing more of the enemy than had died by the Israelite swords. Joshua was everywhere. Finally he encountered Caleb, whose sword was dripping with blood, and his face was smeared with gore.

"It's getting dark," Caleb yelled. "They'll get away."

And then God spoke to Joshua very plainly. Joshua was stunned, but he obeyed God without hesitation. He raised his sword toward the setting sun and cried out with a voice that everyone close to him heard, "O sun, stand still over Gibeon, O moon, over the Valley of Aijalon."

Caleb stared at Joshua. He had seen miracles by the hand of Moses, but now Joshua was God's man. He looked up at the sun, shading his eyes, and grinned. "If the sun stands still, we'll kill them all!"

And the sun did stand still in the sky, and the men of Israel fought until they could barely stand.

The day went on and on, seemingly forever, and finally

Caleb came and gave his report, barely able to speak. "They are all defeated, Joshua. We won."

"What about the kings?"

"They've hidden themselves in a cave."

"Go, bring them here."

Caleb gave orders, and a few hours later the five kings were brought. Joshua, still bloodied, called his soldiers so that all might see. He said to his captains, "Come here and put your feet on the necks of these kings."

The five kings were made to kneel, and the captains of Israel went around and put their feet on their necks.

Joshua was exultant and said to his captains, "Do not be afraid; do not be discouraged. Be strong and courageous. This is what the Lord will do to all the enemies you are going to fight."

Then Joshua struck and killed the kings and hung them on five trees, and they left them hanging until the sun went down.

———

When the soldiers returned from the battle, Ariel rejoiced at the sight of her father and brother. She hugged them both and began to demand the details of the battle. She listened with delight and shock at how hailstones had fallen from the sky and how the sun itself had stood still.

Finally Caleb said, "The one flaw in our victory is Othniel."

"Othniel?" Ariel said. "What happened to him? Is he dead?"

"I wish he were," Caleb said in disgust. "He ran away and left his fellow soldiers."

"I can't believe it," Ariel said. She looked at Ardon and asked, "Did you see him run away?"

"I saw him," Ardon said. "He ran like a rabbit. He's a coward. A disgrace to Israel."

CHAPTER

24

The camp was filled with music and singing. The soldiers had returned triumphant, having suffered few losses. Joshua had declared a feast, and the smell of cooking meat laced the air as the soldiers were embraced by their families.

Rahab was as excited as anyone else. She joined in the celebration and fed some of the soldiers who had no family.

Late that afternoon she saw Phinehas and ran up to him, exclaiming, "What a wonderful victory!"

"It is indeed." Phinehas smiled broadly. "The Lord has delivered them into our hands—exactly as it was in the days of Moses!"

The two stood talking about the battle, and although Phinehas had not been there, he had heard all about it from Joshua and Caleb and some of the other captains. Finally he shook his head sadly. "Too bad about Othniel."

"Othniel?" Rahab said, worried. "Was he hurt? Is he dead?"

"No, he's not dead, but he's a disgrace."

"What did he do, sir?"

"In the heat of battle he ran away—and left his fellow soldiers to fight the battle themselves." Phinehas shook his head sadly. "I think a lot of that young man, but that was a very bad thing to do."

Oman was standing beside Rahab and spoke up. "Well, I like him even if he did a bad thing."

"Try to help him, won't you, Phinehas?" Rahab pleaded.

"I have tried," the priest said, shaking his head, "but he's beyond help—beyond my help, at least."

"Did he tell you why he ran off?"

"No, he's too drunk to talk. I don't usually give up on people, but Othniel is a lost cause, I'm afraid. I have no hope anymore that he'll change."

———

All night long Rahab thought about Othniel. She had liked the young man ever since the first time he had come to her house in Jericho. At that time he had been far more friendly than Ardon. Her family had also learned to appreciate his good humor and cheerful ways during their difficult time.

Finally Rahab knew she had to do something. She went to Caleb's tent and lurked outside until she saw Ardon leave and start walking among the tents.

"Ardon," she called out and ran to him.

He turned to her and said, "What is it, Rahab? You look worried."

"It's about Othniel."

"You heard about that? I suppose everyone has. Soldiers don't forget a thing like that. A man can be very bad, but if he stays and fights, he's accepted. That's all we have to depend on when we're in battle—the fellow on our left and the fellow on our right. Othniel ruined himself forever by running away."

"I'm so sorry for him."

"Save your grief for somebody else. Some of our men probably lost their lives because he left his place."

"Don't you ever forgive?" Rahab demanded suddenly.

"He's no man, Rahab. Forget about him."

"I feel sorrier for you than I do for him. You have no gentleness and no forgiveness, no goodness in you."

Her words sparked an angry reaction in Ardon, and he said, "Be quiet, woman! You don't know what you're talking about! The kind of life you've led, you're not fit to judge anybody else!"

"I did lead a bad life, but I've learned about Jehovah. I've learned that He's forgiving."

"He's also a God of judgment." Ardon's words were hard, and his eyes even harder. "I hope," he said, "that God strikes me dead before I fail Him and my family like Othniel has."

He turned and walked off, his back stiff. Rahab watched him go with grief in her heart. She found that she had spoken the truth. "He's worse off than Othniel. He's hard and has no pity on anyone. Othniel may lack a lot of things, but at least he has a heart."

PART FIVE

LAND OF MILK
AND HONEY

CHAPTER
25

Battle had become a way of life for Israel ever since crossing the Jordan. The battle of Jericho had been but the opening of a curtain on the great drama which they now participated in. Every day was filled either with a battle, preparing for one, or recuperating from one. Wounded men were brought in and had to be cared for, and burying the dead was a day-by-day occurrence. The wailing of women weeping for their husbands or brothers or sons had become so common in the camp that it was like any other part of their daily lives.

For Rahab the struggles were not as hard, for she had no relatives to lose in battle. But despite that, she still was caught up in the daily life of the camp. It was a common sight to see Rahab helping with the wounded, and she gained some reputation as a healer. She was especially good at comforting the families of those who had lost their men. There was something gentle and compassionate in her countenance that gave the people confidence in her.

During this period Rahab was constantly concerned about Othniel. As the days went on in the seemingly endless fight, she thought about him more and more. At night she would often dream of the young man, and a feeling slowly grew in her that she somehow should be a help to him. She had not seen him at all lately, for he had left the camp.

One early afternoon the feeling that she should do something about Othniel grew stronger, and finally she could no longer ignore it. She made her way to Phinehas's tent and found him instructing a group of young men. She waited patiently without interrupting, and finally, when Phinehas dismissed his class, she approached and bowed low before him. "Master, may I speak with you?"

"Come in, Rahab," Phinehas said. "I've just finished a class. Here, sit down and tell me what you've been doing." Phinehas smiled. "I hear good things of how you are attending the wounded and comforting the survivors of those who were lost in battle. That is a good thing."

"I wish I could do more. It grieves me that the men of Israel are being lost."

"Yes, it is a sad thing"—Phinehas nodded—"but it is the price we must pay." An odd expression crossed the priest's face, and he shrugged his thin shoulders. "Our people expect to walk into a land of milk and honey and have it handed to them on a silver platter. But Moses knew better than that. I myself heard him talk many times about the battles that were sure to come. Very few things in this life come easily."

The two sat there talking, and finally Rahab brought up the subject that had become so pressing to her. "I've been concerned about Othniel, Phinehas."

"I can understand that. I feel the same way."

"He needs a friend. He's lost everything."

"Indeed he has. It's always a shame to see a young person throw away great potential. Othniel could be almost anything he wants. He has so many fine qualities."

"Why has he thrown them away?"

"Who can say why a person does such a thing? One man goes right and serves God and is faithful, while another takes the wrong turn. Each of us every day are making choices like that."

"Do you know where he is? I haven't seen him since he left the camp."

"Oh yes. He's not far away. The rumors come drifting in." Phinehas shrugged. "There's a local tribe that stays on the outskirts of our nation. They are scavengers, more or less, dwellers in tents. Raise a few cattle and sheep. Not an admirable people, but they've taken him in, I hear." He looked at her keenly and said, "I thought that I should go, but I've neglected it. I think it would be a good thing, however, if you would go talk to him. Maybe you can have some influence on him."

Rahab smiled. "I don't know whether I can or not, but I can never forget how he and Ardon brought us out of Jericho. They saved our lives."

"Well, it was only right. You saved their lives first. If you find him, tell him that I still care for him and value his friendship. Try to do something for him. He has so many fine qualities, and he's throwing them all away."

As Rahab came to the village where Phinehas said she would find Othniel, she felt a sense of disgust. The children were ragged and thin, almost like miniature wild dogs. They glared at her suspiciously, and one of them picked up a rock and threw it at her. It missed, and she ignored the boy.

An old woman was stirring something in a pot. She was dressed in rags and had very few teeth. She bared her yellow fangs that were left at Rahab as she approached. "What do you want?"

"I'm looking for a man named Othniel."

The woman laughed a high-pitched wavering sound. "Oh yes, the drunkard. He's over there. You won't get any sense out of him, though. We thought he'd help us, a strong young man like that, but he's no good."

"Thank you." Rahab nodded. She made her way to the tent that the old woman had indicated. Ignoring the stares of other villagers, she ducked low and went inside, and for a moment had to stop while her eyes adjusted to the darkness. Finally she was able to discern a figure lying next to the wall of the tent. "Othniel?" she called.

"What . . . who is it?"

"It's me, Othniel. Rahab."

Her eyes had adjusted better now, and she moved closer as Othniel sat up. In the darkness of the tent she could see his haggard features indistinctly. He obviously had not cut his hair or bathed or taken any care of himself personally. A rancid odor rose from him, and his voice was thick as he spoke. "What do you want, Rahab?" He reached over and picked up a wineskin, tilted it, and she watched as he squirted a thin stream of liquid into his mouth. He swallowed it and then sat there staring at her dully.

"I've been worried about you for a long time, so I came to see how you were."

"You can see. How do you like it?"

Rahab knelt down so she was on the same level with Othniel. Flies were swarming in the tent. One of them lit on his upper lip and began crawling, but he did not even bother to brush it away. He was that drunk.

"I've come to see if I can't persuade you to come back home."

"Who sent you?"

"No one. I came because—"

"I know it wasn't my uncle or my cousins. They hate the sight of me."

"No they don't. You shouldn't talk like that. Nothing would please them more than to see you come home."

"I'm sure they'd love to have a drunk come home and live off of them."

The bitterness was harsh in Othniel's speech, and his eyes were grim. He sat there listening as Rahab tried to convince him that he was capable of better things. Finally he shook his head. "Go away, Rahab. I'm no good, and I never was."

"There's good in you. I've seen it."

"Well, I haven't seen it, and Ariel hasn't seen it."

"People can change, Othniel."

"I'm glad you believe that, but I don't."

"I have to believe it, because I've changed."

Othniel took another long drink of the wine. It was almost flat, and he frowned and hurled it across the tent. "Well, maybe you have, but I've had plenty of chances to change and I never have."

"I think it was Jehovah who helped me to change. The Lord has been working in my heart, and I think He wants to work in yours."

"Jehovah doesn't care anything about me."

"You know better than that. Phinehas says that Jehovah loves everyone."

"How could He love a drunk?"

"How could He love a harlot?" Rahab said sharply; then her voice softened. "That was what I was, but He's preserved me. He used you and Ardon to bring me out safely from that city with my family. And since then He's blessed me greatly. He wants to do the same thing for you." She leaned forward and put her hand on his shoulder. "Jehovah loves you, and I believe in you."

Othniel fell silent while Rahab continued to speak, pleading with him. She saw, after a while, that there were tears in his eyes. He did not attempt to wipe them away, and they encouraged her. "Our God is a loving and forgiving God. That's His nature, Othniel. You know that far better than I."

"That may be true for you but not for me."

"It's true for everyone."

"Rahab . . . I can't go back again. I'd be too ashamed."

"Shame is sometimes a good thing. We have to go through that after we have sinned, but as we bring our shame to God, He forgives us. You must come back, Othniel. You have to."

"I can't do it, Rahab, I can't!"

Rahab then sat down on the floor of the tent. "Othniel, you may as well make up your mind to do it. I'm going to stay here until you call upon God and then go back to your home. Now, unless you throw me out, I'm going to pray and ask Jehovah God to forgive you for your sins and to give you a new heart." Without preliminary she began praying. She had prayed often enough for Othniel in the privacy of her tent and oftentimes out tending her new flock. Now she poured her heart out to God, saying, "God, save my friend from what he has become. You're the great, the almighty God. You delivered a whole people out of Egypt. You can deliver this one person from the bondage that has come upon him. Open the door, Lord, and let him come out. . . ."

Rahab did not know how long she prayed for Othniel, sitting and weeping in the gloomy darkness of that stinking tent. Finally, when she lifted her head and wiped her eyes, she saw Othniel was sitting up straighter. He was looking at her in a dazed manner, but his voice was clearer.

"I'm glad you came," he whispered. "While you were praying I made a decision. I made a vow to God. I'm going to give myself to Jehovah and be what He wants me to be."

"Oh, Othniel, how wonderful!" Rahab exclaimed. "Come. Now you've got to go home with me."

She stood to her feet, and Othniel slowly followed suit. He looked down at her and smiled shakily. "It's going to be hard. Nobody's going to believe me."

"They'll believe what you *show* them, and you've made a vow. Now, let's see what God can do."

Caleb and his family had enjoyed a fine meal of roasted lamb cooked with spices and fresh bread. There were also a few wild greens Ariel and the servants had gathered. Now Caleb,

Ardon, and Ariel were sipping wine and nibbling at the grapes that were on a silver dish.

Caleb was speaking while Ardon and Ariel listened. "The battles aren't going to get any easier. As a matter of fact, they're probably going to get harder."

"But we've won every battle," Ardon said.

"Yes. And we've lost good men. There are at least ten more kingdoms that have to be conquered before we possess this land, but we can do it. This one coming up is going to be especially hard, though. You'll have to encourage your men greatly."

Ardon nodded. "I'll be—" He broke off at the sound of footsteps outside, and then a man entered the tent. Ardon stared at Othniel, and his glance drew the eyes of Caleb and Ariel. "Well," Ardon said harshly. "I'm surprised you had the gall to come back, Othniel."

Caleb got right to his feet and stared at Othniel. His nephew's face was drawn and he looked thin, but his eyes were clear.

Ariel was watching also, and there was a great bitterness in her. This man had disappointed her more than any other person. "Why have you come back, Othniel?" she asked. "Did you run out of wine?"

Othniel shook his head. "No, I didn't run out. I came back," he said, speaking slowly, his eyes fixed on Caleb, "to ask your forgiveness, sir. I've brought shame to my family, on my father's name, and on you. And on all of you." He waved his hands. "So there's nothing I can do about the past, but I ask you to give me a chance to redeem myself."

Ariel got to her feet, her face flushed. "How can we believe you? You've failed everyone who has trusted you."

Ardon was even harsher. "Your name is rotten among the troops, Othniel. The worst thing a soldier can do to his fellow soldiers is to run away. He leaves a hole in the line in which the enemy can come. There are men among our troops that have threatened to kill you themselves if you ever came back."

Caleb remained silent while his daughter and son spoke harsh words to Othniel. He was watching the face of the young man, searching for something. Finally he said, "You have been a disappointment to me, Nephew. Why do you come now?"

"As I said, Uncle, just give me a chance."

"All right," Caleb said firmly. "I will give you one final chance to redeem yourself. You will serve as the lowest soldier in the toughest troop in our army. You've been spoiled all your life, Othniel, and you've failed at everything except being a prodigal. But you will serve Captain Benzai, and I will give him orders to make life as hard for you as he can. My fondest hope is that you will survive long enough to die a soldier's death and wipe out the shame that you've brought to your father's name. Now get out and wait until I finish, and I'll take you to Benzai."

Othniel said quietly, "Thank you, Uncle." He turned without another word and left the tent.

"You can't trust him, Father," Ariel said angrily. "He'll just hurt you again and all of us."

"That's right," Ardon said. "He'll run the first time he has to face the enemy."

Caleb turned to face the two. "When I was a young man," he said slowly, "I performed a rather disgraceful act. Everybody in the family was disgusted with me except one uncle. He believed in me. If he hadn't, I wouldn't be standing before you right now. I probably wouldn't even be alive. I'm giving Othniel one small chance. It might kill him, but it might also make a man out of him."

———

Captain Benzai was sitting down, casting lots with some of his fellow soldiers. As Caleb approached, he immediately got to his feet, a tough, burly man with features battered from many a battle. "Commander," he said. "What can I do for you?"

Caleb motioned Othniel to come forward, but he kept his

eyes on the face of Benzai. He saw recognition and also disgust. "I see you recognize my nephew, Captain."

"I know him," Benzai said in a curt voice.

"You're going to take my nephew and make a soldier out of him." Caleb smiled grimly at the expression on Benzai's face, but he did not hesitate. "I want you to make him the lowliest recruit in the whole army. Give him every dirty job that comes along. Work him until he drops and then work him some more. Do whatever you must to make a soldier out of him. Show no favoritism just because he's my relative. You understand me, Captain?"

Benzai grinned. "Are you giving me a free hand, Commander?"

"I am. I know what you can do, Benzai. I'll never question your methods. If he dies by them, I'll never say a word." Caleb put his gaze on Othniel, waiting for a protest, but Othniel's face did not change. He nodded to Benzai and the other soldiers and said, "I'll leave him in your charge."

As soon as Caleb was out of sight, Benzai scowled at Othniel and called out, "All of you men come here!" He waited until those men within hearing distance gathered around, forming a circle around Benzai and Othniel. "We have the most famous runner in history here. Some of you witnessed what a fine runner he is. He ran away and left his companions in the lurch. So we know he can run away, but now the commander has told me he wants us to change him so that he runs forward. So I'm giving you orders. All of you, be as tough on him as you please."

A howl of pleasure and yells of excitement went up from the crew. They were a tough-looking bunch. As Caleb had said, they were the toughest unit in the entire army.

Tobiah, a giant of a man with snaggle teeth and a scar running all the way from his eyebrow down to his neck, stepped forward. "Just let us have him, Captain. He can't run from us."

"Don't kill him," Benzai said. "But anything else you have

to do to make something of his rotten carcass is fair." He reached out and cracked Othniel across the cheek with his hard palm. Othniel was driven sideways and sprawled in the dirt.

"Get up!" Benzai said. "What are you doing lying down? You think this is a rest camp?" He turned and winked at Tobiah, then left.

Tobiah reached down, grabbed Othniel, and pulled him to his feet. He slapped him across the face with two ringing slaps and grinned. "You know what I think, runner? I think you'll not last until the battle comes. And even if you do, you'll do your running at the enemy. If you try to run away"—he pulled a gleaming knife from his belt and held it to Othniel's throat—"I'll kill you myself." He sheathed the knife, pulled his sword, and nodded at the sword that Othniel wore. "Now, let's see what you can do with that fancy sword, runner. . . ."

CHAPTER
26

Ardon brushed the flies away from his face, and the effort was almost too much for him. He had slumped down beside a spring and had drunk deeply from the cool water. The past six days had been filled with marching and battles, and the entire army was exhausted. They had defeated Libnah, but now Joshua had sent word that they were going to attack Horam, the king of Gezer, without a single day's rest.

A fierce hunger gnawed in Ardon's belly, but in order to eat he would have to get up, and he was too exhausted to even do that. He heard footsteps and looked up to see Captain Benzai coming toward him.

Benzai was thinner than usual, worn down by all the fighting. Now he fell facedown and drank thirstily from the spring. When he had finished, he rolled over and sat up, wiping his mouth. "That was good," he said. "I had quite a thirst."

"How many dead and wounded did you have in your company?"

"Too many. How about you?"

"We lost some good fighters." Ardon glanced over east in the direction of Gezer. "We could use a rest."

"That's what I said, but Caleb and Joshua say different, and they're the commanders."

Benzai unhooked a bag from his belt, tilted it up, and drank some of the wine. He handed it to Ardon, who took a few swallows then handed it back. "How big an army do you think we'll be facing at Gezer?"

"Nobody knows. Joshua doesn't seem to care. He just finds the enemy and runs us right at 'em. I always thought this was a land of milk and honey. That's what the prophets all said, but all I can see is fighting and blood."

The two men sat quietly, almost too exhausted to talk. Finally Benzai groaned. "I've got to go see that the men get something to eat. You know," he said after he rose, "I don't believe in much of anything, especially in men, but that cousin of yours—Othniel—he fooled me."

"What's he done now? Run away again?"

Benzai laughed. "No. That's what I thought he'd do, but I put him up in the front line right next to me. When it came time to charge, why the fool ran ahead of the rest of us. He hit their line all by himself, slashing and yelling like a demon. I didn't believe it. Neither did the other men."

"I can't believe it either."

"We treated him rough, rougher than we should have maybe. Let him do the dirtiest work. Worked him until he couldn't stand up. I figured he'd run away, but he didn't. I told the men to cut him down if he ran." Benzai rubbed his chin thoughtfully. "Don't know as I ever saw a soldier do any better. You never know what's in a man, do you, until you see him in battle."

"I can't believe it, Benzai. He ran like a rabbit the last time I saw him in action."

"Well, now he's like a man possessed."

"You'd better watch him, Captain. He's let us down more than once."

"He acts like a crazy man when the battle starts. I wish I had a thousand more like him!"

The battle had raged all day, and now that the sun was down, Othniel was fighting alongside Tobiah. Othniel's mouth was dry, and he had a slight cut on his left arm. His right arm was almost dead, for he had struck many blows. Now he suddenly heard a shout of alarm, and Tobiah grabbed him by the arm and said, "Look. They're sending in fresh troops over there to our right. We can't stay here!"

"We can hold 'em."

"No, we can't. There're too many."

Othniel narrowed his eyes. "Look," he yelled. "There's Captain Benzai. He and some of our fellows are trapped up there."

Tobiah stared and shook his head grimly. "They're lost," he said.

"No, they're not."

Tobiah stared at Othniel, who had leaped to his feet and was running, yelling, and waving his sword.

Tobiah laughed and yelled to the rest of the men. "Come on, you weaklings! Would you let a running coward like that have all the glory?" He jumped to his feet, and the men threw themselves into the battle. The action swirled, and men fell, bled, and died, but finally the men of Israel drove the enemy back.

Benzai was on his feet but wounded. He sat down and shook his head. "I'm dizzy." He turned to see that Othniel had come to kneel down beside him.

"Are you all right, Captain?"

"I'll live," he said grimly, then grinned. "What were you trying to do, commit suicide? You had no chance against the enemy."

Othniel grinned also. There was blood on his face and his garments were spattered. "I don't want to have to break in another captain," he said.

Benzai studied the young man and laughed. "Well, it was a

noble charge, my boy. Your uncle Caleb will be proud when I tell him of it."

———————

Ardon had been on the left wing of the army. He had fought until he could barely stand and finally had been attacked by three soldiers that he had managed to beat off, but one of them had given him a bad wound, ripping the flesh in his side. Some of his fellow soldiers had joined in to kill them, but then he had slumped down. One of them stopped, but Ardon waved him on, crying weakly, "Go on. Don't wait for me."

After that he had passed out, and when he awoke, the sunlight was fading. The action was somewhere over to the left, and he thought he heard the cries of triumph. "I hope those are our fellows," he muttered. He got to his feet, and his head swirled. He staggered, caught himself, and dropped his sword. When he bent over to get it, he fell headlong. For a long time he lay there, feeling the blood seep from his side. He pressed his hand against the wound, knowing he would bleed to death if he didn't get help. Getting to his feet, he started back but discovered he had lost his sense of direction. "Which way is the camp?" he muttered. He was unable to decide and then desperately took the way he thought would be most likely. Twice he fell and each time crawled back to his feet. Finally he was shocked when he heard a woman's voice.

"Who's there?"

"I'm a wounded man."

In the moonlight he could see the shape of the woman now. "Are you a Hebrew?" she asked.

Ardon knew that if she were one of the enemy and he said yes, she would kill him and he would be unable to stop her. At least she would call for help. But he could only say, "Yes. I am a Hebrew. Who are you?"

"I'll help you. Come."

"I can't go far."

"Our camp is over here. Everyone has run away because of the battle." The woman came closer and looked down. "You're wounded?"

"My side."

"Come." She touched him then, and he smelled the musk of her perfume. She took his left arm and put it over her shoulder. "Lean on me," she said strongly. "You have to get to the tent."

Ardon did not remember much about the trip to the woman's tent, except for a great deal of pain. She could only half carry, half drag him until finally she said, "There. There's the tent."

She led him inside and said, "Lie down now."

He did not need that command, for he collapsed on the spot. As he drifted unconscious he wondered if he would ever wake. *Maybe this is death,* he thought, and then the blackness swallowed him.

"My name is Mardiah. What is your name?"

"Ardon."

"That's a funny name."

Consciousness had swarmed back to Ardon, and now he had found his upper garments removed, and the woman had worked over his side. "I had to sew you up," she said.

"It's all right. I'm weak as a baby," he complained.

"You lost much blood, but you'll be all right. You need to drink as much as you can." She lifted his head and pressed a cup to his lips. He discovered he was thirsty and drank eagerly.

When he lay back, she said, "You will be all right. You will not die."

"I need to get back to our camp."

"How will you go? You can't walk."

"I guess you're right about that."

"You are a handsome fellow. Are all Hebrews as good-looking as you?"

Startled, Ardon looked up at the woman. She was sitting beside him, and he saw that she had taken off her outer veil that most desert women wore. She had a strong face and a light olive complexion. She was bold and attractive, with well-shaped, deep-set eyes that studied him carefully.

"I suppose I'm average."

Mardiah laughed. "How many wives do you have?"

"None."

"Well, I have no husband. He was killed by a bear a year ago. Maybe we'll do something with that."

Ardon was so weak he could hardly make sense out of the woman. She was laughing at him, and he saw that she had white, even teeth that showed brightly against her olive skin. He did not fail to notice that she was a shapely woman, too, but then he began to lose consciousness.

"Don't go to sleep. You must eat much. Make new blood."

She pulled him up and fed him like a baby. Then she said, "Now you sleep. We'll make you strong again. . . ."

———

Mardiah had a teasing, light way about her, and as he grew stronger, Ardon was more and more aware of what an attractive woman she was. She had dressed his wound, and every day she washed him off. "I like clean men," she said. The first day he did little but sleep, but the second day he felt much stronger. He got up and walked and discovered that his strength was returning.

Mardiah was pleased with him. "You are a strong man," she said. "Here. You must eat and drink more."

Finally the evening came, and she came with water in a dish of pottery. "I must look at your wound and wash you off."

She carefully washed the wound and nodded. "It is good.

You are healing. Now I wash you off, but first you must have something really good."

"What's this?" Ardon said, sniffing at the cup she gave him.

"Very special wine. Make you feel very good. My uncle, he makes."

Ardon took a swallow and gasped. "Strong," he whispered.

"Drink it all. It make you feel much better."

Ardon drank the entire cup and almost immediately felt the effects of it. "That's the strongest wine I ever had."

Mardiah was busy cleaning him off and was dipping a cloth in the water. She began to bathe him, and as she did, she was watching him with a strange light in her eyes. "You like this?" she whispered.

"You've been very good to me, Mardiah."

Mardiah pushed him back. "Lie down," she said. Mardiah continued to run her hands over his body, and Ardon discovered that whatever she had given him to drink had done something else. It had increased his desire. He had been aware that she was a beautiful woman, and from her speech he knew she was a woman of easy virtue. Now suddenly she threw the cloth down and pressed herself against him. "You are a strong man, and a strong man needs a strong woman."

Ardon started to push her away, but his hands encountered the full, round curves of her body, and then he murmured, "No. This isn't right."

But the woman was insistent. Her lips were seeking his, and her hands were busy. "Yes, it is right."

And then Ardon, who had been judgmental of other men, found his control slipping away. With a hoarse cry he seized her, and she laughed with pleasure. "It is the way it should be. A strong man and a strong woman." And then she brought herself against him.

CHAPTER
27

Ariel lifted her head and cried out, "The army! They've come back!" Jumping up, she ran outside and joined the women and young people who came streaming out. They all ran toward the edge of the village of the camp, and there they saw the soldiers, coming back rank on rank. She saw Joshua at their head and Caleb, her father, over in front of his unit. Quickly she ran toward Caleb and cried out, "Father, you're back!"

"Yes. We had a great victory. One less enemy to conquer."

She threw her arms around him, and he hugged her back.

"Well, we made it back, Commander," said a voice behind her.

Ariel turned to see Captain Benzai, his arm bandaged and looking more battered than usual, but he was grinning broadly. "I guess we showed them whose land this is, didn't we?"

"Yes we did. Your unit performed nobly."

"You haven't heard all of it," Benzai said. "You know that nephew of yours that you told me either to break him or make a soldier of him?"

"Othniel? What about him?" Caleb asked sharply.

"Well, I tried my best to break him, but he just wouldn't break. He's the best soldier in this army."

Ariel stared at Benzai. "You can't mean that, Captain Benzai!"

"I wouldn't be here if he weren't."

"What do you mean?" Caleb demanded.

"I got myself in a mess, just me and four other soldiers. They were swarming all over us. There was no chance at all. And then that wild nephew of yours made a charge all by himself. He was so crazy that everybody decided to follow him. So they pulled me out of trouble. He's a wild man," Benzai said with a shrug. "He's a lot like you, Commander."

Caleb did not answer for a moment. He looked down at the ground, and when he looked up, Ariel saw that he was smiling. "That's the best news you could have brought me."

"Well, I gave you the good news first. Now the bad."

"What's wrong?" Caleb asked.

"It's your son. Oh, he's not dead, but he got separated from the rest of the army. Pretty badly wounded, but he's okay."

"Where is he?" Ariel said quickly.

"He's at the rear of the troops. The wounded move a lot slower. We were anxious to get here."

"But he's all right, isn't he?" Ariel said.

Benzai scratched his head, and both Caleb and Ariel saw that he was puzzled. "Well, the wound was here on his side. He found somebody to patch him up. Sewed him together as neat as any woman could do with a needle and a thread. That's all right, but there's something wrong with him. He's not himself."

"What do you mean, Benzai?" Caleb demanded.

"Well, it's like he's dreaming or something. You'll have to see it for yourself, Commander. He's not the old Ardon."

"I want to see him right away."

"Yes, sir. I'll have him brought to your tent."

Caleb and Benzai moved away, and Ariel was greeting all the soldiers she knew. Since she was the daughter of one of the commanders she knew a great many of them. Suddenly she stiffened when she saw Othniel moving into the camp. He saw her and hesitated. She did not really want to speak to him, but she was anxious to get news of Ardon. She moved toward him and said stiffly, "Hello."

"Hello, Ariel."

"I'm glad you're safe, but I hear that Ardon has been wounded."

"Yes. I've been trying to talk to him."

"What do you mean *trying* to talk to him?"

"Well, he won't talk." Othniel shrugged his shoulders as if baffled. "I don't understand it. Of course, I'm not his favorite person. Maybe he'll talk to you."

"Where is he?"

"Come along. I'll take you to him."

Ariel followed the tall soldier. They passed by many that were wounded, and she wanted to ask more details but felt uncomfortable. Finally he said, "There's the wounded moving along there. Look. There's Ardon."

But Ariel had already seen her brother. She ran quickly toward him. He was walking slowly with his eyes on the ground. "Ardon!" she cried. "Are you all right?"

Ardon glanced up, and Ariel was shocked at the expression on his face. He had always been an alert man with quick eyes, but now his eyes seemed dead. He did not answer her, and she said, "You're wounded?"

Ardon just said, "I'm all right."

"What's wrong, Ardon?" She tried to catch his eye, but he looked down at the ground and refused to speak. She continued to ask questions, but he simply moved around her and headed for the camp. He did not lift his eyes except from time to time to see where he was going.

"What's wrong with him, Othniel?"

"I don't know. I've never seen anything like it. Before the battle he was tired but nothing like this."

"It's like he got a wound in the head."

"He'll be all right. I'm sure of it."

Ariel, once again, wanted to speak to Othniel to commend

him for his courage in battle. But she had been disappointed by him too many times. "I must go with him. I'm glad you're safe."

She turned and caught up with Ardon. She spoke to him again, but he did not even look in her direction, and she became fearful. Somehow this was worse than his physical wound!

———————

"It's been two weeks, Father, and he's no better."

Caleb looked at Ariel and for a moment did not answer. "I know. He's like a dead man."

"Doesn't he say anything to you? You're his commanding officer and his father. Something must have happened."

"I've asked him every way I know how, Ariel, but he doesn't answer. It's like he's blocked out everything. He only speaks when he wants something, and have you noticed he can't look us in the eye?"

"It's like he's hiding something," Ariel said. "That's not like him."

"He's not fit to go back into battle," Caleb said.

"No. You can't send him out to fight. Not like this."

"He insisted on going but he's weak. I had to command him to stay."

"Yes. You must make him stay at home."

The two were seated in their tent, and after a time Caleb said, "Well, I'm proud of Othniel. I've got the report from many of his fellow soldiers. They say that charge he made was like nothing they ever saw. It was like he's a man without fear. Captain Benzai's made him an officer."

"It's hard to believe, isn't it?"

"We've got two different men on our hands here. My son and my nephew. They're not the men they were when they left here."

Ariel asked timidly, "What will happen to Ardon?"

"Who can say?" Caleb shrugged. "I've seen men like that a

few times. It's like the battle takes something out of them. But time will help."

———

Rahab had been sitting outside her tent talking with Romar when she saw Ariel approaching. She rose at once.

"Have you seen Ardon, Rahab?"

"Why, no. But I'll help you look." The two women began to go through the camp. Rahab cast glances at Ariel from time to time, and finally Rahab said, "Everyone's so proud of Othniel. Wasn't it wonderful what he did?"

"I suppose so."

The coldness of Ariel's tone shocked Rahab. "What's wrong? You know it was a brave thing. Everyone says so."

"I'll never trust him," Ariel said, her lips drawn into a line.

"You're wrong, Ariel. He's come so far. He's not the same man he was."

"To me he is."

Rahab was shocked at the young woman. She had grown very fond of her, but she recognized that there was a hard streak of pride, and now she said as gently as she could, "You're wrong, Ariel. You need to forgive. We all do."

Ariel changed the subject. "I've got to go take some supplies to my father. He didn't take enough."

"But there's a battle about to take place."

"I'll be careful. If you see Ardon, see if you can talk to him."

"I'll try, but I'm probably the last person he'd want to talk to."

———

The sheep were nuzzling at the bubbling water as it ran over the stones. It was a favorite time of the day for Rahab to bring the sheep down to the stream. They were foolish creatures, but she was absurdly fond of them.

She looked up to see a figure, and shock ran through her as she realized it was Ardon walking toward her. She immediately left the sheep and called out, "Ardon, Ariel's looking for you!"

Ardon gave her one quick glance, then looked away. "I'll find her later."

"She was going to take some supplies to your father."

Ardon shook his head and would have turned away, but Rahab saw a desperation in his face. "Wait," she said. "Talk to me, Ardon. What's wrong?"

"Nothing."

"Of course there is," Rahab insisted. She moved around and tried to catch his glance, and when she did look into his eyes, she was shocked at the emptiness she saw there. This was not the man she had known. That man had been confident, filled with pride and enthusiasm. This man was like a walking corpse.

"Something's wrong, and you need to talk about it."

"I can't tell anyone what's wrong with me. Can't you understand that?" Ardon's voice was hoarse and his face was stricken.

"Ardon, we all need to talk when we have problems." Rahab could not imagine what had come into Ardon's life to bring him to this. She began to speak about his need for getting close to his family, and finally she said, "You obviously think you've done something wrong. But God is forgiving no matter what we do."

Ardon shook himself as if a hand had wrung him. "Why do you try to comfort me, Rahab, when I've treated you so terribly?"

"Why, I want the best for you, Ardon. You've taken care of me and my family."

"You know it was because Joshua commanded me to do it. It wasn't my choice."

"But you did it, and I'll always be grateful to you and Othniel for bringing me out of Jericho and saving my family."

"You're the one who saved us."

Rahab moved closer and put her hand on his arm. It was

the first time she had ever touched him. "You're a grief to your father and to your sister. They're worried sick about you. And I'm worried too."

Ardon laughed. At least he made a sound like laughter, but there was no joy in it. "If you knew what's in my heart, Rahab, you'd despise me."

"No, I wouldn't."

"You don't know. Just leave me alone." He wrenched his arm away and broke into a run.

As Rahab watched him go, a great love for the man that had been building burst upon her. "Why, I love him!" she said. "And he's in terrible trouble." She turned slowly and walked back to the sheep, but her heart was crying out to God for this man. He had treated her badly, and she knew it. There was no hope that he would ever see her as anything but the harlot she had been in Jericho, but still she cried out to God, "Lord, he needs your help. He's lost without it. Whatever is in him, help him with it."

Ariel had brought two servants with her, and each of them were leading three donkeys heavily laden with food for Caleb and his men. The way was rough, but Ariel was thinking of her brother. Her heart had broken over whatever it was that had seemingly destroyed him.

The sun was high and beat down upon her, and overhead some birds of prey circled far over to her left. But after one glance she ignored them.

"We must hurry. I want to be back before dark," she called to the servants.

Five minutes later one of the servants let out a terrified scream. Ariel, who was in the lead, turned to see that a group of wild-looking men had suddenly appeared. One of them swung his sword and cut down the youngest of the boys. The other boy attempted to run, but he was caught and pierced with daggers.

Ariel started to run, but she knew it was hopeless. Strong hands seized her, and she whirled around to face the cruelest eyes she had ever seen.

"Well, we have a beauty here, my fellows. Come. We have to give her to the captain, but after he's through with her, he'll give her to us. You'll like that," he laughed.

Ariel knew that death would have been preferable to this. She could not even scream as rough hands pulled at her and led the donkeys away deeper into the desert. She was in the hands of the most merciless men she had ever seen.

CHAPTER
28

Othniel looked up sharply as his uncle came bursting through the door of his tent. One look at Caleb's face, and Othniel jumped to his feet. "What's wrong, Uncle?"

"It's Ariel...!" Caleb's face was twisted with worry, a look Othniel had never seen. Caleb had always been so strong, so sure of himself. But now a dark cloud of anxiety was revealed in his eyes. "It's Ariel...." he stammered again, his words terse and his lips drawn together into a straight line. "She's been captured by the enemy."

"Captured! How could that happen?"

"She was bringing us some food supplies when she was taken on the path."

"How are we going to get her back?"

"I'm summoning the army. We're going to make an attack right away. I'll kill every man of them if I have to!"

"But, Uncle," Othniel said quickly, "we can't do that." His mind was working rapidly, and he shook his head. "If we attack, they may kill her. You know that happens all the time."

"I thought of that," Caleb said, great anguish in his tone. "But we've got to do something."

"It'll have to be a small operation. We'll have to take a small group, track them down, find out where she is, and then wait for our chance. We'll steal in at night and take her."

Everything in Caleb urged him to strike quickly, with a large force, but taking a deep breath, he forced himself to speak slowly. "Yes. That would be the thing to do. I'll choose my men."

"You can't go," Othniel said.

"What do you mean I can't go? She's my daughter."

"After Joshua, you're the most valuable person Israel has. Joshua's our leader, and he looks to you. If we lost you, we'd lose far too much. I'm going."

"You? Why, that would never do."

"I know you don't think much of me, Uncle, but I've changed. Please. Let me choose a dozen men. We'll get started as soon as we get our weapons together and a little food. We'll bring her back. God won't let us down."

It took some convincing, but Caleb finally nodded reluctantly. "I'd give anything to go myself, but I can see that would not be wise." He put his hand on Othniel's shoulder. "I trust you, nephew, to bring my daughter back."

"I'll do everything possible. You know how we've always been friends, Ariel and I. I have a great fondness for her."

"I didn't know how much I loved her until this came up. Now, go at once!"

———

Othniel had gone through the ranks of soldiers in his mind, and quickly he sought out the twelve he had the most confidence in. Calling them off to one side, he outlined the critical situation and said, "It's not going to be a battle but a raid. I've got to have men who can move quietly. We'll have to do this by stealth. Now get your weapons ready. We're leaving at once."

Othniel turned to get his own weapons and stopped short. Ardon had appeared and had obviously been listening. "I'm going with you, Othniel."

"That wouldn't be wise, Ardon. What are you doing here?

You haven't recovered from your wound yet." He wanted to say, *You're not in the right frame of mind either.* Ardon's behavior disqualified him from going on a critical raid like this.

"I rushed here as soon as I heard about Ariel's capture—Phinehas came with me." Ardon shook his head, determination etched on his features. "I'm not going to argue about this. I'm going with you to get my sister back."

"All right. You understand the danger, and you understand what we must do. You'll have to obey my orders this time, Ardon."

"As long as I'm with you, that's all I ask."

"Good. Get your weapons. We'll be leaving at once."

Othniel quickly gathered his weapons, but on his way back to lead the men out, he encountered Phinehas.

"I heard what's happened to Ariel," the priest said. "I wish I were a soldier so I could go with you."

"You have a more important job."

"What is that, Othniel?"

"You must pray to our God to give us wisdom and strength. Unless He helps us, our task is hopeless."

"Nothing is too difficult for Jehovah. I will pray, and I will call all the elders of Israel. We will all fast and pray until you bring Ariel back safely. Go now, and may the God of all mercies go with you!"

Ariel struggled in the grip of the largest of her captors. He was a blunt-faced individual with eyes that literally glowed with evil. He laughed at her as she struggled fruitlessly. "You can fight all you want to, you delicious little Hebrew, but it will do you no good." He laughed at her and winked over her head at his companions who were watching, grinning broadly. "A tasty little bit, would you say?"

"Yes," returned one of his lieutenants, a squat, muscular individual with a scarred face. "Shame we have to give her to our commander. Why don't we just not tell him?"

Ariel's captor, the leader of the band that had captured her, scowled. "That's what I'd like to do, but if he found out about it, he'd skin us and leave us for the vultures." He ran his hand over Ariel's body and laughed at her tremors. "There'll be plenty left for all of us when he gets through with you."

He dragged her to a tent. Night was coming on now. He shoved her inside and said, "You'll stay here until our king comes. He likes young women like you. Some say his taste is a little crazy, but he's the king after all. Don't try to get away or you'll regret it."

Ariel had fallen to the floor of the tent. She lay trembling as her captor disappeared. Her strength was gone, for the fear that had gripped her from the moment she had been seized had been like an open wound. She could only lie there, covering her head with her arm and weeping.

Finally she sat up and looked around. Only a tiny candle burned to give light. It was obviously the tent used by the soldiers, for there was little in it except some sour-smelling garments, a water bag, and a few morsels of food that she could not even think of eating.

She listened to the rough laughter and jeers outside her tent. Most of the talk was about her, about the soldiers telling each other what they would do to her, each one getting more vile than the last.

All her life Ariel had been pampered, and the pride that had come with that was a natural thing. There in the darkness of the tent, with almost all hope gone, Ariel could not help but think of how badly she had treated people all of her life. Her behavior suddenly became crystal clear to her, and now that death and worse was facing her for the first time in her life, she saw herself as she really was. She remembered the incidents when she had been needlessly cruel to servants, and memories of how she had always demanded her own way no matter what the cost to others trooped through her mind. She tried to shut out the memories but couldn't, and finally she covered her eyes with her hands and moaned, "I've been terrible all my life." Desperately she longed for a chance to live and to become a different woman, but there seemed no chance of that now.

The night wore on endlessly, and the soldiers' voices finally faded as they lay down to sleep. One time her captor came, looked in on her, and leered. "We're going to have a good time with you. You'd better rest now because you won't get any sleep later."

The threat brought new waves of fear to Ariel. She began again to try to pray. She thought of Othniel and how badly she had treated him—always taunting him for his weaknesses—and now the image of his face clearly formed itself in her mind. She remembered a time when she had broken one of her father's favorite vases. Caleb had been upset, and she had told him that Othniel had broken it. She had watched Othniel get beaten with a cane and had laughed at him when it was over.

Finally, as the light of the candle flickered and threatened to go out, the daughter of Caleb began to pray. It was a broken prayer, and the words were barely formed. It was more of an endless moan as Ariel wept over her life. She began to cry out in her spirit. "O, God, I have been so terrible. My sins are before me and before you. Forgive me my transgressions . . . for the way I have treated you . . . and for my pride and the way I have treated others."

───────────

Othniel had driven the men hard. They had picked up the trail easily enough, for the enemy had made no attempt to hide it. The best trackers had pointed out the small footprints that had to be Ariel's, and they had followed the trail hard until the light failed. That night Othniel assigned Akiah, the best tracker and one who moved as quietly as a cat, the task of finding the camp and coming back with a report. Akiah had grinned crookedly and left at once.

The next day at camp Othniel led the men forward at a slower pace. He was fearful that the enemy might have left guards out. From time to time he cast a glance at Ardon, who had spoken not half a dozen words since they had left. The son of Caleb kept to himself, his face a mask, and Othniel was worried about him.

When the sun began to sink in the west, Akiah came running up, his eyes bright with excitement. He pointed over in the direction from which he had come. "They're up ahead," he said. "I've been watching them. They've got Caleb's daughter in a tent."

"Did she seem to be all right?" Othniel demanded quickly.

"They let her out to walk, and she seemed all right. But they put her back in the tent. I think they're saving her for something."

"Describe the camp to me," Othniel commanded.

Akiah began to draw a rough sketch in the dirt of how the tents lay. "Right here in the middle is the tent where she's kept," he said. "The other tents are scattered around, so we'll have to go through them to get to her."

Othniel studied the rough drawing in the dust and questioned Akiah more closely. Finally he asked, "How many are there?"

"Twenty, perhaps—maybe more."

"We can take them," Blaniah spoke up eagerly. "We hit them hard with everything we've got when they're least expecting it."

"They might kill her right off," Ardon spoke up. "That's the way they do things."

"Ardon is right," Othniel said. "If we can get her out without a fight, it would be better. Less danger to her."

"I don't know how you can do that," Akiah said. "She's right in the middle of the camp."

Othniel's mind was working quickly. "We'll get as close to the camp as we can. Are there sentries out, Akiah?"

"Always a couple."

"We'll have to silence them. Then I'm going in. I'll get Ariel and bring her out. We may get fortunate enough to get her outside the camp before they notice."

"What if they do notice?" Ardon said.

"Then we'll fight to the last man," Othniel said.

"I'll go in and get her. She's my sister," Ardon volunteered.

"No, you won't." Othniel had never assumed authority over Ardon, but he knew that his cousin was not himself. "I let you come, but you're under my command. You'll stay with the others. Is that understood, Ardon?"

Ardon stared at Othniel, but deep in his heart he knew that he was in no condition to carry out the delicate task of getting Ariel out of an armed camp. "Yes. That is best."

"We'll wait until everyone is well asleep. Then, Akiah, you and another will go silence the sentries. When you have taken care of them, I'll go in and get her."

———

Since the soldiers were leaving her alone, Ariel had some slight hope that she might be rescued. But it was only a small flicker. For two days the soldiers had taunted her, and the last thing she had heard was that the king would be here, without doubt, by noon the next day. She could not bear to think about what would happen then.

She had tried to sleep, but sleep would not come. Almost without ceasing she had prayed for Jehovah to deliver her. She had heard the priest speak of Abraham and his great faith, and she had tried to summon up faith, but it was very difficult to do, trapped as she was.

The hours seemed to creep by on leaden feet. It was very late now, past midnight, she knew. Suddenly a slight sound caught her attention and a rustling at the door of the tent. Anxiously she drew herself up and waited, thinking it was one of her captors. The candle had burned out. The only light was from the moon outside. A figure was there bent over and creeping in, crawling toward her. "Stay away from me," she whispered fiercely, knowing this would avail nothing.

"Ariel, I've come for you."

Ariel's heart leaped for joy! "Othniel, it's you!"

Othniel was there beside her and whispered, "Don't speak. We've got to get you away."

"I prayed that you'd come."

"We're not out of this yet. We've got to—" He stopped when a wild shout outside broke the silence. "We've got to fight our way out," he said. "Stay close to me."

As soon as the two stepped outside, it was like stepping into a wild storm. The enemy soldiers were leaping to their feet, and the silence of the night was shattered by the clanging of swords and the screams of battle-mad men.

In the darkness it was hard to see, but by the light of the fire that still burned, Othniel made out the forms of his men as they hacked and slashed at the enemy. Ardon was in the middle of it all, his sword cutting down the enemy like ripe wheat before a scythe. He had no care for himself but threw himself against a group of enemy soldiers in a suicidal fashion.

"Stay here. We'll have to kill them all," Othniel said, shoving Ariel back into the safety of a clump of trees. Whirling, he drew his sword and joined in the battle.

It was a fierce battle, worse than any Othniel had ever known, but it was a brief one. The enemy soldiers were cut down and several of his own men were killed, but in what seemed like no time he heard Akiah shouting, "That's it! The last one!"

Othniel was breathing hard. His eyes fell on Ardon, who lay still almost buried beneath a pile of his enemies. "Ardon!" Othniel shouted and ran forward. He pulled the bodies of the enemy aside and found that Ardon's face and body were streaked with blood. "Ardon, are you all right?" He got no answer, and suddenly Ariel was there beside him.

"Is he alive?" she cried.

Othniel put his hand on Ardon's throat. He felt an erratic pulse and said, "Yes, but he's in bad shape." He lifted his voice and said, "Make a litter. We've got to get away from here. We'll have to carry the wounded."

Ariel stood back and watched as the men quickly fashioned litters for Ardon and two other wounded men. Then when Othniel said tersely, "Now, back to the camp quickly," she put herself beside Othniel. Several times on that difficult journey back to the camp of Israel, she wanted to speak to him, to thank him for what he had done. But he scarcely looked at her and said nothing.

He hates me for the way I've treated him, she thought. She had to fight against her own pride. She wanted to speak, but her old pride kept rising up in her, and she made her way with the small group back to the camp without saying what she really meant to say to Othniel.

CHAPTER
29

Dawn was breaking, but the light from the east seemed pale. Ariel leaned forward to stare into her brother's face, and a twinge of fear came to her. He was so still! She laid her hand on his cheek, and the heat of his flesh disturbed her even more. Turning to her left, she dipped the cloth into a vase filled with water, wrung it out, and then laid it across Ardon's forehead. He did not stir.

Two days had passed since the raiding party had returned, and Caleb's joy had been great at recovering his daughter. But his fear for her had been replaced by an anxiety over Ardon. He had stayed close to the camp, not going out in the usual campaigns during this period. He was so deeply troubled that he could barely speak, and Ariel had learned how much the stern old man, who had found so much favor with God, loved his son.

And what did Ariel herself feel? She had slept very little, choosing to remain by Ardon, watching him and caring for him as best she could. There were others in the tribe who were better suited for this, and she allowed them to come, but she kept her station hour after hour. Caleb had said, "Daughter, you're going to wear yourself out. You need to rest." But she found that she had trouble resting even when she lay down and tried to sleep.

Picking up a fan made from woven reeds, she fanned her brother's face. It was hot in the tent, and she thought once of having him moved outside in the breeze but had decided against it. She fanned slowly, thinking back over the terrible events that had taken place since she'd been captured. Mostly she thought of those hours alone as a captive when she had remembered her past life. The passage of time had not erased the memories of her life that had come to her when she thought death was imminent. She had used much of the time sitting by Ardon to think over her life, and two things struck her with surprising force. The first of these was the recognition that she had not been a good woman. She thought over the years how she had used her position as the daughter of the great Caleb to get her own way. There was no way she could avoid the memories of how proud she had been all of her life. She had taken advantage of everyone and had always sought the very best of circumstances for herself. This disturbed her greatly, and again and again she prayed to God to forgive her and to change her.

Somehow she felt that this prayer had been answered, and she was determined to be kinder and gentler in her dealings with others. She resolved to bring before God every day her behavior so she would not fall back into her old ways.

The other feeling she could not shake off was more difficult for her to analyze. It concerned Othniel, and somehow guilt was mingled in with her memories of him. Part of this was because she well understood that she had treated him abominably all of her younger life. This was part of what she had been, a woman of haughty pride, but there was more to it than that. From the time he had appeared in her tent, and perhaps even before that, her feelings for Othniel had been so confused. She had almost hated him when he had failed the family, but she had come to recognize now that there was a different element there. She didn't want him to fail because of a deep affection she had for him.

How long this affection had been there she found it impossible to say. She went back over her life and recognized she had always admired his cheerful spirit, his madly good looks, his willingness to always help others. But this was not all the story. As she lay in the tent waiting for death, she realized that her feelings for Othniel were much deeper than she had supposed. Part of the reason she had treated him so badly when he had failed was that she so desperately wanted him to succeed. She realized that this was part of her affection for him. But how deep did that affection go? For two days now she had struggled with this, and she realized that it was not the affection one had for a relative but that a woman had for a man she cared for.

Why didn't I see this before? Though he's always been with me, a part of my life, I never thought of him as a man I might love. But that night when he came out of the darkness to save me from death, I knew my feelings for him were deeper than I'd ever imagined. He not only was the one who saved me, but he was the one I learned to care for.

She sat there as the morning light grew stronger, and the hopelessness of her feelings for Othniel became clear to her. *He could never care for me,* she thought, *not after the way I treated him.* She resolved to throw all of her energy into caring for her brother and put Othniel out of her mind.

The battle to win the Promised Land, the land flowing with milk and honey, occupied everybody in the camp. Rahab had formed the habit of meeting with a group of women early in the morning to pray for the men who went out to fight. The battles went on constantly, and she had learned that prayer had brought her some consolation.

She left the group early one morning and was on her way back to her tent when Caleb suddenly appeared. She bowed before him, showing him reverence, and greeted him. "Good morning, sir."

"Rahab, I have a favor to ask of you."

"Anything, master."

"I'm afraid my son Ardon is not doing well, and my daughter is wearing herself out nursing him. Please go help her. You're reputed to be a good nurse, good with men with wounds. I'm worried sick about both of them."

"I will go at once and do all that I can."

Rahab went back with Caleb to the tent, and when she stepped inside, she was shocked at Ariel's expression. Her face, usually so fresh and beautiful, was almost gray with strain.

"This will never do, Ariel!" Rahab exclaimed. She went over and pulled the young woman to her feet. "You go at once and rest!"

"Rahab, I can't. I must stay with Ardon."

"You can't help him if you get sick."

"I can't sleep."

Rahab felt the girl's body trembling. "It will be all right. God is not going to let him die."

Ariel clung to Rahab and began to weep. "Why does God let such terrible things happen, Rahab? My brother is not a bad man."

Rahab had thought of this many times herself. Now she held the girl and said gently, "Sometimes, Ariel, we are like naughty children who won't heed their parents. I think God gets our attention by letting something very difficult happen in our lives. That's the time we all look to God. I believe that God had to get Ardon to a place where he would be willing to listen."

Ariel looked up and tears were running down her cheeks. Her voice was faint and trembling as she said, "And you think that's true of me as well, don't you?"

"It's true of all of us, Ariel. You're not happy. You've had an easy life, but now you're discovering that there's more to life than pleasure and ease. Jehovah is knocking at your door, in a manner of speaking. Now the question is, will you open the door and let Him come in?"

Ariel wept with wild abandon. "Yes. That's what I want more than anything else."

"Come. We will pray and then you will sleep. I will take care of your brother. Never fear."

Rahab leaned over when she noticed Ardon stirring. His eyes opened, fluttered for a moment, and she whispered, "It's all right, Ardon. You've been hurt."

Ardon stared at her, but there was a wildness in his expression behind his sunken eyes. Rahab had never seen anything quite like this and felt fearful. "Do you know me, Ardon?"

"God is the judge. He will not forgive."

The words startled Rahab. "No. That is not right. He is the judge, but He does forgive."

"God will not forgive me."

Rahab tried to calm Ardon as he began thrashing around. She captured his arms, and he was so weak she was able to hold them down. His eyes were wild and staring, and she spoke to him gently until he finally passed into a state of unconsciousness. Rahab began to pray. "O Jehovah, almighty and everlasting God, touch your servant Ardon. Heal whatever is in him, and may he make his peace with you."

Even in his unconscious state, Ardon tossed fitfully until his fever went down. Rahab sat beside him the whole time. Once when Caleb came in, she said, "I think, sir, that God is dealing with your son."

"He's been a good son."

"What we think is good," Rahab had said, "may not be what God demands."

Now as Ardon opened his eyes again, she saw that the wildness was gone and she said joyfully, "You're much better, Ardon. Here. You must drink."

She held the cup while he quickly drank. She let him have only a little, however, saying, "A little at a time or it will make you sick."

For the next hour Rahab gave him small drinks of water and was finally able to get him to eat a little of the broth she had kept for just such a time.

She continued to sit beside him, and after a long while he turned to look at her. "I wish I had been killed in the battle," he said. His eyes were clear now but filled with misery.

"Ardon, you don't wish that."

"I do. I'm not fit to live."

Rahab knew at that instant that something had come into Ardon's life that had taken from him all of the assurance he had always had. She knew of his years of careful listening to the Law and his delight in studying it with the elders and the priests. She knew of his devotion to the things of Jehovah, the sacrifices, the sacred feasts, his reverence for the priesthood, but now that was all gone. Nothing seemed to be left in him but a great emptiness and despair.

"Why would you think God would not forgive you?"

"I cannot even speak of it. I thought I was a good man, but I was wrong."

"Ardon, God knows all about you. I think He knew you before you were born, and I know that He loves you. Moses learned that God was a God of tender mercies."

"His mercies are not for me!"

"They are for everyone who will come to Him and confess."

"God can't love me!"

"Why not?"

"I'm a sinner, that's why!"

"Don't you know that all men and all women are sinners? God is so pure, and we all fail Him in so many ways. I know a great deal about that myself, but all people have evil in them just as I have, just as you have."

Ardon grew quiet as Rahab spoke. He watched her face and

saw the peace and the joy that was in her and thought of the woman he had brought out of Jericho. Finally he whispered, "I'd give anything to have your peace."

"If you want to have peace with God, you must confess what's on your heart."

"I . . . I can't bear to think of it."

"Whatever it is you've done, you're not the first man to do it. There are no new sins. There are only the same sins. And, Ardon, I'm not sure that any one sin is worse than any other."

Ardon began to toss restlessly. His lips twisted in agony, and he moaned under his breath.

"Just say it, Ardon," Rahab urged him. "It helps to tell another human being. If you can tell it to me, you can surely tell it to God."

Ardon gritted his teeth so hard she could hear the sound; then he turned to look at her, his face a mask of pain. "I have been so judgmental of others, yet I have behaved worse than any man."

"What did you do? Speak it out."

"I . . . I committed fornication with a woman."

Rahab then understood the deep agony that was in Ardon. He had been so harsh in his judgment of those who had committed this sin, and now he himself was guilty of the same sin. She took his hand and said softly, "Now. You have told me."

"You hate me, I know."

"Of course I don't hate you. How could I hate you when we're all the same before God? But you must confess it to God and ask His forgiveness."

"I can't! I can't even bear to think of going to God with this terrible thing."

Rahab knew she had no power over this man, and she prayed in her heart, *O God, give me a word of wisdom that will draw him to you.*

Instantly she knew what to say, thrilled with a great joy that God was speaking through her.

"I've been studying one of the songs Moses gave to his people. He said, 'You have set our iniquities before you, our secret sins in the light of your presence.'"

The words seemed to cut through Ardon like a knife, but Rahab added quickly, "He knows our sins, but even so Moses prayed, 'Satisfy us in the morning with your unfailing love, that we may sing for joy and be glad all our days.'" She continued quoting the joyful song of Moses that she had committed to her heart and finally said, "Don't you see, Ardon? Moses was a man, and he must have known sin or he could not have prayed like this. But God forgave him, and He will forgive you. Just call out to Him and ask Him. Tell Him that you have sinned. You're not going to surprise Him. He already knows, but you will make Him happy, I think."

"What do you mean, Rahab?"

"I think God knows great joy when we bring Him our sins and beg for forgiveness."

Ardon stared at her for a moment and then began to cry out to God. Great tears ran down his cheeks, and Rahab sat beside him silently. He held her hand tightly, and finally he began to grow quieter. When he was absolutely still, Rahab leaned to look into his face. "You have done all a man can do. Do you feel that God has forgiven you?"

"Yes. I know now the peace that you have felt." He turned to face her. "But I have wronged you dreadfully."

Rahab shook her head. "That's all in the past. Let us look to the future. God has forgiven you. Now there is no guilt. It has gone away. Never think of it again except to give thanks to God for what He has done!"

CHAPTER
30

"It's so good to have you home, Father."

Caleb turned and smiled down at Ariel. "It is good to be home. It seems like life has become just one battle after another." Indeed, that was true, for the children of Israel were moving from one Canaanite kingdom to another. God seemed to be striking their enemies so that oftentimes they fled out of pure fear. True enough there were other enemies to conquer, but Caleb said now, "I know it seems like the battles will never be over, but they will be one day. This is truly the land of promise."

"The land of milk and honey, Moses called it."

"That's what the Lord called it." Caleb nodded. "And it is a good land."

The two were walking through the tents of the tribe of Judah, and almost every family had a man in the army. Many of them spoke to Caleb, and there was an air of happy expectancy among the people.

Othniel appeared from over to Caleb's left, and he called to him. "Nephew, come here, will you?"

Othniel came at once. He gave Ariel a quick glance and then turned to Caleb. "Yes, sir?"

"I just wanted to ask how the men seemed. Are you satisfied with them?"

Caleb and Joshua had agreed to make Othniel a commander in the army of Judah. He had proven to be a man worthy of their trust, for time and again in the battles he had distinguished himself by his personal courage and by his astute use of troops.

Othniel smiled briefly. "They're ready for the next battle whenever you lead us, sir."

"Fine, fine. Now, walk along with us here."

"Really, sir, with your permission, there are some things I need to do."

Caleb was surprised but nodded. "Well, I'm sure you're busy getting ready for the next battle. I just wanted to tell you how pleased Joshua is with you."

"That's good to hear. I'll see you later."

"That was strange," Caleb murmured. "He seemed almost embarrassed." He turned to Ariel. "You two haven't been having another one of your fights, have you?"

"No, sir, of course not."

"Well, I should think not. After all, he was the one primarily responsible for getting you back from those villains. I owe him a debt of gratitude forever for that."

"He . . . he doesn't seem to be the same man."

"Well, of course not. He's not a boy any longer. Don't tell anyone I said this, but Joshua and I aren't getting any younger. Sooner or later we're going to have to step aside. And, you know, I think that young fellow might be just the fellow to lead Israel."

Ariel turned to stare at her father. "You really mean that, sir?"

"Well, he had a bad beginning, but he's become a leader of men. And his attitude toward Jehovah is good now. I was a little worried about that." He suddenly asked, "Why doesn't he come around anymore? You two used to do all sorts of things together. I think you must be having some kind of an argument."

"Not really." Othniel had indeed stayed away from Ariel during those times when the troops were not in battle. Ariel had tried desperately to find some way to express her gratitude to him, but he seemed so distant and did not seek her out as he once had. "He's just too busy for a woman, I suppose."

Caleb was caught by this. He studied his daughter's face and saw that she was not as filled with joy as he was accustomed. "You seem to be troubled, Ariel. Anything you can tell me?"

Ariel forced herself to smile. "No, I'll be all right."

Caleb wanted to say more, but she turned and began talking of other matters. *Something has gone wrong between those two,* he thought. *That's a shame.*

The three figures outlined against the blue sky were of differing height. Ardon was the tallest, between the other two, with Rahab on his right and Oman on his left. They were laughing and talking as they walked through the knee-high grass. Oman was holding on to Ardon's hand, tugging at him and shouting, "Hurry up, Ardon!"

"I'm coming as fast as I can. You've got to be careful with an old man," Ardon said, grinning. He glanced over at Rahab, who was watching the two of them with a smile. "Beautiful day for shepherds."

"Yes. Good for the sheep too." She glanced ahead to where her small flock was ambling along, headed for the stream. They were stupid animals, but they had at least learned where the stream was. Now they paused long enough to nibble at the tender spring grass, and she murmured, "They're such beautiful creatures."

"Beautiful. I've never called them that," Ardon said, laughing. "And they have less sense than any creature I've ever seen."

"You like to eat them, though," Oman piped up.

"Right enough, Oman. Let's eat one tonight." He winked at

the boy, knowing that Rahab was tenderhearted when it came to her animals. "Which one do you want to butcher, Rahab?"

"I don't want to talk about it. We don't need any more meat, anyhow," she said stiffly.

Ardon laughed. "Come on, Oman. I'll race you to the stream."

Rahab watched as the two made for the stream. Ardon was shortening his steps and her nephew was running for all he was worth. It gave her a warm feeling to think about how the two of them had become such friends.

Ardon had become a new man after his meeting with Jehovah. Very few days went by without Rahab thinking of that time when he had called on God and confessed his sin. She had been expecting that Ardon would never mention it again, but he did quite often. He had not told anyone else that she knew, but many times he had remarked to her, "It was the most wonderful moment of my life, Rahab, when I did as you said and confessed my sin to God. It was like I had a huge boulder on my shoulders and it rolled off and I could stand up like a man again. He seemed to delight in telling her about this, and he also was quick to tell her how much he owed her. "I can never repay you," he often said.

But Rahab would never take credit, saying, "It was all God's doing."

The three reached the stream, and Ardon brought out the string and fishhooks. As Rahab watched the sheep from a slight hillock, Ardon and Oman began to fish. The sound of their voices came to her clearly, and Rahab once again marveled over the wonderful change in Ardon.

The morning passed, and the two caught several fish, but finally Oman grew sleepy. He curled up in a ball and fell asleep almost instantly. Ardon sat beside him for a while; then he turned and came over to stand beside Rahab. "I'm afraid I wore the fisherman out." He smiled.

"It does me good to see him have such pleasure. You're so good for him, Ardon."

"Well, he's good for me too." He glanced down at the sleeping form and smiled. "Someday I'd like to have half a dozen boys just like that one."

"All at once?" She smiled at him mischievously. "That would be hard on your wife."

"Well, not all at once, of course." He saw that she was teasing him and laughed. "One at a time."

The two stood there, and a feeling of peace lay upon them. The clouds drifted overhead silently. From far off there came the whistle of a shepherd signaling to his sheep. The breeze was warm, and finally she said, "I wish it could always be like this and you didn't have to go to war anymore."

"That day will come, but it may be a while."

"Isn't it amazing how God has led our people to this land and given it to them? I think so often how He promised it to Abraham, and Abraham had no idea that this would all happen."

"He was such a man of faith. I admire him greatly," Ardon said.

The two began to walk around, idly keeping their eye on Oman as he slept, but finally Ardon said, "You know. I've been worried about my sister."

"I'm so glad you got her back from the enemy. It was a miracle she escaped unharmed."

"Yes, but she hasn't been the same since then. I don't know what's wrong with her. She was always such a happy girl, and now her face is long. She hardly ever laughs."

Rahab said, "I think she found out something about herself during that time."

Ardon turned to face her. "Like what?"

"She had always had her own way and everything in life had been easy for her, and suddenly she was faced with either a terrible death or slavery. She found out that we can lose everything that we treasure in a moment."

"You think that's what's happening to her? But why would it make her so glum and unhappy?"

Rahab had an idea of what was happening to Ardon's sister, but she did not feel it was her place to speak of it. "We'll just have to pray that she'll get over it."

The two were quiet for a time, and finally he said, "Let's sit down here." He sat and Rahab sat closely beside him. He was quiet for a while, and she said, "You're not saying much, Ardon. Is something wrong?"

"I think there might be."

"But you're doing so well. Your wounds are healed. Your father's so happy with you. You're on your way to becoming a leader in Israel. What's wrong?"

He turned to her and studied her face. The light was kind to her. He studied her eyes, which were widely spaced and colored a deep violet that seemed to have no bottom. They were still the most unusual eyes he had ever seen. He said in a guarded tone, "I'm wondering if you could ever forget about what I did."

"What do you mean, Ardon?"

"The sin I committed with that woman."

"You must put that out of your mind, Ardon," she said warmly. "I have."

"Have you really?"

"Of course. Let me tell you what I do. Sometimes thoughts of things in the past that I did come to me, but I keep a little box—oh, not a real box, of course. Just a box that I make up. When those thoughts come, I open the box and I put them in and I shut the lid and I say, 'I repented of that, and I've made the sacrifice. I saw the lamb that died and the priest that sprinkled the blood on the altar and that prayed for the sins to be gone. It's all over.' You have to think like that, Ardon."

Ardon was quiet for a time, and then he said, "I might as well confess something else to you. Another wrong."

Rahab turned to face him fully. He looked handsome and tanned and fit as he sat there. His body didn't have an ounce of surplus flesh. She knew the young women of Israel eyed him often, and he had turned down innumerable opportunities to take a wife. "I can't think of what that would be."

"Well, I've always felt that you were a beautiful and desirable woman. That's why I was so cold to you for so long, Rahab. I felt desire for you. And I guess I have to ask you to forgive me for that."

"To forgive you for being a man?" She smiled. "Don't you know that I have felt the same way toward you?"

Her words shocked Ardon. "You have?"

"Of course. There's a fine line between being attracted to a person and engaging in lustful thoughts. I admit it's hard to keep these thoughts in their proper place, but I was drawn to you from the moment you came into our house."

An intense quiet seemed to surround the two. Ardon could not move for a time, but then he smiled. He took her hand in his and said, "I owe you everything, Rahab."

Rahab met his glance and saw something in his eyes that only a woman can see. She put her hand on his cheek and said, "I've always cared for you, Ardon."

He reached out and pulled her close, kissing her on the lips. She leaned against him, and he held her tightly. "Then, let's start right where we are and forget the past."

"Yes. We don't know what the future holds, but we have today."

"I want you for my wife, Rahab."

She hesitated, and he leaned back to look in her face. "What's wrong? Don't you want me for a husband?"

"People will talk. They know my past."

"Let them talk," he said, leaping up and pulling her to her feet. "Let them say all they want to. I want to marry *you*, not them." He grabbed her, swept her off her feet, and swung her around, laughing as she cried out in delight.

"Why are you hugging her, Ardon?"

Ardon stopped and lowered Rahab until she stood on her own feet. They both turned to see Oman standing there. "Because she's pretty and sweet, that's why."

"Well, why are you hugging him?"

"Because he's pretty and sweet."

"He's not pretty, Aunt."

Rahab laughed and looked up into the face of the man she wanted to spend her life with. "Yes he is," she said, and when their eyes met, something passed between them. They knew, each of them, that they would never forget this day on the hillside when they found each other.

CHAPTER

31

The news of the coming marriage between Ardon, the son of Caleb, and Rahab of Jericho brought a mixed reaction among the tribe of Judah. Some were shocked and could not seem to forget Rahab's past. Others who had watched the woman's growth into a true Israelite were happy about it.

Ariel was one of these. She had seen the change in her brother's life, and when he had told her and her father how it had happened, both of them eagerly welcomed Rahab into their family.

Caleb was happy, for he longed for grandchildren. He was so enamored with the idea that his thoughts suddenly turned to his daughter. A scheme came to mind, and being a man of action he immediately proceeded to put it into place. The only thing he said to Ariel was simply, "I'm going to get grandchildren from my son and Rahab. I'd like to have grandchildren from you too, daughter."

"You will ... someday," she had said, surprised by his straightforward words.

"You wouldn't mind having a husband, then?"

"Well, every woman wants a husband," she had replied and thought that ended the matter.

But it did not, and it was to be brought home to Ariel with a shock very soon.

Caleb had called together the men of Judah to encourage them in their warfare. He had given a rousing speech and at the end, when they were done cheering him, he said, "I have one more thing to say of a personal nature." A quiet fell on the crowd, and Caleb turned and smiled at his daughter Ariel, then lifted his voice. "Some of you may not know that Joshua has agreed to give me my part of the new land that will be ours. Hebron, our father Abraham's old homeplace. He has also agreed to give me Kiriath Sepher. Some of you soldiers know this land. It is occupied by a tough group of our enemies. It's going to be difficult to conquer, but I'm going to make it worth the while of one of you." He smiled again at Ariel and continued. "Whoever conquers Kiriath Sepher in my name, to him will I give my daughter Ariel in marriage."

A buzz of talk arose, and those standing closest to her saw that Ariel had turned pale. The announcement had taken her totally by surprise.

As soon as Caleb dismissed the troops, she turned to him and said, "Father, you can't do this thing! I can't marry a man just because he does as you say."

Caleb had spoiled Ariel all of her life, but his mind was made up on this matter. He laughed at her fear, saying, "This will settle it for you. You won't have to weed out all the men who've been trying to get you to marry them. Now the best man will get you."

"But it may be a man I don't love."

"He'll be a good soldier of Judah, and you can learn to love him. I've given my word, Daughter—you heard me. There's no backing down."

Ariel felt sick. Some of the soldiers, good men though they were, were not men she would ever learn to love. Some of them already had two or three wives, but her father, who loved her dearly, was a man of his word. He would never back down now.

Ardon and Rahab were walking along holding hands, talking about their upcoming marriage. Ardon broached the matter of a husband for Ariel. "I don't think I was ever as surprised as when my father promised Ariel to the man who takes that country in his name."

"You weren't as surprised as Ariel," Rahab said. "She turned absolutely pale and then begged him to change his mind."

"He'll never do that. As far as I know, my father has never broken his word."

"But think of some of those men. Suppose old Gehazi took his men and won that place? Why, he's hideous."

"He's tough, though, and as a matter of fact, I heard him boasting that he was going to be the man to win Ariel."

"He wouldn't win her," Rahab said. "I think Ariel would kill herself before she'd give herself to a creature like that."

The two spoke for a long time, and finally Rahab stopped and faced Ardon. "I want to tell you something about your sister."

"About Ariel? What is it?"

"I think she cares for Othniel."

Ardon laughed loudly. "No, no, you couldn't be more wrong. They've picked at each other since they were children. And you know how angry she got at him when he became a drunk."

"I know all that, but she wouldn't have become so angry if she hadn't cared for him."

"Well, I don't understand the ways of a woman, then. She certainly kept it covered up. Are you sure she cares for him?"

"Yes."

Ardon thought for a moment, then said, "I take it you're asking me to go to Othniel and tell him he needs to be the one to conquer Kiriath Sepher."

"I don't know whether he cares for her or not, but if he

does, now's the time to show it."

"I'll talk to him, but it would be a miracle if those two ever got together."

————————

Othniel was surprised when Ardon came to speak to him, and even more surprised when he understood what Ardon was saying. The two men were standing facing each other just outside of Othniel's tent. As soon as Ardon began to speak, Othniel stared at him.

"Othniel, I have the feeling that Ariel cares for you. There's no one I'd rather have for a brother-in-law and no one my father would rather have for a son-in-law than you."

"Have you lost your mind, Ardon! We're talking about Ariel here. You know she doesn't care for me."

"Rahab thinks she does. She's a good woman, my sister. It's hard to know what women are thinking. Why don't you go to her? Tell her what you feel."

"To give her a chance to laugh at me?"

"If you care for her at all, now's your last chance."

Ardon left immediately, and Othniel could not get the conversation out of his mind. He brooded over it all day, and then later that night he said, "I'm going to find out about this one way or another." He made his way to Caleb's tent and waited outside until he saw Ariel come out. He immediately went over to her and said, "I need to speak with you, Ariel."

Ariel was surprised. "All right, Othniel."

"Not here. Come over where we can be alone."

Ariel was shaken by this. She had no idea what was on his mind. Ever since her father's announcement, she had hardly slept. Three men had already vowed that they were going to conquer the land and claim her, and two of them were absolutely hideous. She couldn't stand the sight of them.

Othniel drew her aside and said, "I wanted to talk to you about your father's offer."

"I think he's lost his mind giving me away to just any man."

Then Othniel made a big mistake. "You've been spoiled all your life. It's time you settled down, Ariel. Now, let's talk like adults. I am thinking of conquering the land myself."

If Othniel had spoken to her gently, things might have been far different. But his harshness grated on Ariel's nerves, and she could not stand to hear another word. "Go away! I don't want to talk to you."

Othniel stared at her. "Why not? We've always talked."

But it was too late. Ariel's nerves had given way to anger. "You're nothing but a weakling, Othniel," she cried, not meaning a word of it. "I know you better than any of them. You couldn't conquer a sick cat, much less Kiriath Sepher!"

Othniel responded just as angrily and made a rash decision. "I'm going to take that land, Ariel, and then I'm going to come back. And everybody's going to expect me to marry you. But I won't," he said grimly. "I'll throw it in your face and laugh at you and tell everyone you're no woman for a real man." He whirled and stalked away.

Stunned, Ariel began to weep. "Why did I do that? Why did I speak to him like that? I'm such a fool." Sobbing now and not able to face anyone, she ran off. She wandered outside of the camp for over an hour, wondering if she could redeem the situation.

"Why am I such a fool?" she said bitterly. "He's proven himself, and all I've proven is that I'm a stubborn vixen with no sense at all. He'll do exactly what he says and I'll be humiliated in the eyes of all Israel."

CHAPTER

32

During the weeks that followed the quarrel between Othniel and Ariel, the two did not speak to each other. More than once Ariel wanted to go and ask forgiveness for her hasty words, but in all truth she had no opportunity. She learned from her father and from others that Othniel had obtained permission from Joshua to lead a small army against Kiriath Sepher to take it for the glory of Israel.

Caleb had been delighted with this. He had exclaimed to Ariel, "That's wonderful! Now you'll have a husband that will be a pride to all of us."

Ariel wanted to tell her father of the quarrel and how Othniel was taking on this task simply to humiliate her, but she could not bring herself to do so. She was utterly miserable and grew more withdrawn as time went on.

———

Ariel was listlessly working on a scarf that she was weaving on her loom when she heard approaching footsteps. She looked up as Rahab burst in, her face alight. "Othniel is back with the army! And the scouts have told what a wonderful victory he's had. He won the battle, and he's come to claim you, Ariel."

But to Rahab's great surprise, Ariel burst into tears. She got up and threw herself on her sleeping pad.

"Don't you understand? He's come to claim you for his bride."

"Leave me alone," Ariel moaned. "Don't even talk to me."

Rahab could not believe what she was seeing. She came over and put her hand on the young woman's shoulder. "What is it, Ariel?"

"He doesn't love me."

"I think he does."

"No he doesn't. You'll see. It's going to be awful!"

"You must go out to greet him."

"I can't."

"You must! Come. Your father's waiting. It's a great moment of victory for Othniel. You mustn't deny him that. It'll be all right."

Rahab persuaded Ariel, and finally, after washing her face, Ariel forced herself to go out. Her father was waiting for her, grinning from ear to ear. "Well, he's back, and he's won the battle. Now I'll be waiting for those grandchildren of mine."

Ariel tried to smile, but it was a pitiful attempt. She was glad when Caleb turned to greet the vanguard of the army.

Othniel came up and bowed low before his uncle. "The battle is won. Kiriath Sepher is yours, Uncle."

"I knew you could do it, my boy. It was something I saw in you long ago." Caleb stepped forward and embraced Othniel. Rahab noticed that Othniel did not so much as glance at Ariel, and this troubled her.

Caleb cried out, "We're going to have the greatest banquet ever held in Judah! You will be the guest of honor, Nephew. There I will make the public announcement that you and my daughter Ariel will be married."

A cheer went up, but Othniel's face did not change. He merely said, "Thank you, Uncle," and then he turned to look at Ariel for the first time. She was staring at him wide-eyed. He waited for her to speak, but when she did not, he nodded briefly, then turned and walked away.

"That was a strange thing," Ardon murmured to Rahab. "They act like they've never seen each other before."

"Something is wrong," Rahab said. "Ariel won't tell me what it is."

"I'll see if I can get it out of Othniel, but he can be a tight-lipped fellow when he chooses to be."

———————

Rahab was helping Ariel prepare herself for the banquet. She had a new gown made out of blue silk, and she looked beautiful in it. But her face was stiff, and she had cried herself sick.

"What's wrong with you, Ariel?" Rahab said. "You're going to be a bride."

"No I'm not. He's not going to marry me."

"What are you talking about?" Rahab said, staring at the girl. "That's why he conquered Kiriath Sepher."

Suddenly it all began to pour out from Ariel's lips. "He did that because he was angry at me. You know what he told me? He said he was going to go conquer that place and then come back and refuse to marry me. He said he was going to laugh at me and tell everyone I was a spoiled brat—which is what I am, Rahab."

Suddenly Ariel was weeping again, and Rahab put her arms around her. She waited until the worst of the weeping was over and said, "Listen, if God means for you to have Othniel for a husband, it will come to be."

"It won't be Othniel I'll have for a husband. He hates me."

Rahab stared at her and then said, "I'm going to talk to Othniel."

"It won't do you any good."

Rahab left at once and went to Othniel's tent. She called his name, and he stepped outside. "I have to talk to you, Othniel."

"Go ahead and talk," he said stiffly.

"Ariel tells me you plan to humiliate her."

"That's right. I do."

Rahab was taken aback. "But why?"

"You don't know everything that happened. She's a spoiled brat and always has been. She doesn't care about anybody but herself."

Rahab wanted to shout at the young man, but she saw he was wound up tight. She began to speak gently. "She has been spoiled, but right now she's a very frightened young woman. All her life she's gotten her own way, but something happened to her when she was captured. She's told me about it. And when you appeared to rescue her, she knew that Jehovah had sent you. She loves you, Othniel. There's a goodness in her that the right man can bring out."

"Well, I'm not the right man," he cried, "and I wouldn't marry her if she were the queen."

———

The banquet was noisy, and wine was as common as water. Everyone knew what the purpose was, but that didn't seem to matter. Caleb had spared no expense. Now he stood talking to Joshua, and Joshua nodded happily. "It'll be a good thing, this marriage between Othniel and Ariel. Both from the tribe of Judah. You should have some wonderful grandchildren out of that pair."

Caleb was somewhat nervous. "I don't know what's the matter with Ariel. She's sad. I went to see her and she was crying. That worries me."

"It's a good thing for a young virgin to be scared and nervous," Joshua said.

"I didn't know you considered yourself an expert in these matters," Caleb said.

"It just shows good breeding," Joshua said.

"Well, I hope you're right. I'm going to get my daughter

now and make the announcement."

"She'll be all right. You'll see."

Caleb went to get Ariel. They were having the banquet in the largest tent available, and the crowd overflowed. When he reached his own tent, which he shared with Ariel, he called her name and then he stepped inside. She was waiting for him wearing the new dress, and he said, "You look beautiful, daughter. As beautiful as your mother when I married her." He stepped closer and saw that her face was tense and her lips were trembling. "What's wrong?"

"Father, what if he won't have me?"

"Won't have you! Don't be foolish! He fought for you. Come, now. You're just having the fears that all young brides have."

Ariel saw there was no hope of getting out of this. She took her father's arm and accompanied him out of the tent. When they entered the larger tent, her name was called out and a pathway opened. She saw Othniel standing there and would have given anything to be anyplace in the world other than here. She knew well what he was going to do, and there was no way to avoid the humiliation that was about to happen.

Othniel stood stiffly waiting as Caleb brought Ariel into the tent. He was wondering, *How did I ever get myself into this? I don't hate her. I've been a fool. She's frightened and I've made it worse.*

As he watched Ariel, his mind brought back many memories of the childhood pleasures he had shared with her. They had always been the best of friends while growing up. He realized that he was the one who had gone astray and had shamed the family and that, somehow, he was blaming her for this.

Fixing his eyes on her face, he knew that she was terrified. Her eyes were enormous, and he was shocked when he saw tears glimmering in them.

Why, she's scared to death of me! That's not what I want.

As Ariel approached Othniel, she saw through her tears that his face was tense, and she prepared herself for what she knew was coming. Yet she could see that he was not angry, that there was a strange look on his face and something in his eyes that she had not seen for a long time. She remembered once when he had hurt her quite by accident and it had nearly broken his heart. He had that same look on his face right now, and she could not understand it.

Then she and Caleb were in front of Othniel. "Here is your bride-to-be, my son," Caleb said.

Ariel raised her eyes to meet those of Othniel, and she saw not anger or wrath but tenderness. He reached out and took her hands, and she was shocked. He dropped to his knees, kissed her hands, and looked up. And she heard him whisper, "Will you have me, Ariel?"

The world seemed to turn over for Ariel. She looked into his eyes and saw that instead of anger there was love! With a glad cry she pulled at his hands and he came to his feet. "Yes," she said. "You will be my husband as long as I draw breath."

A great cheer went up, and Ardon leaned down and said to Rahab, "Oh, I knew from the first it would end like this. I guess I know women pretty well."

Rahab wanted to laugh, but she knew she could not. Her husband was the most ignorant man concerning women she had ever known. "I'm sure you do, husband," she said meekly.

And then the music began, and Ariel was drawn close as Othniel embraced her. She looked up and the tears were gone and her eyes were filled with joy. "Are you certain about this, Othniel?"

"Am I certain? Why, I fought a war for you. Now," he said, and his eyes were laughing down at her, "I've got so much invested in you that it's going to take a lifetime to get my full value out of you."

"Do you think I'm worth it?"

He pulled her closer and said, "You're worth it, Ariel— worth it all!"

EPILOGUE

The early-morning sun bathed the village in a pink glow as Rahab, with a small boy by her side, made her way to the well at the central plaza. After lowering her large clay jug into the water to fill it, she hoisted the heavy container to her shoulder for the walk back home, looking forward to making the morning meal for her family.

"Mother, come quickly!"

Rahab looked up to see her oldest daughter running down the cobblestone street toward her. "What is it, Kaliah?" she asked as her daughter arrived out of breath. "What has happened?"

"It's Bezalel, Mother. We got word that he needs to see you right away . . . he says he doesn't have much time."

Rahab nodded. "All right, I'll gather my things and be right there. Take little Boaz home and prepare the meal for the family."

Rahab hurried home to prepare a basket of medicinal herbs and soothing ointments to take to the home of old Bezalel. She knew there was not much she could do to stop the progression of the disease that was claiming his life, but she could at least offer him comfort and try to ease his pain in his dying hours. While she worked, her mind recounted all the years since she had first left her home in Jericho and become a daughter of Israel.

The Israelite army had long since conquered the land of Canaan, promised first to Abraham and then to his descendants over the centuries. Now the twelve tribes had been allotted their places throughout the land and had settled into towns and villages, stretching from the northern hill country to the southern deserts and the western sea. Rahab's village was located just outside the ancient city of Jerusalem, where Bezalel lay dying.

Rahab thought lovingly of her first husband, Ardon, the son of Caleb, who had died some years ago, leaving her to care for several children by herself. She had grieved deeply over the loss of her first love, but she had peace in her heart knowing that he was safely in God's care now and that she must attend to her family, who needed her more than ever. While she threw her energies into caring for her own children, and for those in her village who were sick or in need, another man came into her life whose name was Salmon. Rahab smiled at the thought of her second husband. He was a loving and caring man who had lost his own spouse and who, too, had been left alone with growing children. It did not take Rahab and Salmon long to marry and unite their two families into one. Rahab felt so blessed by Jehovah, who provided for her even in the midst of death and loss. Within the first year of their marriage, an additional blessing from God, a beautiful little boy they named Boaz, was born to them.

"Take care of the children, Kaliah, until I return. I don't know how long I'll be. This may be Bezalel's last day."

"I will, Mother," Kaliah said as she gathered the children to the table for their morning meal.

––––––––

Rahab walked swiftly along the dirt road into Jerusalem. It was close to midday by the time she arrived at the home of Bezalel. A servant woman welcomed her in and led her to his bedside, whispering quietly that his time had come and he was insistent on talking with her.

She wondered at this as she drew close to the dying man's side and gently took his hand in hers. "What can I do for you, Bezalel, my friend?"

"May the Lord God of Israel bless you, daughter." Bezalel

could barely whisper the words, but his smile was radiant as he looked up at her.

"He has done that for me every day of my life since I became a believer in Him," Rahab said, returning his smile. "What blessing can I bring to you this day?"

"Sit down here," Bezalel said, indicating a small stool by his bed. "I would like you near me in these last moments I have on this earth. I am not afraid of the future, for I know into whose hands I am returning, but I have one last task I must accomplish before I go to my true and everlasting home."

"Is it something I can help you with?" Rahab wondered what else the old man could possibly need to do, since he had been a faithful servant of Jehovah all of his life, carrying out the building of the magnificent plans for the tabernacle of God given to Moses in the wilderness.

"Help me sit up," Bezalel said hoarsely.

Rahab leaned over the old man and carefully helped prop him up so he could look directly into her eyes.

With shaking hands and fumbling fingers, he reached inside his tunic and pulled out the gold medallion he had shown Rahab many years earlier. "Help me take this off," he whispered.

Rahab gently lifted the medallion on its leather strap off from around Bezalel's neck and stared at it once again. "It is so beautiful," she murmured. Then looking up at Bezalel, she asked, "Would you like me to take this to the person of your choosing? Has God told you who it is to be?"

Bezalel lay back against the pillows, his eyes closed, breathing hard from the exertion of removing the medallion. After a moment he opened his eyes again, and gave her a look that astonished her in its depth. It appeared that the wisdom of the ages was reflected in the eyes of one who had seen so much of God's miraculous dealings with His people.

"It is for you ... Rahab." Bezalel could barely speak, but his eyes focused on her in such a way that she could not question his sincerity, nor his sanity. This was not the decision of a demented, dying man—it was the wish of the ever-mysterious God of Israel.

Rahab was stunned. She, a woman—a woman with a sordid past, no less—was being given this incredible honor of carrying on the line from whom would come the Redeemer of the world. She did not know what to say. She could only weep as she stared at the image of a lion, strong and powerful, on one side of the medallion. Warm tears of joy slid over her cheeks and dripped onto the precious gift in her hands as she turned it over to look at the beautiful lamb on the other side. Strength and power, balanced by meekness and humility. It was indeed a great mystery, but a privilege she could not begin to fathom.

Tears streamed down her face now as Rahab lifted her eyes to Bezalel to thank him. But when she looked on his face, she saw that he had already gone. His eyes were closed, and his breathing had stopped so silently, she had not even witnessed his passing from this life into the next.

Slowly she put the leather strap over her head and tucked the precious medallion inside her tunic, close to her heart. She fell to her knees by the lifeless form of Bezalel and raised her eyes and hands toward heaven. "Blessed be you, O Lord, God of Israel, God of all creation. You alone, O Lord, have given us life everlasting. May your humble servant be yours forever."

———

Now faith is being sure of what we hope for and certain of what we do not see. This is what the ancients were commended for. . . .

By faith the prostitute Rahab, because she welcomed the spies, was not killed with those who were disobedient. . . .

These were all commended for their faith, yet none of them received what had been promised. God had planned something better for us so that only together with us would they be made perfect.

—Hebrews 11:1–2, 31, 39–40